I, YEVISH

THE

IRONMASTER

Also by Author
  BURNT TAVERN ROAD
  CAPE ISLAND
  THE SMOKE OF SUMMER

For Suzanne, Sarah, Helen, Jonathan, and Charlie
—my nieces and nephews—all distinguished artists
and writers.

Library of Congress Catalog Card Number
92-093593

ISBN: 0-9626330-6-2 (Paperback)
ISBN: 0-9626330-7-0 (Hardcover)

Acknowledgement

This is the fourth book of mine that Bob
Waldmann typographed and made
camera-ready for printing. His artistic
input and enthusiastic support over the
past four years have been indispensable
to me. And so a special thanks to
Bobby for the whole Harrah Saga—from
a grateful author.

Published by
I. Yevish Books
Box 366
Cape May Point, New Jersey 08212

Manufactured in the United States of America

Part One

MISALLIANCE

WEDDING NIGHT

On her wedding night in Atsion, Cassandra threw her husband out of his house.

Standing in his nightshirt, Edward Blount pounded on the door of the ironmaster's mansion, pleading with Cassandra to let him back in. But his wife of a few hours was deaf to his cries. Unlike Cora Botts, Widow Sizemore's daughter, Cassandra knew all along that a marriage was consummated in bed. She was prepared for this. It was clearly the price she had to pay for becoming Mrs. Edward Blount.

This is not to say that Cassandra did not have qualms about what was coming. Plainly she felt like a whore. It did not matter that in some fashion any woman who entered into a marriage contract was a whore. But women who married money bore the stigma even more. And Cassandra had married money.

When the pounding continued, Cassandra weakened for a moment and thought to unlock the door. But the vivid recollection of her husband's pink flesh and soft limbs made her hesitate. She might bear him physically. After all, he was a gentleman and gentlemen were notoriously soft. What she could not bear was his sexual appetite. He breathed and snorted after her like a pig in a feeding trough. His usually placid face was transformed into a blunt-nosed snout dripping with passion. And his hands—were there two or four?—moved in all directions. How could a woman stand it? After Nathaniel Harrah, the love-making of her wedding night seemed like a wallow in a bog. Nathaniel Harrah was a reserved man, a patient lover. And his patience drove her into his arms. Edward Blount drove her to distraction. His pawing lasciviousness, his pasty kisses utterly repelled her. And Cassandra could not for long suffer being repelled.

So she pushed her husband out of her bed. And when he went downstairs to pour himself a glass of wine to soothe his feelings, she followed him. Opening the door to the main entrance, she asked him to leave.

"But this is my house, Cassandra!" He shook so violently that he spilled half the wine in his glass.

"I want you to leave," she insisted.

"In my nightshirt?" He tried to close the door but was pushed from behind onto the north portico. The door was slammed shut after him and bolted.

"Cassandra!" he shouted. Blount was near apoplectic. Cassandra could not see his face, but she pictured it violently

4

flushed, with spittle dripping from the mouth.

"Cassandra, open up!"

Cassandra fell back against the door. She was rather astonished that she had gotten him out of the house. She had wanted him out. But even as she insisted on his leaving she did not believe she would manage it so easily. As she leaned against the door and felt the vibrations of Edward's repeated poundings and heard his hysterical, frantic calls, she discovered that she had an outrageous sense of satisfaction. She was still married but she had not yet quite bartered herself. Her flesh was still intact and her self-respect, which had taken a battering these past few hours, was slowly struggling back into her body.

"Cassandra, you can't leave me out here like this! Open the door!"

Cassandra stirred herself and pulled away from the door. The bolt would hold; there was no need to barricade it further. Taking the open stairway to the second floor, she removed some clothes from her husband's closet and crossed the hall to the sewing room. Opening the window overlooking the north portico, she tossed the clothing in a bundle to the path below.

Edward retrieved the bundle.

"Where am I to sleep?" he asked, still in shock.

"At some inn. But not here. At least not tonight. Or any night in the near future."

"But Cassandra—"

"I'll be home to you in a week."

"In a week?"

"Yes, and then we'll talk."

Cassandra made the most of the week she had asked for. She released Edward's cook and sent for Rachel who had secured employment in Jesse Richards's household after the fire destroyed Hostetler's tavern.

Rachel arrived with her bonnet askew and a bag of personal possessions in her hand.

Cassandra greeted her with a kiss.

"I need you, Rachel. I need someone I can trust. I don't know when I can pay you. But it will be more than you earned on Burnt Tavern Road."

"Is something wrong?" Rachel knew that Cassandra had been married only the day before.

"My husband and I have quarreled."

Rachel found the news distressing, more than she could handle. She set her bag down.

"You needn't worry," said Cassandra. "I'll not leave this house. You'll have a permanent place here."

"It's you worries me. You never should have married Mr. Blount."

"And why not?"

"You know that better than I," whispered Rachel.

Cassandra took her bag. No one ever gave Rachel her due. She was as plain as a laundry tub but she was no fool. "Come inside. I'll show you your quarters."

With Rachel in tow, Cassandra arranged for the door locks to be changed. She sent for the locksmith at Quaker Bridge. A stranger to Atsion, the locksmith had no reservations about doing business with her. Who was he to know that it was Edward Blount's house? The locksmith spent the better part of the afternoon on his work. When he was through, Cassandra paid him with one of her wedding gifts, envelope and all.

"May I come in?"

She had not seen Jesse Richards arrive. The ironmaster had left his carriage several yards from the house and come the rest of the way on foot.

"But of course, Mr. Richards."

"You can call me Jesse, Cassandra," said the Batsto ironmaster as he pushed his huge frame into the house and took a seat in the drawing room.

"Don't bother with tea or wine," he added. "I'll come right to the point."

"You've seen Edward."

"Yes. And he's as sorry looking a groom as I've ever encountered."

"That's not my fault."

"Isn't it?"

Cassandra was agitated by the ironmaster's presence. She respected Richards, and she wanted his approval. But how could she explain what had happened? No words could paint a true picture of her wedding night. No man could understand her feelings of revulsion.

"You locked the man out of his own house. And from what I can see you've taken measures to keep him locked out."

"I'll not be treated like a sow," said Cassandra. "Edward may be a gentleman. But in the bedchamber he's just an animal."

In spite of himself, Jesse Richards smiled.

"You're a fetching young woman, Cassandra. Edward might not have been able to restrain himself."

Cassandra flushed. "I'd rather not talk about it."

Jesse Richards abandoned his chair and strode towards the window. "Do you want to dissolve the marriage?"

"I don't know." And in truth Cassandra did not know.

"Then things aren't as bad as I fear."

"They're bad enough," said Cassandra.

The ironmaster turned to face her. "In a way I feel responsible," he said. "It was I—at least Mrs. Richards—brought you together. I thought Edward could do with a little fire. And I believed you could better your station in life. But wedding nights have a way of proving matchmakers wrong."

"I don't blame you," said Cassandra. "You and Mrs. Richards have been good friends, patrons even. I'll not forget that."

"We're extremely fond of you, Cassandra."

"But Edward and I will have to settle our own differences—alone."

"Then you will be seeing him?"

"On Sunday. I told him so."

"He made no mention of that."

"It's true nonetheless."

"In that case I will let you handle the matter. You and Edward. And I hope we will still be friends."

He took Cassandra's hand and pressed it warmly. Then in the center hall he turned the new latch and left.

PATCHING IT UP

On Sunday Edward Blount knocked on the door of his house and informed Rachel that he would like her mistress to join him for a carriage ride. He walked back and forth in front of the north portico until Cassandra appeared.

"Don't you want to come inside?"

"I thought we'd go for a drive instead."

Edward made an effort to show neither anger nor dismay. But it was clear to Cassandra that her husband had not recovered from the indignity of the wedding night.

Cassandra allowed Edward to help her onto the carriage. And she could see that, rather than come to the house for his clothing, he had purchased a new Sunday outfit. Edward wore a maroon coat but no hat, and his light brown hair which was wispy in front was brushed over his forehead. Except for rather heavy jowls, Edward Blount was a pleasant-enough looking man, at least in broad daylight. Cassandra decided it was the passion of their wedding night that had distorted his features and made them grotesque.

Edward drove his carriage slowly. He passed the company store, the old post office (which he wanted the federal government to reactivate), the grist mill, the forge, two of the three saw mills, and the village church on Quaker Bridge Road. Everywhere he went he nodded to the men and women he passed, and he waved to the children. It occurred to Cassandra that this was all done deliberately. She had no doubt word of their quarrel had spread about town. It was not every day that newlyweds parted company. And the affairs of the ironmaster's son were as much a concern of the inhabitants of Atsion as the ironworks themselves. Apparently her husband was determined to show that there was not much substance to the rumors. Cassandra did not hold this against Edward. But she recognized that Edward had his own reasons for taking her for a drive, apart from his fear of entering the ironmaster's house after what had happened last Sunday.

At a clearing on Atsion Lake, Edward drew his carriage to a stop.

"I understand Jesse was in to see you," he said.

"He wanted to know what my intentions were." Cassandra made no move to descend from the carriage.

"And so do I."

"I have no intention of leaving the house."

"And what are your intentions regarding our marriage?"

"That depends on you, Edward."

"On me?"

"I'll not be ill-used by you."

"I meant no harm."

"But great harm was done. I don't know if it can ever be undone."

"You talk as if I wanted to do you an injury. All I wanted—"

"I know what you wanted. And I was prepared to give it to you. But you showed no patience, no tenderness."

"I love you, Cassandra. I—"

"It's not love you're talking about. It's lechery. And I'll not be the victim of it."

Edward could see that a difficult time was in store for him. He could not understand how this had come about. Other men married and bedded their wives, and no more was heard of it. But his marriage was like a breach of the peace. And, unsuspecting, he had walked into the middle of it.

What made things more difficult was that he wanted Cassandra so badly. Even as she sat there remonstrating with him, with no thought of passion in her mind, his own passions were rising. Only now she was dressed to the neck and completely unattainable.

"What do you want me to do?" he asked at last. The little dimple in his chin quivered.

"What do you want to do?"

"I want to return home."

"And you'll wait?"

"Wait for what?"

"Wait for the time when I'm ready for you."

"When will that be?"

"When you've learned to treat me as your wife, not as a Tuckerton hussy."

Edward was too humiliated to make his concession in words, so he merely nodded.

"Good. Now you can take me to lunch at Quaker Bridge."

SEMBLANCES

When Cassandra looked into the mirror of her dressing table that night, she was not pleased with what she saw. It was one thing to marry Edward Blount in the hope that one day she would come to love him. It was another to face the scalding truth. She would never love the man she now called her husband. And his presence in the next room, where he was rattling through drawers to let her know he was there, only pointed up the desperateness of her situation. Edward was in the next room as part of the understanding he had arrived at with Cassandra. In time, if all went well, he would find his legitimate place in the master bedroom. But for Cassandra that time would never come. She had all to do to keep him away from her on their wedding night. How did she expect to hold him at a distance from now on?

What Cassandra should have done, she realized, was not allow the marriage in the first place. But any doubts she had about marrying Edward Blount—and she had them—were dissipated by Nathaniel Harrah's betrayal. Until then she had been torn between leading a penniless life on Burnt Tavern Road with a sometime artist and an outsider, a stranger to the Pines but at least a man she loved, or marrying an ironmaster's son and all that his position entailed. The prospect of ever marrying Edward Blount stood at a considerable distance even then, but at least she could pretend to be his wife.

Now all pretense was gone. Just as Harrah had destroyed any illusion she might have that the two could make a happy life together, with a Gypsy van for a home and a hand-to-mouth existence, so had Edward destroyed whatever illusions Cassandra held that she could carry out her bedroom responsibilities.

But having made this marriage, intolerable as it was, she wanted something to show for her trouble. And it looked to be a great trouble indeed. Jesse Richards and all the new friends she had made would not countenance so quick a dissolution of her marriage. Just what they would countenance, she did not know. She had only her instincts to go by. She had to have something to show; otherwise the venture would be a total loss. And that something would be the ironmaster's house.

For one thing, she had no place else to go. Burnt Tavern Road was gone. Bill Hostetler was on the run. There was precious little he could do for his "daughter." There was only the house. In Atsion the big house was at the center of things. It stood for prestige and stability. Husband or no husband, the house would be just compensation for a bad bargain.

"Shall we dine together tonight?" Edward asked this question the next morning when Cassandra came downstairs for breakfast.

"If it pleases you."

"I thought we might have the manager and his wife join us."

"Isn't it too soon to be entertaining?"

"Too soon?"

"Newly married couples generally want—"

"To be alone?"

"To be free of social obligations."

"Perhaps you're right."

Cassandra did not trust him to be so agreeable.

"On the other hand," she said, "a visit might be just the thing. Why don't we ask Jesse and his wife to join us? Make it Friday night instead. It will give Rachel sufficient time to get things ready."

"What about the manager?"

"He's too close to home, don't you think?"

Cassandra did not quite understand what the manager did at the Atsion ironworks. She knew only that the ironmaster, Edward's father, had gone in retirement to Mount Holly to live with his daughter and that, in name at least, Edward was now the ironmaster. But Edward had made it known that he would leave most of the manufacturing decisions to his manager, Mr. Etheridge, and that he would spend the bulk of his time developing land holdings near Medford.

"Then it's settled. It'll be Jesse and his wife—on Friday. I'll send word to Batsto." Edward was pleased that at least the semblance of marriage was taking shape.

Jesse Richards and his wife arrived late in the afternoon. Sarah Richards was six years younger than Jesse and had borne him six children. The daughter of Reverend Haskins of St. George's Church in Philadelphia, she had never lost her religious upbringing. She was a pious, gentle, reserved woman in sharp contrast to her exuberant, dynamic, larger-than-life husband.

"We'd stay the night," she said. "But we have visitors coming tomorrow morning."

Cassandra had wondered how she would handle their staying over if the matter came up. She was relieved outright to know that no pretense at being married would be necessary that night.

In the drawing room Richards showed her a sketch of the new grist mill being built in Batsto. "Will make us self-sufficient," he said. "Will give us flour enough to bread all of Batsto."

"Even the new mouths to feed," said Mrs. Richards.

"Yes," said the ironmaster, "I understand your friend Molly

Pitchard is with child. I know the girl well. Gave her a pair of silver candlesticks for her wedding. Her husband works on one of my ships.''

With child? Cassandra wondered. Not Nathaniel Harrah's. Then she allowed that it was probably Molly's husband's. They would know soon enough. How quickly a child's face takes form and betrays an uncanny resemblance. Unless the child favored Molly.

"She'll make a good mother," said Cassandra of her one-time friend. "She needs someone to fondle and care for."

"Don't we all," said Mrs. Richards.

"I think it better that young couples wait," argued Jesse Richards. "They should come to know each other before starting a family. There's time enough for little ones once their parents find out who they are."

With these words Cassandra sensed that she had an ally in Jesse Richards, a formidable one at that.

"I couldn't agree with you more, Mr. Richards—"

"Jesse."

"Jesse, then." Cassandra poured some port for the ironmaster and sherry for his wife. It was only as an afterthought that she asked Edward his preference.

"Whatever you're drinking, dear."

"Even hemlock?"

Edward was visibly shaken. "Well, make it port then."

"And what will you do," asked Mrs. Richards, "when Edward goes to Medford to sell that land of his?"

"I'll redecorate the house."

"You don't like Empire?"

"Not all of it. It's too stiff, too formal. I almost prefer tavern furniture."

Jesse Richards burst forth a hearty laugh. "Tavern furniture, Cassandra! My girl, you have the daring of a hussar! I've always said we place too much stock in taste and fashion."

"Oh, the house will be tasteful once I've finished with it. But it may not be fashionable."

"And how do you feel about all this, Edward?"

"Well, Sarah, I really haven't given it much thought. It was my father's house for so long. I never had any notion of changing it."

"How is your father?"

"Quite ill. He insisted the wedding go on without him."

"All these years an ironmaster," mused Sarah Richards, "and then to be stricken. Let that be a lesson to you, Jesse."

"But what else would I do, my dear? A man's work is his life.

Oh, there's time enough for family and friends and parties. But it's the work that gives meaning to things. Where would I be without Batsto?"

"And where would Batsto be without you, Jesse?" interjected Edward gracefully.

"Exactly. That's where the real marriage is. Even Sarah understands that."

"Do I? Well, I suppose I do," said Mrs. Richards, noticing Rachel for the first time. "But I see that dinner is waiting."

The dinner proved to be a quiet affair as both Jesse Richards and Edward were voracious eaters. Conversation gave way to the rattling of dishes and the scraping of silverware against platters. Rachel had served fried chicken, a good choice, as there were legs and breasts and thighs and wings enough for six. And cranberry tarts and coffee filled the hollows that remained.

When the ironmaster and his wife were ready to leave, Sarah Richards embraced Cassandra, then Edward, and wished them well.

Edward responded to this by putting his arm round Cassandra's waist and drawing her close.

"We'll be most happy, Sarah. I assure you."

But Jesse Richards saw that Cassandra could barely suffer her husband's touch, much less his arm. And the ironmaster thought Edward's display of affection under the circumstances unseemly.

"Drop by to see me when you can, Edward."

"I will, Jesse."

"And as you will be busy altering the house, Cassandra, I will drop by to see you."

"Whenever you wish," said Cassandra, moving free of Edward. "You're always welcome."

A WAR OF ATTRITION

"That was uncalled for," said Edward when they were alone.

"What?"

"Your telling Sarah that you're going to make changes in the house."

"But I am."

"What for?"

"I don't like things the way they are. A house should reflect the person in it."

"Shouldn't we wait?"

"For what?"

"To see how things work out?"

Cassandra did not mistake his meaning. "Either you want me to live here or you don't. If you don't, I'll leave tomorrow."

"Of course I want you to live here."

"Then let's not discuss the matter any further."

On Saturday Edward visited his manager, Mr. Etheridge, and spent the day with him at the ironworks. When he returned for dinner, Edward announced the he was leaving for Medford Monday morning.

"Shall we attend church tomorrow?" he asked.

"I'd rather not."

"Why not?"

"I'm not a churchgoer. I told you that when you were courting me."

"But I'd rather not attend alone."

"Then don't go."

"Aren't you being unreasonable, Cassandra?"

"I don't think so."

"But there are appearances to keep up. After all, I am the ironmaster now. It will not do for me not to be seen at church."

"I said you can go alone. You can sit with Mr. and Mrs. Etheridge. You can say that I'm not feeling well."

"What about the next time?"

"We'll worry about the next time then."

Edward studied his wife but was unable to fathom her. "You're a difficult woman, Cassandra."

"Not with everybody," she said. She felt she did not have to explain herself further.

On Monday morning Edward mounted his horse and rode off.

As Cassandra watched from the window, she experienced a feeling of release, a surge of joy. For a week at least she was free to be herself, to undertake whatever project she had in mind.

She felt no sense of guilt about this. She justified all she did on the ground that her husband had misbehaved towards her. She was caught in a terrible vise. Like it or not, she was married. Like it or not, Edward expected certain things of her, spousal rights or whatever they called it.

At the same time, Cassandra was not proud of the way she treated Edward. She did not like herself for demeaning him. But what else could she do? Who was there to turn to? Edward did not look like Nathaniel Harrah, talk like Nathaniel Harrah, or fill a room like Nathaniel Harrah. With all his treachery, Nathaniel Harrah rendered him a Lilliputian to Harrah's Gulliver. But there was no Nathaniel Harrah anymore. He had disappeared into the world outside the Pines. And Cassandra would have sent him away had he reappeared. How could she do otherwise? How could she forgive his duplicity? That Harrah had betrayed her and her feelings for him made any coming together again impossible. Never to say who he was and what he was doing on Burnt Tavern Road— this was what pained her most of all. She had given freely of herself and he had held back on everything.

And so Cassandra turned away from the thoughts that troubled her, and she made a list of pieces she wanted removed from the house and stored away. And through the mails she ordered furniture from a cabinet maker in Philadelphia, including an 18th Century breakfront for the crown glass china and an Old Tavern bonnet-top secretary.

Jesse Richards called on her during the week. Had she mended things with Edward before he left?

"No."

"What's wrong, girl?"

"Everything."

"Everything?"

"I can't stand for him to touch me."

"Didn't he touch you during the courtship?"

"A chaste kiss, no more. He was afraid of frightening me away."

"You can't go on like this," said Richards.

"I know."

"End the marriage."

"I can't."

"You mean you won't."

"I can't because it's all I've got," pleaded Cassandra.

"You can stay with us at Batsto—until you've made a new life for yourself. I've known Edward since he was a boy. But I will do that for you and be glad of it."

"I'm grateful for that, Jesse. Truly grateful for the time I've already spent with you. But I will not be dependent on anyone, even you. I will be the mistress of my own house. I will guide my own life, no matter how difficult the situation seems."

"Then there's nothing more to say."

"But we'll still be friends?"

"Of course, Cassandra."

"You'll not throw me to the wolves?"

"Not while I'm alive."

"Give my love to Mrs. Richards."

"I will." And off he went.

DRAWING BLOOD

When Edward did not return from Medford on the expected day, Cassandra began to think something might have happened to him. A lame horse or an encounter with a highwayman. At first Cassandra pretended concern. There was a commonality of feeling among people, wasn't there? And Edward was now legally kin. But then Cassandra dropped all pretense, despising herself for her hypocrisy. The truth was she wanted him out of her life. The hard truth—and this she would not admit to herself—was that she wanted him dead. With Edward dead, she would be free of her marriage and mistress of the iromaster's mansion. To free herself of him while he was still alive was too uncertain a business and too painful a struggle.

Edward did not return the next day either. Instead he sent a message to the house.

"This is for you, Ma'am," said the messenger. "It's from Mr. Blount."

Inside the house Cassandra opened the package and found a pearl necklace ensconced in a velvet box. A note lay beneath the necklace.

"I do love you, Cassandra—Edward."

Cassandra snapped the box shut. She took the necklace, the box, and the note and threw them on the trash heap. Then she told Rachel she was going for a ride. "I need some fresh air. I may go to Speedwell."

"The air is no fresher there than here."

"But it's one place I haven't looked yet. And who knows, Bill may be working there."

"Bill Hostetler?"

"Yes."

"Unless there's a tavern," said Rachel, "it's not likely."

"He'll get his tavern yet," promised Cassandra. "All I've got to do is find him."

Edward returned from Medford and when he discovered what had happened to the pearl necklace left again. He was not so much in rage as a state of shock. A few days later he reappeared with a box of chocolates.

"I don't like chocolates," said Cassandra.

"They're not for you, my dear. They're for me."

There now began a war of attrition. Undeclared, it was conducted in earnest. Cassandra's strategy was to deny her husband all the comforts of home—talk, concern, companionship—and, of course, the amenities of bed. Edward's strategy was to be unpredictable. One night he would say he was staying for dinner but would not show up. The next night he would appear unexpectedly. Hadn't he told Rachel he was coming?

After two months of such goings-on, a kind of uneasy truce was established. Cassandra laid claim to the bulk of the house, the new furniture, which was arriving daily, and the master bedroom. Edward settled for the stable; the study, which contained the records of the ironworks; and the guest room. They breakfasted separately, did not take lunch together, but sat at the same dining table for the evening meal. After dinner Edward sat in the second drawing room, sipping sherry, smoking cigars, or munching on a box of chocolates. And Cassandra went downstairs to the kitchen where at the oak work table she reminisced—and Rachel listened— about Burnt Tavern Road. At bedtime Cassandra gave no thought to Edward anymore, though the guest room, where he slept, was just a wall away. She thought only of Nathaniel Harrah and could not understand, despite what had happened at Burnt Tavern Road, why he had never come for her.

One night her recollection of Harrah was particularly vivid. Though she was dreaming, she was certain that his presence was palpable and substantial. She clung to her dream but was impatient to open her eyes and find him.

When she awoke she found Edward hovering over her. And as soon as he saw that she was awake he lay himself down on top of her and tried to kiss her on the lips.

"Get off me!" Cassandra cried, only faintly aware that it was not yet dawn.

He held her arms down and pushed his face against her turned-aside cheek.

"You must be insane!" she screamed, struggling to free herself.

"Not insane enough to live in separate rooms," he heaved. "I'm through with it!"

Edward twisted his body so that his weight kept her left arm down and his right arm was free to maneuver. Ripping at her night dress, he tore it at her breast. His quick movement caused the oil lamp near the bed to flicker.

When his mouth pressed against hers, Cassandra bit his lip and, drawing blood, spat the blood back in his face. Shocked by her action, Edward yielded his grip for a moment. Cassandra wriggled free and toppled off the bed.

Getting to her feet, she seized the oil lamp with both hands. "I'll throw this at your face and burn the whole house down if you come at me again!''

Her husband remained atop the bed on all fours.

"I mean what I say!'' she hissed.

"All right.'' Edward waved his arm and abandoned the bed on the far side of the room. Standing in his nightshirt, he did not seem so frightening a figure as when he lay so close to her.

Cassandra took one hand from the lamp and tried with her shredded gown to cover her breast. Despairing of it, she looked across the room at Edward and shouted, "Here, take your last look of it!'' She let her breast fall free. "You'll see it no more. From this day on I want you out of the house!''

"It's my house, Cassandra.''

"No longer. Take what you want out of it. But the house is now mine. If you ever come back here, I'll see to it you're arrested for sodomy.''

"Sodomy!''

"Yes, I'll tell the whole town you've committed sodomy. How does that sit with you, Mr. Edward Blount? Yes, from now on I'm Cassandra Trescott. And make of that what you will!''

Edward was astonished by what he saw. But even he knew that his tenure at the ironmaster's house was at an end.

"I curse the day I met you,'' he said, making for the door.

"No more than I,'' shouted Cassandra. "Go straight to the devil!''

When he left, she found herself shaking and surrendering to tears. But once it dawned on her that the war of attrition with her husband was over, her tears gave way to short bursts of laughter and finally to one continuous run of giggles and gasping for breath.

REALITY AND UNREALITY

Jesse Richards did not desert her. Edward's departure from Atsion did not prevent him from seeing Cassandra or extending invitations to parties at Batsto. He even sent his carriage to fetch her.

With the onset of winter and the closing down of the ironworks until April, the ironmaster's mansion was aglow with warm fires and strong liquors and lilting music. And Batsto itself, normally dirty and dusty and covered with cinders and ashes from the furnace, was now white with virgin snow. The barns outside the main house lay like winter sheep burrowing in the snow drifts. The general store, the skeletal corn crib, and the frozen-wheeled grist mill looked like ghostly figures of another time. Only the sheep shed and the stone silage pit retained any color. And there was black smoke from the wheelwright and blacksmith shop.

But Cassandra loved it. For her, winter was a repurification. The heat, the filth, the passions of summer were filtered clean by the cold, bracing air of January and February. And if her feet were numb under her carriage blanket and her ears were half-frozen by the wind, she could nevertheless feel the spirit within her rejoicing. It was all over. The mistakes of summer were behind her and she had the keen sense of a new beginning. The ironmaster of Batsto had stood by her and had plucked her from an uncertain doom. Now she was a guest at his house and a centerpiece at his parties.

Mrs. Richards was not all that happy over Cassandra's separation. She thought Edward Blount to be as fine a young man as she knew and he was distantly related to her sister-in-law. But she, no less than Jesse, went to a great deal of trouble to make Cassandra feel welcome and to include her in all the evening's festivities. She saw to it that she had dancing partners, made new acquaintances, and enjoyed the music and the outdoor frolicking in the snow.

If Cassandra had any concern, it was over money matters.

"I've had numerous letters, even threats of legal action over the furniture," she confided to Jesse. "I've even had trouble putting meat on the table."

"Edward left you no money?"

"None."

"Let me speak to him in Medford when I go to the Bank."

A week later Richards brought her good news. "Edward's agreed to an allowance. It should be more than enough for your needs."

"In return for?"

"In return for nothing."

"But I don't understand."

Richards wore an infectious smile. "Oh, he didn't do it willingly. But when I told him I'd call in his notes—"

"You have his notes?"

"Indeed I do. He's been dealing heavily in land speculation. Anyway, when I told him I'd call in his notes, he became very agreeable."

Cassandra took the ironmaster's arm. "How can I ever thank you?"

"By not spending all the money on that jughead tavern."

"How did you know about that?"

"There's very little I don't know about this part of the woods. Billy H, he calls himself. The least he could do was change his name."

"What do you think of its prospects?"

"The tavern? It'll keep him out of mischief. And put food in his belly. But little more. It's rather out of the way."

"That's just fine for Bill."

"I quite understand."

And so it went till Nathaniel Harrah found her.

They say that dreams have the pinch of reality. At least Cassandra heard it said; she could not remember where. But to Cassandra dreams were unreality. For in her dreams Harrah was forever returning on horseback or on the driver's seat of his artist's van. With a single sweep of his arm he somehow wiped Edward from the face of the earth. With hardly a gesture he made Bill and the Burnt Tavern reappear as they had stood before the fire. And in intimate embrace he confessed that Benjy was not hanged, only an effigy. Yes, Benjy was alive, though banished from the Pines. And Bill was tavernkeeper once more. And she and Harrah were free to marry. And as a wedding gift Jesse Richards would present her with the thirteen-columned ironmaster's mansion at Atsion.

But, of course, Harrah did not return. For weeks, for months, she expected him to swoop down on Batsto when she was staying there and later at Atsion. She never intended to hear him out or to forgive him for what he did, but she fully expected him to make some attempt to explain himself. He owed Cassandra that much.

No, dreams did not have the pinch of reality. Dreams were a taunt. Dreams were a bog where a path should be. And so Cassandra hated the night almost as much as the days of her new life.

Cassandra never could figure out what went wrong when she finally saw Harrah. Maybe reality was a taunt too, just like dreams. At the sight of him, her heart stopped. Oh, how she wanted things to be the way they had been on Burnt Tavern Road. But everything they said worked against them.

"Yes, married. And at the same time, not married," she admitted. And she admitted a few other things too, things a woman shouldn't admit to her lover. But she could not build a new life on lies, so she made a clean breast of it.

All this proved too much for Harrah. He was undone by the revelations, the hard truth. It was with new eyes that he now saw Cassandra. The love that had once dwelt there was all but extinguished. In its place was hurt and anger and cold resentment. She had no choice but to send him away.

"Leave now," she said, "and maybe some day you'll come back. But if you do, let's not talk of Burnt Tavern Road and the things that divide us. Let's not talk at all."

And so at the end he tipped his hat. A tip of the hat and a meeting of the eyes. That was all. He had no more for her than that, and he left.

Cassandra must have relived this day a thousand times. His image was always before her, and that meeting of the eyes. And in her sleep she could dream of nothing but his parting on horseback. It was an anguish, that parting—a deep, bitter anguish—and it pierced her heart like a bullet.

But slowly the wound began to heal. It was tissue badly scarred; it never really gave her any relief from the gnawing, hollow pain. But it was enough to protect her psyche from further hurt.

Besides, she had the house to keep her busy. It was in a constant state of alteration. Furniture moving, carpentry, and new wall paper patterns prevented one from knowing just what the house looked like. But only in this way was Cassandra able to remove any vestiges of Edward Blount.

Morever, she had made a reputation in Atsion. She was the Pinelands girl who had somehow unsurped the "big house." Used to tend bar and wait on tables. But now she was a woman to reckon with. From appearances the house was all hers. There were even a few who called it "the ironmistress's mansion."

Cassandra heard this whispered in the general store. The ironmistress's mansion with its thirteen iron columns. If this was the ironmistress's mansion, then Cassandra was the ironmistress. So be it. Only why wasn't Nathaniel Harrah there to share it with her?

Part Two

HARRAH'S NEW LIFE

PORTRAITS DON'T LIE

Harrah had taken a page out of Hostetler's book and bought a tavern at Cooper's Point. The cedar-board tavern was well-placed, standing near the ferry and the livery stable and flanking a store and a dozen or so dwellings nearby. Harrah had been offered the business before he went looking for Cassandra. But despite the good price, he had put off buying it until he returned empty-handed and heartsick from Atsion, Atsion where a married Cassandra had made a shambles out of mistaken notions and misunderstandings. In a Camden bank he plumped down his savings, signed a few notes, and consummated the deal.

"Ale and Table" proved to be a moneymaker from the start. With additional ferries dragged into service for the spring and the summer and a run of hot days bringing people over from Philadelphia for the day, passengers crowded into the bar. There were some nights Harrah counted more than he had made in a month in other employment. And he was not half trying. The only thing he did differently from his predecessor was to serve a free lunch of German sausages with the drinks. So spicy were the sausages it took several mugs of ale to put out the fire.

In a matter of months Harrah found himself free to leave the tavern in the care of hired help. And he ventured into Philadelphia to see the new Railway Station in Germantown.

Harrah in the past few years had followed with great interest reported experiments with iron tracks and railway cars. He had heard in 1830, before he went to the Pines, of the celebrated contest between a horse and Peter Cooper's steam locomotive outside Baltimore. The engine, *Tom Thumb*, had lost the race to the big gray stagecoach horse harnessed to a railroad car. But the point had been made. Steam power, already at work on side-wheel boats, was the way of the future for hauling freight and passengers.

And in England the Stockton and Darlington Railway and later the Liverpool and Manchester Railway had demonstrated that the iron horse was not only feasible but could reach speeds of twelve to thirty miles per hour! Harrah remembered reading one newspaper account of Robert Stephenson's famous locomotive, the *Rocket*. "It seemed indeed to fly, presenting one of the most sublime spectacles of mechanical ingenuity and human daring the world ever beheld."

All this fired Harrah's imagination, as engineers were said to fire their boilers. And he went to Germantown to see for himself.

He discovered that he had visited at an opportune time. Not

only were the Germantown and Norristown Railway cars and coaches in view, little more than green stagecoaches on rails; but an exhibition of locomotive models from England, Scotland, and Wales was on dazzling display.

His mind was agog with all the mechanical doodads and ingenious devices he found on the models. The main attraction of the exhibition was a copy of George Stephenson's 2-2-0 *Planet*-type locomotive and tender. The blue-barreled boiler had a protective outside frame, cylinders inside the smokebox, a steam-dome, and a water-jacketed firebox, with the cranked axle and driving wheels nearest to the firebox. Its finely fluted chimney rose like a golden tower, its shine complementing the wheel spokes and the boiler bands.

"All the handles that get hot are ivory," one man observed.

"I still prefer copper," commented his companion who had an attractive woman on his arm.

"Notice the feed pumps. They are driven off the main axle and the springs and frames are above the axles."

"I hear the reversing system is difficult to operate."

"No more difficult than ours."

"Do you know this man?" the young woman asked her escort, indicating Harrah.

Harrah looked up. She was a luxuriant brunette, with big brown eyes, a classic genteel face, lovely shoulders, and an inquiring gaze. Harrah thought she looked familiar but he could not be sure.

Her escort turned round.

"No, my dear."

"Then perhaps he knows me."

Her escort introduced himself. "My name is George Brookens of the Germantown and Norristown Railway. This is my sister, Mrs. Pierot."

"Georgina Pierot," his sister added.

"Delighted. And I'm Nathaniel Harrah of Cooper's Point."

Satisfied that he had executed the necessary formalities, Brookens felt that he could leave his sister alone while he continued to inspect George Stephenson's locomotive.

"You seem to be staring at me," Mrs. Pierot said with a pretty smile.

"I believe I did your portrait once."

"My portrait? Mr. Thomas Sully painted my portrait. And a handsome sum I paid for it."

"Mine was a charcoal sketch. Done on Burnt Tavern Road. But I'm not surprised you don't remember it."

"Burnt Tavern Road? Last summer? Of course, I remember.

I was on my way to get married when you did it. But you look more prosperous than you did then."

"I am. Then I was an itinerant artist working in a tavern. Now I am a tavern owner."

"Still, Mr. Harrah, I'm flattered that you recognized me."

"How could I forget a face as pretty as yours?"

Mrs. Pierot blushed a smile. "I have a confession to make," she said. "My husband likes your portrait better than Mr. Sully's."

"You're sure it isn't the price he prefers?"

"No, it's the quality. He says your portrait shows more character than the oil painting. And I'm inclined to agree with him."

"I would doubt that very much."

There was now a challenge in Georgina Pierot's smile, a challenge that had the faintest suggestion of taunt.

"Then you shall see them and judge for yourself. Do you have a carriage?"

"No, I came on horseback."

"Then let me see whether I can borrow my brother's."

She left him for a moment and could be seen talking with George Brookens. The gentleman took a second look at Harrah, then, satisfied with what his eye took in, he nodded.

"George will go home with a business acquaintance," she said upon her return. "If you will take the reins and drive, I will show you the way."

Nodding, Harrah tied his horse to the rear of the carriage. Then he climbed aboard and waited for directions. He did not know what to make of Georgina Pierot, but he was not about to turn down so handsome an offer.

After a long but pleasant ride which took them from countryside to the streets of Philadelphia, Mrs. Pierot called a halt to the carriage. She pointed out a red brick residence on Elfreth's Alley, one of several row houses on a cobble-stoned street, and declared it to be hers. Harrah somehow had expected more, a large colonial mansion with extensive grounds. But he said nothing as he helped the young woman down and turned over his mount and George Brookens's horse and carriage to a boy who took them to a nearby livery stable.

"When I was first married," said Mrs. Pierot, "we moved into a large house on Germantown Avenue. But in no time at all my husband lost a considerable sum at cards. So we now live here."

"The place is quite handsome," remarked Harrah.

"But a step down, I assure you."

In the narrow vestibule of the house Mrs. Pierot took his hat. "I'm afraid we're without servants just now. They grew tired of not getting paid and left without notice. But I can get you some tea. Or coffee, if you prefer."

"Nothing yet."

"Ah, you're impatient to see the portraits."

She ushered him into the drawing room and Harrah immediately caught sight of the Sully portrait hanging over the mantelpiece. A fine example of stylized art, with dashing brushstroke and brilliant color, it was almost flawless. If it had a fault, it was perhaps too pink.

"It was done three months ago. Do you like it?"

"Very much."

"I'm glad."

She led him upstairs to the bedrooms.

"At first we thought to put your portrait in the guest room. But my husband did not want me, even in charcoal, to spend the night with anyone but him."

"A proper sentiment."

She opened the door to the bedroom which struck Harrah as too small for the furniture installed there. A bonnet-top secretary, a cherry wood chest-on-chest, a Sheraton washstand with bowl and pitcher, an empire chair, and a massive bonnet-canopied four-poster—all vied for a place in the chamber. The effect was one of heirloom elegance but crampedness.

"We had a magnificent master bedroom on Germantown Avenue, one that was spacious and airy. This, I am afraid, is little bigger than a maid's cubicle."

"But your portrait seems in place somehow," said Harrah.

He studied the charcoal portrait, framed on the mantel wall, which he had not seen in a twelvemonth. Though nothing more than line and shadow, the drawing seemed to leap out of its paper. A paean to youth and beauty, the face was astonishingly perfect. Though she wore a starched bonnet, Georgina Brookens emerged as the eternal female, soft, fetching, and desirable. At the same time there was no denying an enigmatic, spiritual quality about her. It was not so much in her eyes as in the cast of her extraordinary cheekbones. Such lovely contours could be nothing but spiritual as they dipped gently into luminescent flesh and just the right curve of jaw. Yes, it was probably Harrah's best effort, the one flawless work in his short-lived career. "Inspired," Cassandra had said at the time in a fit of jealousy.

And it disturbed Harrah to think of all that had happened since he had done the portrait. Transformed from an itinerant artist to a jack-of-all-trades at Hostetler's tavern, he was now himself a tavernkeeper. And she, unhappily married to a man with an apparent weakness for cards. At odd moments during the year, Harrah had wondered what difference his life would have made had he fallen in love with the girl of the portrait instead of Cassandra. Not that he preferred her to Cassandra; he did not. It was just that Georgina Brookens represented the other side of the coin in his fantasies about women. Dark where Cassandra was fair, full-bodied where Cassandra was slim, genteel where Cassandra was uncultivated, cool where Cassandra was impetuous—though Cassandra's fire burned cool—Georgina Brookens put his imagination in blast.

"The truth is, I should have thrown your portrait away," said Mrs. Pierot suddenly.

Harrah was taken by surprise. "Why?"

"It's only a reminder of what I was, what I might have been. And the thought pains me."

Harrah knew what Mrs. Pierot was talking about. All portraits had the seed of discontent in them, a seed harvested by time. Maybe this was why Cassandra steadfastly refused to have her portrait done. Why perpetuate one moment at the expense of all others?

"I was still innocent then," said Mrs. Pierot. "I was full of faith in the future and in providence. I believed that only good would happen to me because I was good. If I had a fault, it was self-righteousness."

"That's not a fatal flaw," said Harrah. "The years have a way of patching it up."

"It's kind of you to say that. But even a year has taken its toll. The girl of your portrait was full of expectation. The woman you see now has already known bitter disappointment."

Harrah was at a loss what to say. He merely watched as Georgina Pierot gracefully swung her gown to a side and sat her fine woman's figure down.

"I can't have children," she confided. "At least I haven't been able to until now. And of course my husband is an habitual gambler."

He was aware suddenly that she was sobbing. Her splendid woman's figure was pulsating with grief. Instinctively Harrah put his arm around her.

"There's no need for that," he said.

She responded to the softness of his voice. "I know." But she continued to sob and in waves and tremors to give way to her emotions. She stood up as if to shake her wretchedness, and Harrah offered her his handkerchief. But she found that she had to lean on the bed to control her tears.

"You may wonder why my husband wasn't at the exhibition

today, why my brother had to escort me.''

"I gave it no thought."

"At the last moment he heard of a game of cards at some hotel on Market Street. He disappeared quicker than a wink. Fortunately George had stayed the night with us and he insisted I go anyway.''

Although Harrah was not quite embarrassed by these revelations, he was not particularly keen on having them go on.

"I'm sure he will be home soon," he said. "And much as I enjoyed seeing the portrait again, I'd best be going.''

"Soon? If he returns home by tomorrow afternoon I'd be very much surprised. You see, if he wins he plays until he loses. And when he loses he gets very drunk. I'd very much like you to stay awhile. I can't promise dinner but I'm sure there is a cake in the cupboard and I can prepare a pot of tea.''

Harrah sensed that what he said now would shape more than the evening. His inclination was to leave. But, apart from the fact that he dreaded dining alone and spending the evening in his lodgings, he knew that Mrs. Pierot was in a wretched state. His compassion for her and a sense that somehow his portrait was to blame for her condition persuaded him to reconsider.

"Very well, I'll stay. But only for a little while."

Mrs. Pierot smiled through her tears.

"I'm so glad," she said. With that she kissed him on the mouth and left for the kitchen.

Harrah was transformed by the kiss. Until now he was a bystander in a domestic scene, with one of the partners absent. But now he saw himself in a position to fulfill half-forgotten fantasies. Though he had never admitted this to Cassandra, he had at the time of the drawing given much thought to the portrait and the young woman who sat for it. For a change, he had been rather impressed with his skill; not at all critical. And he did not doubt that he was inspired. In fact, it had been a week or more before he finally put the portrait and its subject out of his mind. To see it come alive again, to be able to embrace it after all this time was an opportunity not to be missed.

Mrs. Pierot returned carrying a tray. Her body was pitched slightly forward, accentuating her gown at the waist and the curve of her stomach and swinging her breasts forward. She set the tray down on the empire chair which she pulled to the side of the bed. Then, seating herself on the bed, she invited Harrah to join her.

Harrah had no thought for tea or cake, though he was hungry. He could think only of the splendidly supple figure that was settled snugly beside him. But he made an attempt at eating.

"Aren't you hungry? You barely nibbled at the cake.''

Harrah looked at the tray but said nothing. Putting his cake down, he fixed his eyes on Mrs. Pierot. The weight of her bosom rounded its softness even more and the shine of her gown's fabric added to its luster.

She leaned over to pour the tea.

"Don't bother," said Harrah. "I'd much rather—"

Mrs. Pierot looked up at him. "Not now," she said, removing his hand from her breast. "Next time, but not now."

Harrah withdrew.

"I'm not a trollop," she said.

"I know that."

"When I kissed you, it was for your kindness. I couldn't bear to be alone tonight."

"I understand. But your kiss—"

"Yes?"

"Led me to believe—"

"That I wanted affection? Well, perhaps I did."

"I did not mean to offend you."

"I wasn't offended. I did say 'next time,' did I not?"

"So you did."

"Will I see you tomorrow?" she asked.

"I'll have to get back to the tavern. I'm expecting a big delivery."

"I see." She took his hand and tenderly kissed it. "Then it will have to be now after all."

RAILROAD MAN

The next time Harrah saw Georgina Pierot was at the "Ale and Table." He had just finished supervising the unloading of a shipment of casks, with a team of fetlocked Clydesdales looking on, when he caught a glimpse of her between the traces.

"Georgina! How did you get here?"

"By ferry, silly. I couldn't wait until next Wednesday."

He took her arm. "It's too hot to be standing in the sun."

He took her inside, but he was somewhat embarrassed by the nature of his trade. "It's not iron or railroads," he said, apologizing for the noise and the ceaseless scraping of chairs. "But it's a livelihood."

"If it's railroads you're interested in—and why else would you be at the exhibition—I could get my brother George to meet with you."

"Well, the interest is there. But I'm as thirsty for capital as I am for ale."

He signalled for a mug and indicated wine for the lady. "What I said isn't altogether true," he confessed. "I'm doing quite well for the short time I've been here."

"I have no doubt." She placed her hand on his arm. "I've missed you."

"It's only been a couple of days."

"Much too long," she whispered.

"Wednesday will come soon enough."

"Will it? You may not know that I'm a sea captain's daughter."

"Really?"

"Yes, out of Barnegat."

"I know the place."

"But widow's walks are not for me," said Georgina. "Do you fathom my meaning?"

Even amid the crowded tables and the smoke-filled bar, Georgina looked untouched by the wash of humanity that filled the tavern. Her skin glowed with a pearly luster and her gown was sky-blue fresh.

"Is there a private place, a room we can go to?" she whispered.

"Only my lodgings," said Harrah.

"And where are they?"

"Just next door. But it's mid-afternoon."

"What better time?"

He scarcely locked the door of his sitting room when she embraced him and fixed her mouth on his.

"Tell me you're not pleased to see me."

"That," he said, "would be a damnable lie."

She kissed him again, but when his hand reached for her breast she backed away.

"I have only two good gowns. It wouldn't do to soil them." Saying this, she disappeared into his bedroom.

When Georgina came out again, she didn't have a stitch of clothing on.

"Well," she said. "Are you going to remove your shirt and your boots? Or is there going to be a wall of cloth between us?"

Harrah did as he was bid and followed her into the bedroom. Sometime later, when he was already slipping out of her, she threw a sheet over the lower half of her body and lay back with her arms folded under her head. Naked from the waist and swelling at the breasts, she looked like a graceful ship's figurehead. And, of course, there were those classic facial features, enough to drive any man to sea.

"Would you like to meet with George?" she asked with love and contentment in her voice. "He might advise you on the railroads." She smiled as his hand found her breast again.

"Won't he be suspicious of our relationship?"

"George is a gentleman. He would suspect nothing—even if he did."

"All right."

"Wednesday, then."

"But I thought Wednesday was our day."

"And so it will be," she said, feigning a kiss, "after we meet with George."

"The railroads are the stagecoaches of tomorrow," George Brookens said as they took lunch at the City Hotel. "There won't be a town of any consequence that doesn't have a railway passing through it."

"And so what do you advise Nathaniel?" asked Georgina.

"So it's Nathaniel now."

"Yes, Nathaniel Harrah. It's always been my name."

"Well, Mr. Harrah. I'd get hold of every dollar I could beg, borrow, and pilfer. And I'd invest it in railroads. Why, in ten years you won't know the country. There'll be as many railroads as there are canals."

"But don't you see a danger in them?" said Georgina.

"Oh, you've been reading those Philadelphia posters, have you?"

"Well, they say frightening things. There was an explosion

which demolished a train in Charleston.''

"Of course there was. The idiot fireman tied down the engine's safety valve! How else was the steam to escape!''

"What about the minister of Parliament who was struck down by a locomotive? Near Liverpool, I believe.''

"How many more men have been struck down by runaway horses!''

"I'm just relating to you what I read,'' said Georgina.

"I understand,'' said George Brookens who had none of his sister's good looks and resembled her in no discernible way. His hair was a nondescript brown, combed to a side. His face, though clean-shaven, was stubbled with whiskers underneath the skin. And his eyes were neither blue nor hazel, just a muddy wash on a couple of yellowing egg shells. "And there are a couple of horror stories you haven't mentioned yet. Such as barns being burned to the ground by the locomotive's hot cinders. Such as cows being unable to give milk. Such as women suffering miscarriages at the mere sight of a steam-driven railway car. I've heard them all. These are the same stories that were told when the big blast furnaces were built in Jersey and steamboats first plied the waters.''

"But the stories enjoy wide currency,'' said Georgina. "And people tend to believe them.''

"All the same, the age of railroads is upon us. Look, Harrah. Only last year the Camden and Amboy Railway opened its first section of track. You should have put your money into that instead of a tavern.''

Harrah tended to agree with him.

"But it's not too late. Railroads are springing up all over. In Albany and Baltimore, even in the South. I'll wager that whoever plunks a dollar down on them will come away with ten in five years.''

"My husband has nothing to show for it,'' said Georgina.

"Your husband has his own form of locomotion,'' said her brother. "His vice has gotten the best of him, not the railroads.''

"Well, Nathaniel, what do you think?'' Georgina asked when they were alone once more.

"I'm just as confused as ever.''

"Wasn't George helpful?''

"Of course he was helpful. My dilemma is where to go, where to begin. For some reason I don't want to stray far from Cooper's Point, from South Jersey.''

"Do I have anything to do with that?''

Harrah was embarrassed. "You? Of course, Georgina.'' He was

embarrassed because at this moment he was thinking of someone else.

"That's what I wanted to hear," she said, taking his hand. "I think we could be happy together, Nathaniel."

"You're not happy now?"

"Of course not. How could I be happy married to Gerald? I want a man who will be a good provider. I don't want to be dependent on my brother for the few luxuries I have."

"What makes you think I'd be a good provider?"

"You're looking into railroads."

"And you think railroads are the answer."

"I haven't heard of anything better."

"And what if I remained just a tavern owner?"

"It would make no difference. That is, if it makes no difference to you. But I suspect it does."

Harrah squeezed her hand. "You're a beautiful woman, Georgina. But there are several problems. To begin with, you're married. I haven't heard any talk of a divorce."

"I haven't heard any proposals of marriage."

Harrah smiled. "That's true." He released her hand. "And then there's your brother, George."

"What has George to do with us?"

"I don't know. That's what bothers me."

Now it was her turn to smile. "George is a railroad man. It was you who expressed interest in the railroads, remember?"

Harrah did not remember. But it did not matter. He had her pretty eyes and marvelous cheekbones to look at. Besides, it was Wednesday.

ELFRETH'S ALLEY

So long as he was in company of Georgina Pierot, in intimacy or otherwise, Harrah was content to be nowhere else. But the moment they were apart—she in Philadelphia; he at his tavern at Cooper's Point—her hold over Harrah was less than compelling. The fact of her marriage—with the possibility of her husband popping up at any time—disturbed him. But more distressing was her lack of occupation. By her own admission Georgina Pierot was not likely to have children. Nor did she pursue a calling of any kind. Used to servants, she did none of her own housework. She managed, of course to get about town and to read the newspapers and to take the ferry to Cooper's Point (for which he was eternally grateful). But she had too much time on her hands. And there was in her outlook a disposition to be idle.

She did not sew, she did not paint, she did not wait table. Georgina was best at sitting—sitting for a portait, as she did last summer—or sitting on his lap with no thought to her nakedness.

Harrah had no serious complaint about this. But he despaired how things would be once she was past the childbearing age, past being beautiful and perhaps going to fat. Would she still intrigue him then? Or would all that he was experiencing now be little more than a sweet memory? Harrah liked his women active, at least committed to something or involved in more than simply playing the lady. Georgina Pierot's only physical activity occurred in bed.

And then the fact of her husband made itself strongly felt.

They had spent the night at Elfreth's Alley when Harrah awakened to a sense of danger. He threw on his clothes and aroused Georgina by shaking her shoulder.

"What is it?" she asked, still in the grip of sleep.

"I don't know, but you'd best get dressed."

"You're just anxious to leave me."

"It's not that at all."

"Then let me be."

"I really think you should get up."

She pulled aside her sheet, revealing herself once more, the smooth ivory thighs, the dimple just below her stomach, the full, red-nippled breasts. And Harrah was sorry for his apprehensions. Still, he did not stop her when she threw her robe on.

"I just have a feeling your husband will be walking in."

"Much too early for him," she said.

"In any case, I must be going." He stood up and reached for his hat.

"Won't you have a cup of tea before you go?"

"Nothing, thank you. Just a kiss."

Still half asleep, she saw him to the door.

Harrah met Mr. Pierot as he was leaving. Pierot's head was down and he was drawn to the point of emaciation. He seemed totally preoccupied. Though he wore a hat and a fashionable coat, he was unshaven and in wrinkled trousers.

"Why, Gerald!" said Georgina in excellent possession of herself. "This is Nathaniel Harrah. Mr. Harrah is in Philadelphia to meet with George. A year ago he did the portrait you're so fond of."

"Did he stay the night?" her husband asked tartly.

Georgina reprimanded him with a disdainful look. "Yes, in the servant's quarters. I thought you'd be home last night, if not for dinner, at least to sleep."

"You know I'd rather play cards than sleep," he retorted. "In fact, I'd rather play cards than—"

But the expression on his wife's face prevented him from finishing.

Harrah glanced at Georgina to see if she were in any danger from her husband, but she showed no trace of apprehension and signalled for Harrah to leave.

Harrah tipped his hat as he stepped into Elfreth's Alley. "I'm sorry we missed you last evening, Mr. Pierot. I should have liked to talk railroads with you."

"Perhaps next time, Mr. Harrah. There will be a next time, won't there?"

"Not likely. It's not often I get to visit Philadelphia. I run a tavern and it keeps me pretty busy."

"A pity. Not so much for me, as Georgina."

He turned to his wife. "I'll have my breakfast now," he said. "I had a good run last night. But this morning my luck gave out. Still, I'm ahead and that counts for something."

Harrah took the opportunity to bid goodbye to Mrs. Pierot, who threw him a kiss when her husband was distracted. Then Harrah turned and headed for the livery stable.

"ALL FOR THE PUBLIC GOOD"

Harrah planned no more visits to Philadelphia for a time. But he fully expected Georgina to visit him. When in the next few days she did not appear, he began to re-examine his resolution. At last he gave in to his fears about her safety and left word that he would be gone for a few days. Mounting his horse, he turned his back on the tavern and waited for the old wooden ferry to discharge its passengers.

"Hello there! Is that you, Nathaniel?"

Harrah turned to see Georgina in her brother's carriage, rolling down the carriage plank, with George Brookens at her side.

Harrah was both relieved and disappointed. Despite his interest in railroads, he was in no mood this bright sunny day for a business lecture. He turned his horse round and followed the carriage to the "Ale and Table."

"I brought George along so that Gerald would not get the wrong idea," explained Georgina when the three of them were seated inside the tavern.

"He made an awful fuss," said George. "But I backed your story all the way."

"Much obliged," said Harrah.

"And now you can do me a favor."

"What's that?" asked Harrah, not without caution.

"Buy us a drink."

"Of course."

The three of them chatted amiably for a while over apple jack and whiskey, and then George made his offer.

"We're selling some new shares in the Germantown and Norristown Railway. It's a splendid opportunity for you to get into the business. We're going to be expanding our line and I can say with assurance that the state legislature will speed passage of the necessary condemnation acts. If not this year, next."

"Condemnation?"

"Yes, this will enable us to buy up land for the tracks to be laid on. Otherwise we'd have to pay the asking price and we couldn't afford that."

"Is that true in Jersey, too?"

"Yes, but that's no problem. Senator Trowbridge is on the transportation committee. And he's in complete sympathy with the railroads."

"How much is he getting for his trouble?"

"Suffice to say that friends of the railroad will not starve."

37

"I don't like it," said Harrah.

"Don't like what?" asked George Brookens, taken aback.

"I don't like this marriage of government and railroad."

"It's a marriage of convenience," said Brookens. "Without it, we could not grow."

"But for the farmer and the landowner it's a shotgun wedding. What if a man doesn't want the railroads dividing up his farm? What if he has other plans for his property?"

"It's all for the public good," said Brookens, becoming annoyed. "At least in the long run. And it won't hurt your tavern any having the Camden and Amboy Railway at your door."

"Yes, but let's not quarrel over it," cautioned Georgina. "If Nathaniel has doubts or reservations, I'm sure they're justified. Why don't you run along, George? Mr. Harrah will see me home. Besides, you've got a shareholders' meeting this afternoon."

"I'm sorry, Harrah. I trust I was not too insistent."

"On the contrary, you were very informative." But Harrah did not get up to see him go.

"You're a funny fellow," said Georgina, taking his hand. "The railroads are breaking no law. Why should you take on so?"

"They're making the law. That's what troubles me."

"What if they are?"

"I was in government once. In no great capacity. But I didn't like what I saw. It won't do for a country to be corrupted in its infancy. Before it has a chance to come of age."

"All governments are corrupt, my love."

"That's like saying all women are sluts."

"I see," she said, blanching and drawing her hand away. "Maybe they are."

"I didn't mean you, Georgina."

"But in a way you did. You think I want you to invest in my brother's railroad for services rendered?"

"I think nothing of the kind!"

"Well," she confessed, "I can see where it might have looked that way. I don't deny that my brother has been giving me money. There's none to be had from my husband, you know. But that's as far as it goes. I accompany George because he is unmarried and a woman on his arm gives him a certain advantage. More than that—"

"Please, Georgina."

"I just want you to know the truth of it. There's no pretense in me where my affections are concerned. You should know that, Nathaniel."

"I do. And I'm sorry."

"I don't know that you have any money to invest. What's more, I don't care. Have I asked you for anything?"

"No."

"And I won't now. Not even your love, much as I looked forward to being with you today." Two or three tears trickled down her cheek, making Harrah even more wretched than he felt already.

Georgina got up to leave. "You needn't take me home," she said when Harrah rose too. "I believe I can catch George at the ferry." She gathered up her parasol. "Goodbye, Nathaniel." Her voice faded and seemingly trailed behind her as she disappeared in the crush of the crowd.

Harrah saw her but one more time that summer.

COOPER'S POINT

Harrah was visited by two men representing the Camden and Amboy Railway. "We're planning to extend the railroad to Cooper's Point."

"So I hear."

"This should increase patronage by a hogshead or more."

"Could very well be."

"That's why we're asking you to contribute a thousand dollars to help defray expenses."

Harrah rose from his table. "I'll not contribute a rusty nail."

"But you admit the advantage you'll have."

"Let's get this straight," said Harrah. "You're not building the railroad to accommodate the tavern. You're building it to connect up with the ferry."

"Still—"

"I'm sorry, gentlemen. I've got a business to run."

Later that day he discovered that the two men did not represent the Camden and Amboy, or any railway for that matter.

"There's all kinds of speculation going on," said his informant.

"Speculation? It's more like out-and-out thievery," remarked Harrah.

At the end of the week a fair was held announcing the start of the project. And a celebration of sorts took place. A platform was erected for the speakers, railroad men and politicians; and an American flag was draped across the speaker's podium. Stalls were set up. Cakes and pies were sold. And a huge punch bowl, paid for by the railway owners, provided sweet cider to ladies, gentlemen, and children alike. At least a dozen carriages and a few wagons cut deep ruts into the already scarred dirt road that led to the ferry. And a four-horse stagecoach from Tuckerton was discharging its passengers at the door of the tavern. But as the passengers were attracted to the festivities, Harrah stepped outside to listen to the speakers.

A spokesman for the Camden and Amboy proclaimed all the advantages of steam-driven railways and sought to dispel the fears and protestations of their opponents. His speech might have been written by George Brookens. The next speaker, a state senator from the Amboys, painted a glorious picture of railroads bringing the different parts of the state closer together. "An Erie Canal of rail and timbers—only cheaper, faster, and without the burden of having to dig ditches!"

His remarks were greeted with applause. And there was much

milling about to see an artist's rendition of the locomotives and railway cars that would soon make their scheduled way to Cooper's Point—once the funds were in place and the track completed.

But apparently no celebration of the railroads was complete without George Brookens himself and his sister, Georgina. Harrah saw them standing near the speaker's platform. George had engaged a bystander and was no doubt explaining to him the virtues of the Germantown and Norristown Railway which one day would be linked by way of the ferry to the Camden and Amboy. And Georgina cast about her to see whom among the crowd she might know. She was at this time a beautiful but pathetic figure. Her sky-blue gown caught the brightness of the day and more than one gentleman's eye. But she never ventured far from her brother and was never quite free of the role she had to play. Then, as though in response to what he was thinking, she looked towards the tavern and spotted Harrah. She stared his way for a while. It was not an unfriendly gesture but neither did it seem a peace offering. Then slowly she turned and rejoined her brother.

In this brief moment Harrah knew that Georgina was not yet through with him. She might make him pay for his transgressions. She might make him suffer for what she thought he had implied. But she had not ruled him out of her life.

There was, of course, George Brookens to contend with. His sister had a pliant nature. But George, as one might judge from his behavior on this or any other day, was all business. Harrah did not know how many shares George Brookens actually owned in the Germantown and Norristown Railway or even that he owned a significant number of them. He knew only that Brookens was engaged in the business of selling shares to interested buyers. And Harrah had ruled himself out of this group.

Still, he was glad to see Georgina again, however briefly. And when he stepped inside the tavern once more he found that his thoughts of her were warm and kindly.

Some minutes later a boy entered the tavern with Harrah's name scrawled on a message.

"For me?" asked Harrah, tipping the youngster.

"For no one else," he replied, almost by rote.

Harrah unfolded the messsage.

"Don't mind my brother. All is forgiven. Meet me at Elfreth's Alley."

Elfreth's Alley! How significant the name had become for him! Yes, Harrah was pleased by the tone of the note. And he had nothing but good feelings for Georgina. It was good being forgiven by her. It was good being invited again to Elfreth's Alley. But even

Yevish

as he read the note and appreciated it for what it was, Harrah knew he would not visit Georgina again. In the past week he had made other plans.

Part Three

IN SIN

THE LESS SAID THE BETTER

Cassandra saw him as she stepped out of the Atsion Post Office. Dressed in a white coat and brown boots, but with no trace of the dandy about him, he stood in front of his black horse and a buggy that was spanking new except for a coat of white sand sprayed on its underbottom. Yes, he was waiting for her. And when he noticed her he made no move except to indicate the buggy was hers to ride in.

Cassandra hesitated just long enough for her eyes to adjust to the South Jersey sun. Then taking Harrah's proffered arm, she stepped up to her seat and settled in. She waited until Harrah went round and climbed up beside her. And she watched as with a chuck of the reins he jostled the horse into motion.

Hers was not quite a smile. First, seven months. And now most of the summer. It had been a long wait, a long absence. But the important thing was that he was here. She could take comfort in that. She was strangely at peace with herself, even pleased.

And she was in no way disturbed by the faces that turned her way as their buggy rolled towards the mansion. She was looking well, had even put a pound or two on her thin frame. And she now had something to show for her vigil. The man she had given her first love, freely and without condition, had come back. And how elegant he looked! If this was grist for the mill of clacking tongues, so be it.

Harrah said not a word to her. What was there to say? Wasn't it enough that he was back and they were riding down Atsion's main street together? Words would only beggar their actions.

The buggy drew up at the iron-posted ironmaster's mansion and Harrah jumped off to hitch his horse. He then extended his hand and helped Cassandra down.

"You will come in?" she asked.

Harrah looked at the house, her husband's house. But he dismissed any thought of hesitation and nodded.

Though this was no more than Cassandra had expected, she was relieved that it had been decided so easily. She entered the house with a quiet elation. The sense that he was following her was almost too much for Cassandra to bear. Still, she was in reasonable control of her feelings. Why shouldn't she be? For a woman, the situation called for restraint. And over the past year she had learned to rein in her emotions. The twin horses of love and hate would run wild if permitted. Without a steady hand, one or the other would take over and she would be the slave, not the master.

In the drawing room she offered Harrah a chair, but saw that he had already settled into a Hitchcock. Though he seemed at ease, she knew that he had been under a strain, the strain of a long journey and strong emotions.

"Something to drink?" she asked.

He nodded.

"Cognac or Irish whiskey?"

"Aren't they the same?"

"The same?"

"Except for their accents, I mean."

She smiled. There would be no recriminations then. Just talk. Talk of little things. No reminders of the past or of past mistakes.

She shook a little brass bell and Rachel appeared.

"You know Mr. Harrah, don't you?"

Plain-faced Rachel was as ingenuous as ever. "Yes, I know him." She did not mention Burnt Tavern Road. "He was here earlier to look for you."

"He was? I see. Well, get us some Irish Whiskey, Rachel."

"Is Mr. Harrah staying for lunch?"

"For lunch? Why, yes. But I'll look after that. I want you to take the day. Visit friends. Put up for the night with the Higgins Family."

"The foreman?"

"Yes, you know them well enough to spare embarrassment, don't you?"

Rachel tipped her head to a side. "I suppose I do."

"Good. Then you'll bring us the drinks on the way out."

With Rachel gone, Cassandra remembered to put the bell down. "How was your summer?" she asked.

"A mite busy."

"Doing what?"

"Keeping a tavern at Cooper's Point."

"A tavern?"

"I know it sounds odd. What with Bill being in the business and everything. But I left my government post and had to do something. And then I heard of this tavern for sale. It seemed too good an opportunity to pass up."

"Cooper's Point, did you say?"

"Yes, near Camden. It's all one township now."

Cassandra seemed unnerved. "Why, that's almost as far away as Philadelphia."

"It is," said Harrah. "But—But I've sold the business."

"Sold the business?" The news had a momentous effect on

Cassandra. The change in her face was marked. Her blonde hair, always dusky in tone, shone like a silver bowl.

Rachel returned with the whiskies. She was dressed for the street but was reluctant to leave.

"You needn't worry, Rachel. I can fend for myself."

"It's not that."

Not that. Then what was it? Cassandra was tempted to say. But she knew what was on Rachel's mind. Better left unspoken.

She opened the door and almost pushed the woman onto the porch. At the last Cassandra wished her a good day, squeezing her arm as a peacemaking gesture.

Now it was Harrah she wanted to come to terms with. She returned to the sitting room and picked up her glass.

"To old times," she said, not sure this was the best toast to make.

"To a new day," added Harrah, leaving his seat to join her.

"You'll stay for lunch?" The drink was not as smooth as she had hoped, but it warmed her all over.

He nodded.

"And the night, too?"

"And the night, too, Cassandra."

THE IRONMASTER'S HOUSE

It was the first of many nights. And days too in the beginning. But the days gave way to other matters. And with Rachel back, cleaning and fussing about, there was no finding one's way upstairs before dusk to foreshadow the evening.

Rachel retired early, seeing to the doors and the stray glasses and the lamps. But Rachel or no Rachel, the evenings had a character quite their own. From the upstairs bedroom window they could see the glow of the furnace, sparking red flames in the blue night. And the interminable roar of the huge bellows and the puffing fire kept a steady pounding in Harrah's head, like a pulse beat. No need to whisper or be secretive. They could not be overheard. The incessant noise of the irontown was kettle and drum to the hammers of their hearts. And their hearts were locked in a cast-iron embrace.

No complaint of flatness this time. In the course of a year Cassandra had grown to full womanhood. The little weight she had added put skin on her ribs and rounded her breasts. Harrah was not afraid of hurting her everytime he crushed her to him. A certain fragility had given way to firm flesh. And he was no longer afraid of snapping a rib or breaking a bone.

Though Harrah had not engaged in total abstinence during the year—if anything, Georgina Pierot had been a sexual feast—he found he could not get enough of Cassandra. Because there was less of her than Georgina, he wanted more. It seemed like a contradiction, but the spareness of her body somehow suggested greater depths to plumb. Her hips were narrow. Her belly was more flat than rounded. And her arms were still lean and girlish. All the more reason to draw her close to him. There was nothing to impede their coming together.

And Cassandra was totally drawn to him. For her, of course, there had been a famine. Since their lovemaking of the previous summer—moments she cherished then and wistfully looked back on later—sex had become an entrapment for her, something she wanted to avoid at all costs. For sex spelled servitude. In her marriage to Edward she regarded it as despicable, abject surrender, a sacrifice at best, psychological torture at the very least. And she would have no part of it.

With Harrah on the other hand, there was no need to hold back. Every instinct, every desire demanded that she give herself to him as she had done in the past. In his arms she saw instant fulfillment, the gratification of unrelenting longing. And she saw no reason for play or seduction.

They set up housekeeping. It wasn't quite as simple as at Burnt Tavern Road. After all, this was the ironmaster's house with a well-equipped kitchen in the basement, two drawing rooms and a dining room on the main floor, three bedrooms and a sewing room on the second floor, and servants' quarters at the top of a narrow staircase leading to the third floor. And the only servant they had was Rachel who tried to keep out of their way.

Harrah unpacked his trunk and moved in with Cassandra. At her behest he shifted his papers to the bonnet-top secretary, piled his linens into two drawers of the highboy, and hung his clothes in her closet. Later he accepted responsibility for the wine cellar, the meat room, and the ice house.

Every other day he drove Cassandra to the general store where they bought provisions and supplies and a kitchen utensil or two for Rachel. With chores out of the way, they climbed aboard his buggy and rode into the woods. Here they either picnicked near the lake or drove to Quaker Bridge for lunch at Thompson's. Though Harrah had other things on his mind, he never brought them up. This was their special time together, to make up for lost time; the rest could wait.

But Cassandra had no such restraint. She was full of plans for renovating the house. The milk room needed redoing. It had very little light for temperature control. And what did they need two drawing rooms for? That was all right when she planned big parties. Now she wanted something more intimate. And she intended to convert the sewing room into a studio. She had an urge to paint again.

"You don't approve, do you?" she asked.

"I haven't said anything."

"You still think of this as his house."

"Well, isn't it?"

"No, it's mine."

"Yours?"

"The spoils of war, you might say. And it was a war, I assure you. Even the townspeople think of the house as mine."

"So I've heard."

"I'll not give it up," she said.

That's where they left it.

A few days later Cassandra started to clear out the sewing room.

"You might give me a hand," she said.

He took hold of the sewing table, turned it on its side, and squeezed it through the doorway.

"You'll never get it upstairs," he said, pointing to the steep, narrow staircase.

"Then let's break it down and rebuild it."

When Harrah saw that she was serious, he offered a counter-suggestion. "Let's put it in the barn instead."

"In the barn?" She shrugged her shoulders. "Whatever you say."

"When we fix up that studio," asked Harrah after he had carried the table downstairs and stored it in the barn, "who'll sit for whom?"

"I'll sit for you."

"In the nude?"

"No. That will come later."

"Later?"

"Off canvas. I'll not be seen by anyone but you."

"Good enough," said Harrah, drawing her to him. "Then let's complete the job. I never did like sewing rooms."

EDWARD

Cassandra turned the sewing room into a fine studio. She reveled in its northern light. Of course, the window could have been bigger, but it would do for now. Cassandra still had a box of oils among her belongings. And she had ordered a new easel from Philadelphia and some canvas. Meanwhile Harrah made her a makeshift easel with scraps of pine, and she placed a drawing board with paper on it.

"All right," she said. "How do you want me to pose?"

Harrah picked up a piece of charcoal and pulled up a chair. "Three quarter view will do fine."

"But you're out of practice. Why don't you start with a profile?"

"Because I want a three-quarter view."

"And when I'm in the nude?"

"Then I'll want a full view."

Cassandra laughed. "I thought you'd say that."

"So you read my mind, do you?" He began to sketch in her eyes.

"No, just the expression on your face."

"Sit still."

Rachel appeared, nervous and uneasy.

"What is it?" asked Cassandra, rising from her chair.

"It's Mr. Edward," said Rachel.

"Edward?" Cassandra squeezed Harrah's hand. "What will we do?"

"See him, of course."

Harrah spoke across the room to Rachel. "Tell the gentleman we will be down shortly."

"Yes, Mr. Harrah." Rachel took little comfort in what was coming, but at least she did not have to make excuses. She shut the door behind her.

"What does he want?" asked Cassandra, almost frantic with expectation.

"We'll find out soon enough."

"But I never thought he'd come back to Atsion."

"Why not? It's his house."

"I didn't think he would have the courage."

"Apparently he has," said Harrah. "And you mustn't lose yours," he whispered, "at least not on my account."

"But it's you I'm worried about," murmured Cassandra. "It's strange. Alone I'm not afraid of him. In fact, I believe it is Edward who is intimidated. With you here, I find there's too much at stake. I don't want to lose you."

"You have nothing to fear, Cassandra. I'll not leave you. You must know that. No matter what Edward wants."

She nodded in tacit acknowledgment.

They saw Edward from the top of the stairs. He had not removed his hat but he had found a chair to rest his cane and gloves on. Dressed in the latest fashion with a long coat, a white linen vest and shirt and a lace tie, he wore his trousers over his boots. Though his was still the soft body of a gentleman who found only idle time on his hands, there was a look of determination on Edward's face that spelled trouble.

Descending the stairs a step ahead of Harrah, Cassandra returned to her more formidable self.

"What brings you to Atsion, Edward?"

"My home."

"What do you mean?"

"This is my home, this house. It was my father's home. Now I own it. I want it back!" His lip trembled slightly as he said this.

"But it's my home, too."

"There can be no 'too,' not anymore. You're living with another man." He said this without looking at Harrah. "All of Atsion knows this. I can't help that. But I can protect my interests. I'll not let my house support this dalliance of yours."

"Dalliance!" Cassandra colored to her roots. "There's nothing frivolous about our relationship. We're living as man and wife. But you wouldn't know about that! All you know is flesh and how to lecher after it!"

"I don't have to listen to insults! Least of all while you're living in my house!"

"Can I get you a drink?" interjected Harrah, attempting to settle things down.

Edward surprised him by accepting his offer.

"A glass of wine, thank you," So saying, he turned his back on Cassandra and strode towards the fireplace where he rested his arm on the mantel.

As Harrah poured the wine, he recognized the awkwardness of his position. Here he was, living in Edward's house, sleeping with Edward's wife, offering the man a drink from what was probably his own decanter. It was hardly the noblest of situations.

Edward watched Harrah pour. He had from the start been aware of his presence, but he had preferred to deal solely with Cassandra. Now that he had established his claim on the house, he was ready to take stock of his rival. In truth he was filled with wonder about Harrah who seemed amazingly calm as he brought him his glass. How was it that he was able to gain entrée with Cassandra when Edward had met with nothing but rebuffs? Granted he was handsome in his way, Harrah was not so handsome or so wealthy as to outshine an ironmaster's son or an ironmaster's house. Or was there something Edward had missed?

"I'm not giving up the house," said Cassandra even before Edward had swallowed his drink.

"You're not!"

"No, there's too much of me here. The chandeliers, the sofa, the table and all the silver."

"And whose money paid for it?"

"You were my husband. It was your obligation!"

"You had obligations, too. Did you meet them? No, you drove me from my own bed, from my own house. Like a common thief I had to steal away in the night. Was I obliged to pay for your extravagances once you declared yourself free of me?"

"But you did pay," insisted Cassandra, taking a step towards him.

"Yes, I believed that one day you would send for me, that you would come to your senses—in spite of everything. I was told that in time you would assume your proper role as wife and mistress of my house. But my advice proved to be wrong. And now I want what's mine."

"You'll not have it," said Cassandra.

"How can you say that?"

"But I have said it." She clenched her fists, ready to do battle.

"One minute!" enjoined Harrah.

The two combatants pulled back and turned toward him.

"Let him have it," said Harrah.

"Not the house!" pleaded Cassandra.

"Yes, the house. Let him have it. Let him have everything."

"But it's my house now—as much as his. I'm entitled to my share." She was not about to surrender one board, one panel.

"That may be," said Harrah. "But I want you to give it up."

"Nathaniel!"

"We have each other now, Cassandra. We need nothing more—least of all what's his."

"But where will we live?"

"Where? Edward will give us time to find something." He looked at his rival.

"A few weeks, no more," said Blount.

"That should be enough."

"But I can't leave a pauper!" said Cassandra.

"You'll leave as you came. You're no longer his wife." He turned to Edward. "There's one stipulation, however."

"And what's that?"

"You'll get a divorce."

"A divorce?" Edward shook his head in outright rejection. "Why should I smooth the way for you? Cassandra did not make things easy for me."

"This is not a request," said Harrah. "It's a condition. Otherwise you can forget about the house. I know these things take time. But when I see you again the divorce had better be in hand."

WEIGHING THE CHOICES

"It was most generous of you to give the house away," said Cassandra. "Especially as it wasn't yours to give."

Harrah recognized the old caustic Cassandra he had first known on Burnt Tavern Road.

"It was his house when you came here. You've only been a temporary occupant."

"Seven—almost eight months is hardly temporary. Besides, Edward abandoned it."

"You threw him out!"

"It's mine, I tell you. Mine by adverse possession."

"Adverse possession? When did you become a lawyer?"

"You don't have to be a lawyer to consult one."

He could see that she was fuming and that it would take more than argument to cool her down.

"Don't you see, Cassandra? So long as you live in this house, he has a claim on you."

"No, he has no claim on me. Our marriage is over, finished!"

"But he has a right to his property."

"He gave up that right when he left. And he did not come back until now. He turned Atsion over to Mr. Etheridge."

Harrah could see that he was getting nowhere.

"We'll talk about it tonight."

"No, not tonight!" reddened Cassandra. "You're not going to soften me up by putting your arms around me. We'll come to a decision now, not in bed!"

Harrah smiled in spite of himself.

"But I've already told him we're leaving."

"You had no right to tell him. That's why I'm so furious." She paced back and forth, looking for something to vent her anger on. "This house is a part of me, don't you understand? Look about you. Everything you see, I bought."

"With his money. This is Edward's house, Cassandra. Not yours. That's the truth of it, painful as it is."

"But he left, I tell you."

"You threw him out. It's common gossip."

"What if I did?"

"You had no right." Harrah took hold of her. "Does this house mean more to you than I do?"

Her gray eyes looked up at him. Harrah did not have to remind her of the long months of waiting. Everytime she looked at him she saw that. His presence had meant a difference in her life she could not in any way measure.

"Well?"

Wearily she shook her head.

"Then you've got to give it up. Leave the house and everything in it," said Harrah, releasing her. "We'll be richer for doing it, not poorer."

"Hogwash!"

"We'll do it all the same."

"Oh, how I hate you, Nathaniel Harrah!"

"Hate me? For what?"

"For loving you." She turned away from him and went upstairs.

Now that the matter of their leaving was settled, Harrah had to come to terms with himself. He had sold his tavern at Cooper's Point. A thriving business it was; and with the coming of the Camden and Amboy Railway, it brought a good price. Harrah had thought of keeping the tavern, but it sat too far from the heartland of the Pines and from Cassandra. So, instead of a business, he had money in his pocket. But he knew if he didn't invest it soon it would dribble away.

"Where will we go?" asked Cassandra. "What will we do?"

"I've had a mind to go into transportation."

"What kind of transportation? Surely not a stagecoach line."

Harrah could see that she would be critical of any plan.

"No, I've had a hand in that. Went into partnership in Princeton once and lost a tidy bundle. I was thinking, rather, of a small rail line. I've seen these new engines in Philadelphia. They're sturdily built and quite reliable. And they are no stranger to speed. The Pines could use a railroad. But it takes more money than I can lay hands on. Even a partner will hardly spell the difference."

"Then there's no point talking of it." Cassandra still hadn't completely forgiven him for agreeing to give up the house.

At supper, between servings of soup and pickled beef by Rachel, the matter was brought up again.

"Any place in particular you'd like to live?" asked Harrah.

"It doesn't matter," she said. "Where you work will determine that."

"True enough. But you don't see any merit in a railroad?"

"Not while you lack the money for it."

Harrah laid his napkin down. "Do you think Jesse Richards would be interested?"

"No."

"Why not?"

"Because he has his own circle of business acquaintances. And it is just as well he didn't know you're living here."

"He'll know soon enough. Now that Edward knows."

At bedtime Cassandra donned a low-necked nightdress. "Must we leave the house?" she asked. "I'd so love to spite him."

"I thought we settled that."

"You settled it, not I."

Harrah prepared himself for renewed battle.

"If we stay here, you might open a spirits shop," suggested Cassandra. "There's many a thirsty ironworker in this town."

"But the owners frown down on drinking. And it would be difficult to get a license. Besides, we're not staying in Atsion, in or out of this house."

"All right. Then you decide what to do. At the rate you're going, I'll have a babe at my breast. And you'll still be thinking how to invest your money."

"Are you pregnant?"

"No. But it isn't for lack of effort on your part." She smiled. "Or mine either."

That was better. A smiling Cassandra he could deal with. At least on that score.

CASSANDRA'S PLAN

One morning Cassandra woke up in a pool of blood.

"What happened?" asked Harrah when she awakened him.

"I miscarried."

"Then you *were* pregnant."

"Men are so stupid."

"What will you do now?"

She took his hand. "Rest."

"Shouldn't you see a doctor?"

"What for? Time is all the medicine I need."

Harrah was not too happy about this. He had always been a patient lover. And he found that his patience removed any lingering reticence on Cassandra's part, any desire she had to hold back. Stirrings Cassandra had almost forgotten had taken hold of her and demanded their rite. No rivalry now, no dread of a lasting relationship. Just a pure melding of body and mind. But "time" in her vocabulary could be a very long wait. For Cassandra was as rigid in her fetish of cleanliness as a Jewess in biblical times. And Cassandra was all the more attractive when she was wan.

"But you can still be affectionate," she said, embracing him. "So long as you know where to draw the line."

She then proceeded to wipe up the mess.

"I have the answer," she said one day as they went for a drive in his buggy.

"The answer to what?"

"Your new occupation and where we'll live."

He pulled his horse back.

"Well?"

Her earring sparkled with mischief.

"Drive to Burnt Tavern Road."

"But—"

"It shouldn't take long. It's only eleven miles from here."

Harrah shrugged his shoulders and rapped the croup of his horses with the reins.

Though they had driven the distance in silence, Cassandra could not contain her excitement. Her eyes sparkled with merriment; her body pitched forward in eager anticipation. But even when they crossed Quaker Bridge she managed to hold her tongue.

Harrah, on the other hand, fell into thoughtful watchfulness. Burnt Tavern Road conjured up a pile of memories for him. Hostetler's tavern. The smuggling and the double dealing. Benjy

Stride's trail of blood. (Benjy who was now a legend!) The ironmaster's house at Batsto. And, of course, Harrah's life as an itinerant artist and Cassandra's lover. But what did all this mean to Cassandra? And what did she have in mind for the future? He dared not ask.

They reached the Road in less than two hours time. Little had changed from the day Harrah had last seen it. Grass had overgrown the charred ruins of the tavern. George Taylor's barn looked the worse for weather. Widow Sizemore's place was boarded up. Only the crossroads stood out in sharp relief, the woods having been thinned out by a series of fires.

"There it is," he said. "All but abandoned. Except for the smith's shop." He noticed a corral had been attached to the forge, where a few horses grazed. This was the only thing Harrah had not seen before.

He hoped to find out what Cassandra was thinking before he drove any farther. But Cassandra was determined to reach the burned-out tavern. She jumped down from the buggy and ran the remaining hundred yards on foot.

When Harrah caught up with her, she seemed an unduly cheerful mourner at what, after all, was the tavern's resting place.

"We'll build it here," she said. "A new tavern. And you'll be the proprietor."

Though he had been given hint enough from her, Harrah was completely unprepared for the suggestion. Burnt Tavern Road? Hadn't they had enough of the place for one lifetime?

"The coaches still stop here," beamed Cassandra. "There's no reason to think the passengers wouldn't like refreshment."

Harrah remained silent.

"You've money enough to build a tavern, haven't you?"

He nodded.

"It needn't be as big as the last one. As for helpers, I'll be barmaid. And Rachel will cook. You needn't worry about finding someone to wait table. The town will settle in again once the tavern is here. And—"

"And what?"

"And Bill will tend bar."

"Bill Hostetler?"

"Yes."

"When have you been seeing Bill?"

"I haven't. But I've been getting letters from him. Poor Bill's too confined in a jughead tavern. He needs a larger establishment to move about in."

"He told you this?"

"Not exactly. But I know Bill. He'll fade away now that Speedwell is near done."

"What about the authorities?" asked Harrah.

"Are they still looking for him?" Cassandra seemed surprised.

"Maybe not. It's been a while. But it would be unwise for him to apply for a license. You were thinking of him as a partner, weren't you?"

"Only as a silent partner. You will be the licensee. I can get Jesse Richards to sign a petition for you."

So she had it all figured out. Harrah would own the tavern, but Bill would run it. And Cassandra would help out. Like the old days. But what of the damnable prophecy? A name like Burnt Tavern Road could again be self-fulfilling.

"I know what you're thinking," said Cassandra.

"Do you?" He wouldn't put it past her.

"Yes. But you needn't worry. Lightning doesn't strike thrice. This tavern will outlive us all."

Harrah was not averse to the idea of a tavern. With Hostetler's example before him, he had gone into the business himself. And he had found it profitable, handsomely profitable. But he was not sure he wanted to reconstruct the past. Much as he liked Hostetler, he didn't want to share Cassandra. With Bill back on Burnt Tavern Road, there would always be a father about. And Harrah wanted to be husband and father to her—all things.

"He's getting on in years," said Cassandra. "I don't want him to have to fend for himself. Had I stayed on at Atsion, I would have sent for him."

So this was the price Harrah had to pay for her giving up the house! Well, it was not the best of transactions. Burnt Tavern Road would not exactly be a homecoming. Except for Cassandra, he had no sentimental ties with the place. The fire, of course, had changed things. It was almost a purification, a burning off of unhappy associations. Just as the fire had destroyed the tavern and the stables, so he hoped it left no trace of the part he had played in halting the illicit traffic and in bringing Benjy to justice.

Harrah recognized that his had been a devious role, and he took no pride in it. He regretted that he had to be the one to bring the scourge of the law to Burnt Tavern Road. What he regretted even more was uprooting Hostetler from the world he found him in. It was an outcast world, this world of Hostetler's, a world tainted with skullduggery. But it suited Hostetler to a tavern truss.

And though Harrah was not a worrisome man, he did harbor a few fears about revenge or retaliation. He was not insensitive to the possibility that some people might resent his presence on

Burnt Tavern Road and wish him harm or injury. Which people, he did not know; for most of them had gone elsewhere to live and work. But people had a way of showing up at old dwelling places, old haunts. And he fully expected to meet one or more of them again.

But all things considered, it was better returning to the scene of the outrage than having to deal with Edward and what clearly belonged to him. He wanted Cassandra gone from Atsion. If he had to return to Burnt Tavern Road to accomplish this, he had best do it.

"All right," he said after a long silence. "We'll build another tavern."

Cassandra bit her lip, but there was unrestrained joy in her eyes.

"But where will we live in the meantime?" he asked.

"In Dorothea's house. No one has a claim on it now that she's gone. We can all live there. Bill, and Rachel too."

He dragged her into the woods and behind a tree.

"Now, look here," said Harrah, drawing her to him. "It's bad enough Rachel's in the house when I'm doing with you. I'll not have Bill hearing the bed creak."

"Then we'll do it on the floor," she whispered, pulling him close. "The floors are solid oak."

Part Four

BURNT TAVERN ROAD

"THE CROSSROADS"

Jesse Richards agreed to get the tavern a license, but he refused to meet Harrah.

"Not till he marries you," he said. "And then we'll see."

"But how can he marry me when Edward has yet to get a divorce?"

"All the same."

Cassandra suspected Mrs. Richards was behind Jesse's intractability. It was not like the ironmaster to be so stolid. But she pretended that it was otherwise.

"You've gotten rather high-churchy, haven't you, Jesse?"

"I've always had my religious scruples."

"But where's the tolerance you're famous for?"

"I've been tolerant with you, haven't I? And you're not even my daughter! How much toleration do you want?"

Cassandra retreated. She would take one thing at a time. It was enough he agreed to get the license.

"And why do you tolerate me?" she asked, acknowledging the fact of it.

"Why? Damned if I know!" And with that he broke into roaring laughter.

When Harrah saw the rafters going up and the center chimney, he began to marvel. All Cassandra had to do was will the thing and the tavern was taking shape. It was an act of creation, much like having children. Only this time she had planted the seed and the idea grew into being.

The worst part of building the tavern was the winter. Though the Pines had seen little snow, the cold made construction difficult. The ground was stubborn; and digging a cellar proved to be hard on the picks and the spades, as well as on the hired hands.

Harrah did not want to build on the old foundation; it stilled smelled of burnt wood. He thought to cover it over with sand and to start afresh nearer the crossroads. Besides, a new foundation meant a new beginning. And this he felt would take the curse off the place.

Spring broke early, even before the robins arrived. And the tavern stood finished. Nothing fancy like the Franklin Inn or classic like the one in Smithville. Merely solid and homespun as befit the Pines. Only the stables remained to be done. But here Harrah went along with the old foundation. The catacombs had come out of its entombment with its stones intact. Hostetler had built it well; no need to do it over again. And the horses would be provided by the stagecoach line. Either Wixted or his helper could look after them.

Wixted put in an appearance. The blacksmith had been watching the construction of the tavern from his forge. And he had uttered a few words of greeting between hammer blows every time Harrah stopped by. But he never let talk get in the way of flying sparks. This time he hung up his leather apron on the ox-shoeing frame, brushed his coat, and walked down the road to the tavern.

"A fine place, Mr. Harrah. Well-built and convivial, as Bill used to say. Is it true he'll be joining you in the venture?"

"Quite true, Mr. Wixted. He'll arrive here any day now."

"Like old times, then—except there aren't too many of the old timers around."

"Whatever became of Meech?" asked Harrah, more in the way of notation than of interest.

"Drifted away," said Wixted, accepting the chair Harrah offered him. The blacksmith was careful not to mention the blow from behind that Harrah had taken at Meech's hand a while back. No need to disturb old wounds. "Always a drifter was Michael. Bill was the only one able to keep him on hand for any period of time."

"Gone to work at Batsto?"

"For a spell. But not for long. The fellow has no tolerance for hard work."

"Mr. Wixted—"

"Yes?"

Harrah dropped all pretense. "You don't think I returned to Burnt Tavern Road too soon, do you?"

The blacksmith took the bottle Harrah offered and poured himself some rum. Rather painfully he fashioned in his mind what in his hand he so easily fashioned at his anvil.

"No, Mr. Harrah. It's been more'n a year, near two. I'm the only one left of the old road."

"But we may see others from time to time."

Wixted nodded.

"What then?"

Wixted poured himself a second drink. "Should make no difference. Time has done its thing. Bill's put it all behind him—if he's coming back, as they say. And I hold no grudge against you. She was the only one had vengeance in her heart."

The blacksmith pointed to Cassandra who was helping Rachel set up platters on the bar.

"And from the shape of her, I would say she's forgiven you,

63

too."

Harrah looked at Cassandra who was now almost five months pregnant. Yes, Cassandra had forgiven him. Indeed, she had forgiven him many times over. Any breach they had known would be healed by this new bond between them. Of course, she no longer permitted him to come near her, not till the baby was born. But there was no lack of affection between them.

"You're a lucky man," said Wixted. "Women like Cassandra don't forgive easily. No, not easily."

Yes, thought Harrah, he was a lucky man. But how was Wixted able to see this, Wixted who kept to his forge from dawn to dusk? No matter. Burnt Tavern Road, like Harrah, had survived its destruction. And he had lived to see its third coming.

SILENT PARTNER

Hostetler's return to Burnt Tavern Road was clearly a triumph for him. He arrived on horseback, his belongings rolled in a blanket tied just behind his saddle and his saddlebags loaded with keepsakes. When he dismounted, he had his first close-up look at the place and the sign which bore its name, "The Crossroads."

"Fit for a king. Or at least a president," pronounced Hostetler. "By the way, who is President these days?"

"Jackson still," volunteered a bystander.

"King Andrew?"

"The very same."

"Then Mr. Tariff is still his Vice-President."

He greeted Cassandra who was standing at the entrance and held out a hand to Harrah.

"Nathaniel, my lad. It's good to see you. I needn't tell you how good."

Harrah warmly grasped the tavernkeeper's hand.

"And it's good having you back, Bill."

"Yes. Just like old times."

"We delayed opening the tavern for a week," said Cassandra. "When you didn't get here, we had to start without you."

"A last minute delay," said Hostetler. "Just as well." He leaned over to whisper in Cassandra's ear. "A grand opening wouldn't do for a silent partner."

He entered the tavern and subjected it to his expert gaze. It struck him as not too different in design from its predecessor, except that the general room had been reduced in size, with less open space and smaller tables.

"It's cozier this way," observed Cassandra. "And there are fewer rooms to worry about upstairs. Food and drink is our primary concern."

"Then maybe you can fetch a drink for this thirsty traveller."

"By all means, Bill." Cassandra was solicitous of his every word, retreating to the bar to do his bid.

Hostetler took the opportunity to speak to Harrah. "I want to pay my share," he said. "Cassandra wrote me that it was all worked out. A nice gesture. Like the daughter she is. But I want to pay my way. Silent partner or no."

"You can pay us later."

"I've got money in those saddlebags, Nathaniel. Enough to settle accounts."

"Later, Bill. Later."

"So long as you understand."

Harrah nodded agreement.

"How about something to eat?" asked Cassandra after she had set a bottle of rum down on Hostetler's table. "Rachel has a ham roasting on the spit."

"Rachel? So the old girl is still with you. Let me pay my respects." Hostetler rose and, favoring his arthritic leg, ambled into the kitchen.

"Well, how does he strike you?" asked Cassandra.

"Like the Bill of old. Only a mite older. He seems thinner and a bit stiff in the joints."

"Do you think he'll be happy here?"

"I suppose so—if you don't smother him with all that daughterly looking after."

"He can stay with us, can't he?"

"Maybe you'd better ask him what he thinks. I don't know how he'll take to living in Dorothea's house. It holds strong memories for him, I'm sure."

When Bill returned, he was one warm smile.

"Hasn't changed a bit, old Rachel. Still as plain as a bed board. I could barely get three words out of her. But I think she was glad to see old Bill. Not a young filly anymore. But who am I to talk? I saw fifty-seven last winter."

"You'll stay with us tonight," announced Cassandra. "In fact, we'd like you to live with us."

"In Dorothea's house?"

"Yes."

"Well," said Hostetler, "I'll be happy to tear bread with you. But I'll put up at the tavern until I find a place to throw my blanket."

"But why, Bill? We've room enough. Don't you want to stay with us?" asked Harrah.

"It'd be no good. I'd only be under foot. Besides, the house is not without ghosts for me. Time was, I'd tremble at the thought of spending an evening with her. My linen would be so clean, I'd be afraid to move. The dinners we had are still 'graved in my mind. But the time is past for thinking about Dorothea. I want to put her to rest. It's peace we need now. Peace for both of us."

Hostetler pulled out his pipe and lighted up. "Is the old cottage still around? The one I gave Cassandra to live in?"

"It is, Bill."

"Then I'll bed there. 'Twill suit me fine. And keep me out of harm's way—as befits a silent partner."

"But not too silent, Bill," said Harrah.

"No danger of that. Now where's the ham Rachel promised

me? Must be burned to a crisp by now. She's a slow wheel, that girl. And the years haven't made her any faster.''

If Harrah had any concern that Hostetler would play too active a role at the tavern, he could put it to rest. Hostetler slept late in the small cottage Cassandra once called home, leaving the opening of the tavern to Harrah or Rachel. Not once did he take stock of the provisions or count the casks of rum or the kegs of ale. Not once did he wipe clean the painted sign that hung in front of "The Crossroads." Not once did he greet the passengers on the Tuckerton-to-Philadelphia stage run though he did walk out on the old stage road to see the coach go on its rumbling way once the stop was over. Nor did he wear the familiar striped shirt which in the old days was as much a signal that the tavern was open as the United States flag that was flown outside.

When Harrah was busy, Hostetler wandered about outside the tavern, inspecting the overhang, kicking the hitching post, or examining the catacombs of his once proud stables.

"Any plans to rebuild the stables?" he asked one day.

"Not just yet. The corral will have to do, and the open shed."

"A pity," said Hostetler. "We could do with some horses of our own."

"Thinking of breeding again?"

"I've been giving it some thought."

The truth was that Hostetler had lost interest in the tavern. He never said as much, but it was written in his countenance. The old fervor was gone. Cassandra attributed this to a lack of females in the place.

"In the old days there were always pretty girls about. Not that Bill would bed them. But he loved to tease and tickle their fancies. And if the only woman in his life was Dorothea, he was not without admiration for a fine head of hair or a pretty face."

"We could hire a girl or two for the peak hours."

"Where would we get them? Burnt Tavern Road is hardly the bee's nest it once was. And no girl is going to make the trip from Quaker Bridge for a few hours work."

True enough, thought Harrah. Even the runs were not as frequent as before. There were other roads into the Pines now, from different starting points, although none as well-travelled as the old stage road. Still, the tavern was making money.

"Don't you want to see the books?" asked Harrah. "How else can you determine your share?"

"Books don't interest me," said Hostetler. "Unless one is for us and one for the government."

"I'm afraid there is only one set."

"Then I'll take your word for it."

Hostetler passed into the kitchen where he lifted a slice of whortleberry pie off the plate.

"I think I'll go for a ride," he announced. "Maybe to Batsto or Thompson's at Quaker Bridge."

"Sure, Bill."

As he watched him ride off, Harrah was convinced that it was not the tavern Bill found wanting, at least not the tavern itself. What the former tavern owner missed was the smuggling and the illicit traffic that had made Burnt Tavern Road a hub of commerce in the old days. The exhilaration of a new arrival or a new shipment of goods, never knowing quite what to expect, was foreign to "The Crossroads." The taste of danger and of exotic happenings was also missing. A man brought up on outlaw whiskey was destined to find an honest mug of ale a pale brew. Though reformed, Hostetler was not entirely regenerate. And Harrah believed that Cassandra and he rather expected too much if they thought the tavern would hold Bill on the strength of its honest trade alone.

And so Harrah did not trouble himself too much about the man. Hostetler would find something to do, something to amuse him, something to challenge his outcast nature. It was only a matter of time.

"I think I'll ride up to Colt's Neck," Hostetler announced one morning.

"But that's a long way off," said Harrah.

"I'll take my time. Might pick up a few horses and start a stock farm."

"Where?"

"On Burnt Tavern Road. Where else?"

Cassandra opposed the trip. "You can't let him go by himself. He's not a young man anymore."

"He's only fifty-seven," said Harrah. "If he could manage a jughead tavern by himself, he should be able to make it to Colt's Neck. I think he needs something to keep him busy."

"Then go with him."

"Not in your condition, my girl."

"But he worries me."

"He'll be fine."

"MUSTERING OUT"

In mid-winter Cassandra gave birth. Harrah had seen to it that a midwife from Martha had been on hand for better than a week. Upon her arrival Mrs. Lorry was quite proper, quite sober. She offered to help in the kitchen but Rachel would not have it. With nothing to do but wait, she helped herself to a glass of wine, then two or three glasses, and was quite tipsy by the end of the fourth day. At first Rachel took her aside and scolded her. Then Harrah, quietly but firmly, advised the woman that he would see to it she midwifed for no one if she didn't sober up. So sober up she did. And when Cassandra went into labor early Sunday morning Mrs. Lorry with a steady hand helped bring the baby out.

"You have a boy, Mr. Harrah," she announced. "I can't say he looks like you at this point, But he has big hands and feet, and is as unblemished as a new peach."

"A boy!" Harrah managed to contain himself and was deliberate in his climb upstairs. A boy. And all of a piece. What kind of a man would he make one day? And how would Harrah do as his father? These were the thoughts that swam about in his head until he saw Cassandra.

"Well, my girl, you have a son. How does that sit with you?" Cassandra seemed none the worse for the effort.

"I would have preferred a girl. But under the circumstances I'm glad it's a boy. I suppose you're as proud as a peacock."

"Well, proud enough." He embraced the new mother and complimented her on how well she looked. "I thought you would have a rough time of it—in light of the miscarriage."

"A little blood, but no trouble at all. Mrs. Lorry did a fine job after all."

"Yes, she did. We can now take the lock off the liquor closet."

That night Harrah uttered a prayer that all had gone so well. Though not a religious man, he was grateful for the gift that was Cassandra and now for the added gift of a son. It augured well for the future.

And as the days passed Harrah looked for some sign as to what life would be like now that they were three. The fact was Harrah did not know what to expect of Cassandra. Some women, he understood, were completely submerged in motherhood. The baby, the baby—that's all one heard. For years this absorption in offspring was total and exclusive. Other women, especially in wealthier circles, turned their babies over to servants or governesses and, except for a few chosen moments during the day, saw little more of them than they saw of distant relatives.

Cassandra struck neither of these modes. For two hours in the morning and again at feeding time she was everything an infant could want. She washed it, played with it, talked to it, and carried it in her arms. But as soon as the tavern was abuzz with stagecoach passengers, alighting for a rest stop, she was there to carry food and drink. To the casual stranger it was difficult to believe that a new-born infant now shared her bedroom. To Harrah himself it seemed as though Cassandra had yet to experience motherhood.

But at night Cassandra's maternal side took form again, and Cassandra walked up and down with her son, humming "Rosin the Beau," and bathing and powdering him.

"We'll call him Jonathan," she had said that first day. "After your father."

Harrah was pleased, but there was something in the way she said this that suggested the next time the choice of name and sex would be Cassandra's.

For his own part, Harrah had an abiding curiosity about his son. He was not a young father for a first-born, having turned thirty-one in February. And he supposed this accounted for a certain maturity on his part where the baby was concerned. He was not filled with self-satisfaction and preening pride. He loved his baby but he did not want to prejudge his inchoate virtues or his failings. Nor did he want to determine the course his nature or character would take. A confirmed believer in free will, Harrah wanted to see how, unencumbered by a doting father, the infant would grow into childhood. Yet he was not foolish enough to disregard the influence Cassandra and, in her new role of governess, Rachel would have on Jonathan in those early months of his new life. Nor did he dismiss the effect he himself would have on his son in those brief moments when he held him close and talked to him and showed him the pines and the stars.

"You are strange with him," said Cassandra.

"What do you mean?"

"You talk to him as though he were a full grown boy."

"I'm not one for baby prattle."

"But he'll never learn that way."

"He'll learn no matter what we say or do."

"He'll learn what we teach him."

"And what does Rachel teach him when we're both at the tavern?"

Cassandra had no answer for that.

"He'll walk even if we don't teach him," said Harrah. "And he'll talk, too, if he hears people talking."

"It's as simple as that?"

"Yes, he has the instincts of the race. All the rest is refinement."

Some of Cassandra's instincts, on the other hand, were put to rest. Oh, she was affectionate enough and even seductive. She teased Harrah with her smile. She taunted him with her eyes, very gray when she wore a powder-blue gown. And she even stole a kiss or two. But when he caught her in his arms, she wriggled away.

"The hour's not right."

"I've got things to do."

"The baby needs looking after."

Always it was one excuse or another.

"What now?" he asked one night.

"It's my time of month," she replied.

"So soon?"

"I've not been regular since the birth."

"Why don't you see a doctor?"

"What do they know? I know my body at least as well as they do."

"Then speak to the midwife. She has some experience about these matters."

Reluctantly Cassandra agreed.

A few nights later she was playful again.

"Stop teasing me," said Harrah.

"But you're so handsome these days. I can't help it."

"Handsome, am I?" He reached for her gown.

"Yes, my man, it's hard for me to keep my distance."

He pressed her against the wall.

"What did the midwife say?"

Cassandra held on to her nightgown.

"That I'm good for more babies."

"When?"

"Whenever I want. But I need time to restore my body."

"I see nothing wrong with it."

"It's not the weight. I was all baby. It's my figure."

In fact, it was hard for Harrah to see what she was talking about. With the baby born, Cassandra was a young girl once more.

"How many babies do you want?" he asked.

"Just one more. You have your son. I want a daughter."

"Then let's not tarry," he said. He tried to disrobe her.

"Not now," she said, pulling away. "There's a baby next door."

"How do you think he got there?" laughed Harrah.

"But we're not married yet."

71

"We weren't married before."

"I know," she said. "Jonathan's a boy. It's not that important for a boy. But I don't want my daughter to be a bastard."

Harrah retreated to the washstand and poured water on his hands and face to cool off.

"You do understand, don't you?"

Harrah shook his head. Of course he understood. He was not daft. But did Cassandra understand?

MRS. KETTLES

"Who's the new woman you hired?"

Cassandra was stacking the pewter when Harrah put his arms round her waist.

"Mrs. Kettles. I thought Bill might find her to his liking. She used to work for Mrs. Richards. But with the children gone from the house, they've cut down on the number of servants."

"She's hardly the young girls you were talking about."

"No, but she'd make a good wife."

Cassandra slipped out of his grasp and went into the kitchen, "Here, taste a slice of the bread she's baked. Delicious, isn't it?"

"The bread's fine," pronounced Harrah. "But unless I'm mistaken, Bill's not looking for a wife."

Lavinia Kettles was in her early forties. Hers was a handsome face with good color and a porcelain complexion. But she no longer possessed a girlish figure. In fact, she had no figure at all, having no doubt consumed more than a portion of the loaves she had baked. Yet her disposition was flawless. She smiled freely, showing good teeth and had the Irish gift of easy banter, though she insisted she was English, hailing from Middlesex.

"Yes, I lost my husband on the voyage to America. Had a frail constitution, poor fellow. Not like his Lavinia. When my children were grown, I set up a pastry shop on Mill Street in Mount Holly. Then I went to work in the ironmaster's house at Batsto. Mr. Richards himself hired me. It was cheaper than going back and forth to Mount Holly, he said. How he loved my cakes!"

When Hostetler first set eyes on Mrs. Kettles, he dismissed her as an extravagance. "Rachel's cook enough for this tavern, bread or no bread. She'll eat into our profits in no time."

"But the woman's a ray of sunshine," protested Cassandra. "Give her a chance and you will see."

Hostetler knew what Cassandra was up to and Harrah could see that he was not flattered by Cassandra's matchmaking.

"I admit I'm getting on," he confided to Harrah. "But I need no woman to mother me. I've still got some fire left and I'm not going to light it in that stove."

"Don't blame me, Bill. It wasn't my idea. Though she's pleasant enough."

"Too pleasant! With all that banter, she goes on like a running stream. After Thea I don't think I could stand it!"

But Bill was too much the gentleman to be rude to the woman. And when Mrs. Kettles asked to see Burnt Tavern Road, he escorted her up and down the old stage road, pointing out George Taylor's barn, and the site of the old stables, and Cassandra's former studio up the hill. He did not let on where he was living for fear that the woman would want to see the place from the inside.

"It's not Batsto," she said.

"No, it's not. Batsto's always pounding in the ears and billowing smoke and fire. That's why I prefer the Road."

The next morning Cassandra called Bill to a side. "Here's a list of things I'll need at Quaker Bridge. Take Mrs. Kettles with you and let her pick out the fabric."

"Take her with me? I see through your little intrigues, my girl. Let her go to Quaker Bridge on her own."

"Come now, Bill, You won't deny me?"

"I won't deny you. But I won't take her either. I'll go myself."

"What do you know about fabrics?"

"Little enough, I grant you. But I know a great deal about fabrication."

Nevertheless he piled Mrs. Kettles onto the buggy and took off for Quaker Bridge.

When he returned with the fabric, he was furious.

"These amorous women! Don't they know their place? I could scarcely keep her hands off me. Pretending to lurch from side to side when the road was no bumpier than a baby's bottom. If Mrs. Kettles doesn't leave Burnt Tavern Road, I will!"

Cassandra tried to sort things out. "I can't believe he's that angry with her. What is the matter with Bill? All they need is time," she whispered to Harrah.

"I think he means it, Cassandra."

"He'll leave?"

Harrah nodded.

"But she's such a lovely woman."

"To you. But not to Bill. That's the thing to remember. Frankly I think he's past marrying. And if he weren't, his bride would not be Mrs. Kettles."

When Hostetler disappeared early the next day, Cassandra conceded defeat. "I guess we'll have to let her go."

"Back to Batsto?"

She nodded. "Jesse told me that if things didn't work out he would find a position for her in Mount Holly."

And so Mrs. Kettles was packed off to Batsto.

When Hostetler returned three days later, he ventured into the kitchen where Cassandra was slicing a smoked ham.

"I see that Mrs. Kettles is gone."

"You're not sorry, are you?"

"No. But she did bake fine bread."

"Well, it's gone now," said Cassandra. "You will miss her one day. You'll see."

"Not half as much as the bread."

DRIFTING AWAY

The departure of Mrs. Kettles did not solve anything. Hostetler was still a lost man on Burnt Tavern Road. With no smuggling to spice things up, he spent less time at the tavern and turned more and more to horse breeding. But with no prospect of stables soon, he had to hold back on his purchases.

"Look," he said, setting three bags of gold on Harrah's desk. "There's money enough here for stables and a tack room."

"Where'd you get it?"

"Saved it from the old days. Had it buried until now. Just dug it up."

"Smuggler's gold?"

"What's the difference, Nathaniel?"

Harrah leaned back in his chair.

"I can't stop you from building stables, Bill. I know you've got your heart set on it. But it won't be here, near the tavern. Not with that money."

"Then I'll build them elsewhere."

"And leave Cassandra? She wouldn't hear of it. Nor would I. Be patient, Bill. We'll come up with the money in time. And we'll still be here together."

Hostetler fell into a chair.

"It's not that I'm impatient. It's just that I feel my life slipping away."

"We all feel that way at times," said Harrah. "But you've a way to go yet. If things pick up at the tavern, maybe we can start building next year."

Actually Hostetler saw little prospect of things picking up. Better than Harrah he understood what it was that drew people to the old tavern. Harrah relied solely on the stage stops. Any additonal business was pure happenstance. At Hostetler's tavern and Cyrus Earle's before him, there was always the scent of something illicit going on. When one sat down at a table with a mug of ale or a bottle of rum, he knew that much more was taking place in the backroom than the counting of glasses. And this groundswell of activity spelled danger and profit and the tantalizing knowledge that things were being done that the law did not sanction. To defy the authorities was one thing. To make a profit from this defiance added spice to what was already a salty enterprise.

And then there were the girls, saucy and teasing, even a trifle vulgar. Without the girls, the tavern was deprived of a certain naughtiness (and without the Widow Sizemore and Red Corcoran and Michael Meech, a certain bawdiness). That, Hostetler missed most of all. Cassandra ran her tavern like the lady of the house, which she was. This was to take nothing away from her or her good looks. It was merely recognition of the fact that things had changed, indeed times had changed. And Hostetler was of another time.

Though it was becoming more and more difficult for Hostetler to find the stirrup and mount his horse, he pulled up his arthritic left leg and made it a ritual to ride away after breakfast. One day it was to Thompson's at Quaker Bridge, another day to Batsto, and sometimes to Martha Furnace. At Martha, Red Corcoran and his drinking companion Maggie Sizemore had made their home. Though the years had not been kind to either of them, they were never at a loss for talk; and their rowdiness had a bracing effect on Hostetler.

"I don't see how Red is able to work the furnace," he confided to Cassandra. "He's almost never sober. And Maggie's not one for housekeeping. The poor fellow's thinner than that iron fireplace poker. But he's still the taunt he was. And Maggie's still complaining he's taking her by force. After all these years it's enough to split a man's sides!"

"And how's Cora?" Cassandra asked.

"Mrs. Fred Botts has twin young 'uns now. But she still blushes when we remind her of her wedding night."

"And you? How are you these days, forever running off?"

"Biding my time," said Hostetler. "I don't want to be in the way."

"But you're not. The tavern needs you."

"Does it? What for, may I ask? It needs you, Cassandra. But Old Bill, it can do without. It's horses for me. That's what I spend my time on now. And one day we'll have a stock farm, right here in the Pines.

"So long as it's here," whispered Cassandra.

"Oh, I'll not venture far. You're all the kin I have. All the kin I want."

"And," muttered Cassandra, almost afraid of affection, "you're all the father I'll ever want."

OUT OF THE PAST

Michael Meech stepped out of the past and into the tavern. Never a tidy fellow, he was black with soot and unshaven. And much of his brawn had gone to fat. But he was still a powerful man with bulging forearms and knotted biceps. His black hair was wiped forward over a low forehead.

"A bottle of rum here!" he called out, pulling up a chair and banging his fist on the table.

It was at the height of the afternoon stage run, and for that reason neither Cassandra nor Harrah had seen him. Harrah made a move toward the table, but Cassandra stayed his arm.

"Let me handle it," she said.

"No," insisted Harrah, "he's my trouble."

He appproached Meech's table.

"There's no rum for you here," he said.

"No rum? Why not! First Wixted says there's no work at the smith's. Now you say no rum. A fine way to treat an old acquaintance!"

"You heard what I said. I said it plain."

But Meech pretended not to hear. He slapped some money on the table and spread it around. "It's rum I want, not your company. So better get your hands on some."

Harrah reached out and pulled the table from under him.

"Get out, Meech! You're not welcome here."

Rising, Meech tossed his chair aside.

"Not welcome?" His eyes shifted toward Cassandra and the other patrons. "That's a fine thing, coming from you. I've got money and this is a public place."

"All the same."

"All the same? Well, I'll not budge till I get my drink."

Harrah moved towards him. "I said, 'Get out.'"

"No one's pushing me out. Least of all a turncoat!"

Harrah pulled off his apron.

"All right, Meech. If it's a fight you want, let's have at it. Or don't you fight face to face?"

"What's that supposed to mean?"

"I think it's plain enough."

"It wasn't me struck you from behind. I only know what I heard."

"It wasn't?"

"No."

"You're a damned liar, Meech! I say this before everyone

present. And if you want to fight me for saying it, here's your chance!''

Meech turned scarlet. It was apparent he had misjudged his man. Harrah was no longer the shiftless artist he had come to know on Burnt Tavern Road. Meech realized that to some extent this had been a pretext. There had at odd times been flashes of a different Harrah, particularly during the ill-fated raid on the squatters. But Meech was not prepared for the head-on manner that Harrah displayed as keeper of his own tavern.

"Don't push me," he sneered. Meech's sneer had not improved over the years. Only this time it evaporated into a doubtful smile, the hairs of his moustache glistening with sweat. "I'll fight," he said, "but in my own good time."

"And when is that?" asked Harrah.

"Tomorrow. Yes, tomorrow morning. Out on the road, if you're up to it. You can even have your choice of weapons."

"Nathaniel," called Cassandra, "don't listen to him. What's done is done!"

"Stay out of this, Cassandra!"

Harrah again confronted Meech. "What kind of weapons?"

"Ax handles, whips, whatever you say."

"No weapons, Meech. Just bare fists," said Harrah. "I want to get my hands on you."

Meech was not warm to the idea, but in front of so many witnesses he could not easily back down.

"Whatever," Meech said at last and stalked out of the tavern.

Cassandra could not sleep that night. While she was relieved that ax handles and horsewhips had been eliminated from the fight, she did not look forward to seeing her husband brutally beaten or maimed. She knew Meech to be a brawler. She had seen bare-fisted fights before with noses and cheekbones smashed and teeth knocked out. And always the victor was a brawler, someone like Meech, with a long record of fights and conquests. She was also aware that Harrah had been in a fight or two in the old days when he was an agent of the government and later as a tavern owner at Cooper's Point. And she was sure her husband knew something of the manly acts of maim and mayhem. But she feared a confrontation in the street of Burnt Tavern Road, partly for Harrah's safety and partly for the memories it would conjure up.

In the past year or so Harrah had managed to live down his reputation. As the man who arrested Bill Hostetler and brought in Benjy Stride, he had been known as "The Turncoat of Burnt Tavern Road." But very few of the oldtimers who remembered what had happened were still around. And Hostetler had taken the burden of guilt off Harrah's shoulders by becoming his partner. If Hostetler was willing to forgive and forget—Hostetler who had to flee the Road when the agents moved in—then no one had any grievance left. Except Benjy, of course, and Benjy was dead.

But somehow by becoming legend Benjy had achieved a reputation that only his death made possible. The State had hung Benjy, not Harrah—that was the way people saw it. Few, if any, remembered that Harrah had brought him in. Few, if any, cared. The legend itself was worth the price Benjy had paid. Benjy Stride was now up there with Joe Mulliner.

And so there was only Meech. Big, foul-mouthed Meech. He had in the tavern already opened up old wounds by calling Harrah a turncoat. A fight would only spread the poison. What effect this would have on Harrah and "The Crossroads," she did not know. But Cassandra was afraid that Harrah would become a pariah again, forced to leave Burnt Tavern Road and the life they had built together.

"I wish you wouldn't fight," she said when she realized that Harrah too was awake.

"I've got to. And I want to," he said.

"Why?"

"Because I suffered badly at his hands. Not only the pain, but double vision for months. Even now when the weather is raw I feel the wound. And it's been over three years."

"And what will you gain if you fight? New wounds and more pain and more bitterness?"

"Maybe. But Meech will get his share too. Until now he's gotten off scot-free."

"And what if he kicks you? His boots are heavy enough. Or picks up a rock? Or fights foul?"

"Then I'll fight foul, too. But in the end it's his head will be buried in the sand."

Cassandra turned away. "And what," she whispered, "if he raises the old ghosts?"

"I've thought of that," said Harrah.

"Well, what if he does?"

"Then there'll be a haunting."

"Doesn't that bother you?"

"It does. But I've learned to live with ghosts. If I had to do it again, I would. Only I wouldn't wait so long this time to reclaim you."

Cassandra said no more. Resigned to her fears, she lay back in his arms till dawn and at last fell asleep.

When Harrah climbed out of bed, he could take only weak

tea for breakfast. Soaking his hands in salt water to toughen them, he clenched and unclenched his fists. Pulling on a fresh shirt, he took a last look at his sleeping wife and started for the road.

It was a damp, overcast morning. The sky threw a white pall over the Pines, almost hiding them with mist. And there was a ghostly chill in the air that grayed his skin and ashened his lips. Harrah slowly made his way down the well-trodden path that led from Dorothea's house. He emerged from the woods a few hundred feet from the tavern.

On the road he cast about for Meech. But his antagonist was nowhere to be seen. Was Harrah too early? Was the mist playing tricks on him? After a half hour of looking one way and then the other, Harrah was met on the road by Hostetler who had just arrived on horseback from Quaker Bridge.

"Morning, Nathaniel," Bill said in a hoarse voice. "What are you standing around for?"

"I'm waiting for someone."

"Who?" asked Hostetler, pulling on his horse to steady it.

"Meech. I've got a score to settle."

Hostetler took off his hat and wiped his sweatband.

"Meech, is it? Then you've got a long wait."

"What do you mean?"

"I saw him about three miles from here. Galloping hard he was—the other way. Didn't so much as say 'hello.' Not a word. And after all I've done for the son-of-a-bitch."

"Is that so?"

Hostetler trotted ahead as Harrah followed on foot.

"Relieved?" asked Hostetler, turning round and looking back. "Or disappointed?"

"A little of both," said Harrah.

PURDY WELCH & CO.

But the matter did not end there. On the following day when Harrah was returning on foot from the blacksmith's shop, with a new saddle girth in hand, Meech appeared on horseback. Crossing his path, he spat on the ground just short of Harrah's boots.

"Are you ready to fight?" asked Meech. "Or did you give me up for gone?"

Though taken by surprise, Harrah said he was ready. And to prove it he tossed the leather strap across the road and clenched his fists.

"Don't throw the leather away," said Meech. "You may be needing it."

Harrah wondered for a moment what Meech meant. When he saw the horseman draw a coil of whip from behind his saddle, the sour taste of betrayal parched his mouth.

"What's the matter, Meech, chicken-hearted? We agreed to fight bare fists, didn't we?"

"I hurt my fist raisin' ore."

"A likely tale," scoffed Harrah. "But I'll make it easy for you. I'll turn my back if that will help."

Meech understood the insult, even tolerated it. But he did not wait for another. Reaching back, he unravelled his whip and lashed out at Harrah.

Harrah pulled back and the stroke fell short. But in dodging the lash, Harrah lost his footing and found himself sitting on his haunches. He did not sit long. At the next crack of the whip, he rolled over and rushed to his feet. Smarting now, Harrah felt debased and animal, and only vaguely understood why. And then it came to him.

Purdy Welch and Company. He had seen the "Grand Mammoth Zoological Exhibition" on Federal Street in Camden. The striped quagga, the lama, the panther, the jaguar of Brazil—all were on parade. But it was Major Jack Downey's twenty minutes with a Numidian lion and a Bengal tiger that he remembered best. Downey wielded a brutal whip. Its screeching lash forced the lion to the stool and drove the tiger through the fiery hoop. As Downey's strokes ripped through the air, blistering the animals' backs, Harrah had recoiled with pity. The military band and the sixty splendid grays did nothing to ameliorate the pain, the indignity of the lash. If anything, they gloried in the exercise. And Harrah, who detested the naked inhumanity of Major Downing, now saw himself being scourged as Meech dragged his whip along the bleached white sand road, preparatory to striking again.

Finding it cumbersome to attack from his horse, Meech dismounted. But on foot he still wielded advantage and made the most of it. Snapping his whip, he cut Harrah a wicked blow. The lash curled round the soft leather of his boot and Harrah could not shake it free. Pulling hard, Meech brought him down once more but was unable to sustain the whip's hold. Like a Bengal tiger, Harrah sprang to his feet, ignoring the pain shooting up his leg. He caught sight of his discarded saddle girth lying at the edge of the road. Breaking free, Harrah ran towards it. He had almost reached the girth when once more he felt the sting of Meech's lash.

At this moment Cassandra emerged from the tavern, followed by Rachel. The crack of Meech's whip again split the air. Seizing Rachel's hand, Cassandra shouted, "Get Bill!" Then she ran down the road towards the combatants.

"What do you want, Michael Meech?" Her voice was agitated by the jarring impact of running. "Haven't you done enough?"

"Stay away, Cassandra," said Meech. "He deserves every bit what he gets!"

Cassandra pressed forward, discarding her shoes on the way. "You coward! Why don't you fight fair? No man is a match for the whip!"

"Tell that to Benjy. He was no match for the hangman's noose!" Rearing back, Meech lashed out again.

When Cassandra reached the man, she scooped some sand out of the road, then flung it into his eyes. Meech blinked and rubbed his eyes and swore an oath, but it was not enough to stop him. He kept wielding his whip and striking blindly.

Harrah seized the moment. He slipped out of range and reached the saddle girth. Swinging it above his head, he stepped forward and lashed out at Meech, driving him back several feet. But the strap was not long enough or sinewy enough to do the job. Still, Harrah kept thrashing, forcing Meech to give ground. Meanwhile Cassandra continued to scoop up sand and throw it at Meech. Angrily he ordered her to stop. When she ignored him, he wheeled round and snapped the whip in her direction.

This infuriated Harrah. He charged Meech and was upon him before Meech could snake back his whip to strike again. The two men went down, rolling over one another on the sand road. Emerging on top just long enough to rest his weight on Harrah, Meech pressed his arm against the ripple of Harrah's throat. But Harrah would have none of it. He dug his elbow into his opponent's ribs and jostled himself free. As they struggled to their feet, the combatants stalked one another, moving from side to side.

Saliva dripped from Meech's mouth, but he made no attempt to wipe it off. Harrah watched as he waited for an opening.

Meech now swung wildly, completely missing his man and spinning around. Before he could right himself, Harrah's boot landed solidly on his rump, dumping him on all fours, Meech got up only to be greeted by a smashing blow on the mouth. This sent him sprawling again. Struggling to his feet, Meech tried to strike back at Harrah, but all his thrusts were wide of the mark. And each time Harrah slipped past his outstretched arms to smash stunning blows to the head.

Meech or Major Jack Downey of Purdy Welch and Company? It did not matter. So long as Harrah was snapping his head back.

By now Hostetler appeared on the scene. Astride his horse, he called for the men to stop fighting.

"Enough, I say! Michael, Nathaniel, let's end it!"

In the old days, when he was master of Burnt Tavern Road, this would have been enough. But too much had happened since then. Now neither man would call a halt. When Meech finally landed a blow, sending Harrah back on his heels, he bent his head down and drove into his opponent like a battering ram. Harrah grunted as the air was knocked out of him. But he recovered himself and managed to drive his fist into Meech's face, bloodying his nose. Realizing that Meech was more meat than muscle, a figure mightily diminished without his whip, Harrah was relentless. He pummeled his man with sledgehammer blows to the head and face. He all but cracked his ribs with his fists.

Determined this time to put a stop to the fighting, Hostetler tried to dismount but he had trouble disengaging his left foot from the stirrup. A shriek from Meech, as Harrah smashed him just under the heart, startled Hostetler's horse. It turned fidgety and restive. Hostetler tried to calm it. But at a second cry, the horse whinnied and bolted. His foot still caught in the stirrup, Hostetler was thrown backward. Abruptly and violently, he was dragged behind the crazed animal as it sped down the hard-packed road.

"Bill!" Cassandra stifled a scream.

Harrah turned and shouted a halt but the horse would not stop. It tore down Burnt Tavern Road like a runaway steam engine, continuing to haul Hostetler behind it. At every stride Hostetler's body bounced up and down against the ground. About fifty yards down the stage road, Hostetler's leg broke free and he tumbled head over boot in a heap.

Harrah and Cassandra gave chase. When they reached him, Hostetler was clutching his side in agonizing pain.

Wixted came running from the opposite direction. "What

happened?'' At a distance the blacksmith caught sight of Meech wiping the blood from his face with his sleeve.

"Get a doctor," said Harrah as Cassandra cradled Hostetler in her arms. "Get the black doctor."

A SADDLEBAG OF TROUBLES

"How is he?" asked Cassandra when John Witt finished examining Hostetler.

The black doctor never changed. He stood as wiry and angular as ever. And his face looked no older than it did when he first came to Burnt Tavern Road.

"Worse than appears."

"What do you mean?"

"The bruises are bad enough. And the abrasions. But he's got shooting pains in his arm and his shoulder. His heart's had a jolt."

"His heart?"

"Yes, don't move him or feed him till I tell you. If he makes it through the week, he'll be all right."

"Through the week?" Cassandra sank into a chair.

"It's serious, Ma'am. Very serious. He could leave us at any moment. I say the week. But fust night's even more critical."

"Is he awake?"

"He's awake. But he's most uncomfortable. If he lasts the day out, he'll be powerful sore tomorrow. By Wednesday he'll be feeling somewhat better and even thinkin' of getting out of bed. But don't let him. He still has to make it through the week. And then we'll see. I'll be back in a few hours. Got to see a sick baby in Batsto."

When John Witt returned, he found Hostetler asleep, Cassandra at his bedside.

"Well, at least he's still alive," he remarked to Harrah who had followed him upstairs.

Harrah did not know what to make of the doctor whose candor disarmed him. The black doctor was so dreadfully honest as to make Harrah have second thoughts about the truth in such a situation. For what purpose, he wondered. Was the patient any the better for it? Or those that cared for him? It seemed that the truth was only self-fulfillment.

After a thorough examination at his bedside, which consisted chiefly of Witt's pressing his ear against Hostetler's chest and looking at his eyes and tongue, the doctor pronounced Hostetler as roughly the same.

"I'll be back again tomorrow morning. Remember, nothing to eat. A little water if he's thirsty."

The next day it was more of the same. "Except that he's survived the first twenty-four hours. That's one thing in his favor."

But Hostetler's discomfort increased.

"He's still sore," said Witt. "Tomorrow should be a better day."

"I think he's going to be all right," said Cassandra as she emerged from the guest bedroom. "He's sitting up and talking. His voice is stronger. And he kept down the broth the doctor made him. In fact, he wants to climb out of bed."

Harrah recalled that the doctor had said as much. "He still has to make it through the week," quoted Harrah.

"Oh, that he'll do. I have no doubt. Go see for yourself."

Whether this was self-deception on Cassandra's part or wishful thinking, Harrah did not know. But he dared not think what would happen if Cassandra were wrong. All the signs pointed to a rough convalescence. Harrah regarded Hostetler's improvement as temporary at best. What disturbed him most was Witt's demeanor. Usually the black doctor was positive and unrestrained in his professional outlook. Harrah saw none of that at this time.

"How long do you think it will be before he's up and around?" asked Harrah.

"Can't say."

"But he will recover?"

"We'll have to wait and see. Nothin' to do but wait."

As an afterthought Witt sat down in the drawing room and stretched his legs.

"I don't mean to keep you hangin' on this," he said solemnly. "That man was a mighty help to me when I needed it. He mortgaged my land and helped me build a house. Never did complain when I couldn't make the payments. I only jus' paid him back in gold this year—with interest."

"Three bags of gold?"

"That's right. I suppose he told you. Well, I'd like to be able to say Bill Hostetler will be his old self again. Nothing would be more comfortin' to me. But he won't. His heart's bad, like a broken clock. If he pulls through—and I ain't saying he will—he sure as hell won't survive the next time."

Harrah found it difficult to accept this assessment of Hostetler's chances, though he knew it to be true. At the same time he respected the doctor for his insistence on not mincing words.

"I thank you, Dr. Witt, for all you've done. And for your plain speaking. I know it wasn't easy for you. Your professionalism is deeply appreciated."

John Witt rose to accept the hand that Harrah offered him.

"I only wish there was more I could do? There are occasions when even a doctor is no match for what ails a man. It's a mighty humblin' experience. But we can't let it be a discouragement, can we?''

When the doctor was gone, Harrah went up to Hostetler's room to give Cassandra a chance to get some sleep. The poor girl had no more than two hours rest since Hostetler was stricken. She kept to his bedside as though her presence alone would keep him alive. And tired as she felt, she was reluctant to leave when Harrah assured her that Bill would be all right without her.

"But call me if he needs anything."

"I will, Cassandra."

Kissing Hostetler on the cheek, she left.

Harrah pulled up a chair and patted Hostetler on the shoulder. "You're looking pretty sound to me," he began.

"Sound as a Batsto stove," said Hostetler.

"I'm sorry about the fight, Bill."

"Don't be sorry. He had it coming."

"But if we had stopped when you asked us—"

"It would have happened anyway. My leg's been a bother for years." He made no mention of his heart. "Life is a saddlebag of troubles, Nathaniel. No sooner do you grab hold o' one problem than you dig yourself up another."

"It seems that way at times."

"I'm not saying that it hasn't its better moments. But at the last it's a mixed bag. And sometimes the mix is hard to deal with."

Hostetler was more animated than he had been in some time. And Harrah was content just to listen.

"Still, it's all worthwhile, 'specially if you've been a tavern-keeper. In the end it's how we drink the ale that counts. And how we remember it. The memory, you see, is one with the draught."

"And you have your memories?"

"Oh, yes. I remember the early days when I worked in a livery stable in Philadelphia. It was hard, dirty work, with no money in it and the prospects bleak. I vowed I would change my life. So I did. And I remember the great days on Burnt Tavern Road. Yes, they were great days, Nathaniel. I knew I was breaking the law. But the law was stupid, unjust. Stupid as the men who made them. And so I lost no sleep over it. It was the tavern life I loved. Mixing with people, talking with them, drinking, laughing. There's nothing like it in the world. Least for me. The tavern wasn't work for Bill Hostetler; it was entertainment. The few problems attached to it only made the better moments all the sweeter.

"Even Dorothea had her moments. They were few and far between, I'll admit. But there were those times when dining with her, when just being with her in that big house filled my life. I never felt deeply about most things. But I felt deeply about that woman.

And feeling deep has its own rewards. And, of course, there was Cassandra. What a joy she's been over the years. Caring, loving, sacrificing even. Always a thought for old Bill. A man couldn't ask more of his own flesh and blood. That girl has been the summer-tree of my life. The one person that makes me think of myself as having been more than a smuggler, more than a tavernkeeper. Yes, without Cassandra, my journey through life would have come up empty, empty as a keg on Training Day.''

Suddenly Hostetler was fatigued, spent with talking. His face paled and he sank down on his pillow.

Harrah got up to leave.

"I'll see you later, Bill. Better get some rest now.''

That was the last talk they had together. The next time Harrah stopped by his room, he found that Hostetler was no more.

Part Five

A QUESTION OF LEGALITY

A PIECE OF NEWS

It was Cassandra's wish that Hostetler be buried on Burnt Tavern Road, just opposite "The Crossroads."

"Why not a churchyard?" asked Harrah.

"Because I don't think Bill went to church one day in his life."

And so Hostetler's gravesite formed a triangle with the things that had been most important to him in life, the tavern and the stables, whose ruins lay unreconstructed.

It was of some comfort to Cassandra to know when she stepped through the tavern door that Hostetler was nearby. In this way he could still look after her. At the same time she understood that whatever tie she had with Burnt Tavern Road was now broken. With Bill Hostetler dead, whatever life the tavern had known was stilled. Her reason for being there, to provide a sanctuary for Bill's declining years, no longer existed. Without Bill to consider, to sustain her, she and Harrah could build a new life somewhere else.

She did not go into mourning, as Harrah thought she would. Except for the burial, no tears, no wearing of black, no incantations. If anything, Cassandra was more determined than ever to pick up the traces of her life. She owed that much to Bill.

She now turned more and more to Jesse Richards. All her life she had done without a mother. And a mother was not what Cassandra needed. But she could not function without some embodiment of a father to lean on.

Harrah did not object to such a relationship. He fully understood the deprivation of Cassandra's childhood. And he saw nothing in the person of Jesse Richards that might persuade him to change his mind. Richards, though ruddy and handsome for his age, was not a ladies' man. He was every moment, every pound of him, the ironmaster, the father not only of the Batsto Ironworks but of all the men and women who came under his jurisdiction. He was no more threat to Harrah than he was a threat to any of his ore raisers or guttermen or fillermen.

Besides, it was Harrah that Cassandra came to when she wanted affection or closeness. Since his return to the Pines, she could not bear to be without him. She wanted constantly to touch him, to hear his voice, to surrender herself to him. She was not just making up for time lost. She was indulging herself in the bounty of her youth. Though she no longer thought of herself as a girl, she wanted fully to exercise her birthright as a woman. And it in no way seemed a contradiction to her that with Edward Blount she wanted to obliterate sex and with Harrah to foster and even deify it.

Jesse Richards stopped at the tavern. "To see you, me dear. Not to wet my whistle."

Cassandra was pleased. Despite her estrangement from her husband, the tall, ruddy, aging, heavy-set ironmaster of Batsto had never ended their friendship. From time to time he would send her a letter or a small gift or invite her to a party at the Batsto mansion, which Cassandra declined because of Harrah.

"Edward's a nice enough chap, but not for Cassandra," he confided to Harrah. "She's too much the devil for him. He needs one of those delicate creatures who will laugh at his silly stories and spend half the day on her coiffure. Not that Cassandra isn't a handsome woman."

Richards had heard of Harrah's early romance with Cassandra and knew of their living together as man and wife since his return to the Pines. He had never had anything but kind words for his "protegé." Though he had not met Harrah before, he took to the former government agent at once.

"Somehow the tavern suits Cassandra. She's at home here, don't you think?"

Harrah looked across the room at Cassandra who had gone to greet a new arrival. She no longer dressed as a barmaid nor did she wear a blouse and bodice. A tasteful frock with a ruffle at the neck did for her, in keeping with her status as the tavernkeeper's wife.

"It would seem so."

"I have news for you," said Richards when Cassandra returned to their table.

"You've opened a new furnace," she teased.

"Hardly. I'm trying to keep the ones I own afloat. It's Edward. The news is about him."

Cassandra lost all color and Harrah, sensing that he was an outsider in this regard, rose to leave.

"No, stay, Mr. Harrah. This concerns you, too. Edward has secured a divorce."

"A divorce? But when, how?" asked Cassandra.

"I have none of the details, I'm afraid. The important thing is you're free to marry. Actually he's had the papers for some time now. I only just learned of it. I thought it proper that you should know. Apparently the courts have made little effort to keep you informed."

Cassandra stole a quick glance at Harrah.

"I'm grateful to you, Mr. Richards. I expected this would

happen one day. I thought Edward would be the bearer of the news. I dreaded that. I'm glad it was you brought the tidings."

"Yes, thank you," said Harrah. "May I get you some rum or a glass of wine?"

"No," said Richards at first, "I've got to be going." But he saw a look of disappointment on Harrah's face and realized he might take this as a sign of disapproval. "On second thought, a glass of wine might be in order."

Harrah brought the glasses, setting them down in front of the ironmaster. Jesse Richards raised his glass. And then with his arm round Cassandra he drank a toast.

"To you, my dear, the loveliest young thing the Pines have ever known. And to you, Harrah," he added, "the damn luckiest man alive!"

"I'll agree to that," said Harrah, fixing his gaze on Cassandra's gray eyes and then on her golden earring.

TO MARRY OR NOT

"That was good word from Jesse, wasn't it?" Harrah helped Cassandra put things away after the tavern had closed for the night.

"Yes, it was."

"I wonder why Edward kept the divorce a secret."

"I don't know. But, as Jesse said, the court should have notified us."

Harrah, looking for signs, found the choice of the word "us" a comforting one. Though the news was what he had hoped for, he found it disconcerting now that it was here. It was as if Cassandra and he were bonded together while they stood in single opposition to Edward. But with the divorce in hand they had somehow to be rebonded. For their status had loosened, if not come untied.

"Do you find it strange?" asked Harrah.

"Find what strange?"

"Being unmarried."

"A little." She quickly added, "Of course, I haven't been really married for some time."

"That can easily be remedied," said Harrah.

Cassandra smiled, but just faintly.

"Does the prospect frighten you?" he asked.

"I don't know."

"Well, there's plenty of time to think about it." He tried to appear unperturbed, but he was disappointed Cassandra showed such little enthusiasm for the idea.

"Yes, there is no hurry," she said.

The next day Harrah steered away from the subject. He laid in some provisions, asked Wixted to fashion a second spit for the fireplace, and did an inventory of his liquor. In the afternoon he rode to Quaker Bridge for some oysters.

Upon his return he found no change in Cassandra. A kind of depression had set in and he was at a loss to deal with it.

"Is Jonathan all right?" The child had not been feeling well, and Harrah thought it wise to tie in Cassandra's malaise with the boy's illness.

"He's fine now, stumbling about and getting into things. Where were you?"

"To Quaker Bridge. I brought back some oysters."

"What's the occasion?"

"Scottish Independence Day."

"You can't be serious."

"Not entirely. But there is an occasion. As of now, you're scot-free, as they say."

Cassandra almost succeeded in smiling.

"Well, you are, you know. And if marrying again bothers you, put it out of your mind."

"You're upset with me," said Cassandra.

"Not at all. It wasn't a formal proposal anyway."

Cassandra took his arm. "It's not you I'm afraid of, Nathaniel. Surely you know that."

His eyes nodded in agreement.

"It's marriage itself. I didn't make a very good one. I'm not sure I can do better this time."

"You were not to blame, Cassandra."

"Oh, but I was. I set about destroying it from the first day. I was quite impossible. You have no idea. The wonder is I married in the first place."

"It's over," said Harrah. "It's done with. Let's not talk about it any more."

"Yes, it's over," agreed Cassandra. "But I'm afraid it's left its mark." She searched in Harrah's face for some sign that he understood. "I'm not sure that I can do it again. You know that you're the love of my life, the only man I'll ever love. And I know that in the eyes of God we're man and wife—if not in the eyes of the church or the law. And I suppose we should marry for Jonathan's sake. I know all these things. But I can't bring myself to take the final, inalterable step. Do you understand?"

She turned away from him.

"Oh, why am I doing this to you? Now that I'm free to marry, I won't. Oh, Nathaniel, I don't deserve being your wife. I don't deserve that you will have me."

Harrah stepped forward to comfort her.

"Don't take on so, Cassandra." He gently squeezed her shoulders. "We'll go on as before. I want no claim on you. Just your love. If the time comes, there'll be a wedding. If not, there'll still be Cassandra and our very own child. And that's more than enough for me."

But the matter did not end there. Between stagecoach runs and tending bar, Cassandra would offer new explanations and new thoughts on the subject.

"Take Molly—which you did, of course. Would you call hers a happy marriage?"

"I don't know. I haven't seen her all these years."

"But from what you saw then—in Batsto?"

"Forget Molly. Every marriage is different. Just as there are

95

no two taverns alike, the inns of marriage have different signs. From place to place, guests never know what to expect. Still they try."

Harrah picked up four mugs of ale and started for the general room.

"I don't care what other people do with their lives, Cassandra. That's their affair. I care about the life we fashion. If I can make you happy by marrying you, I'll do that. If not, I'll be content to live without a preacher giving us his blessing."

One night while she was rocking Jonathan to sleep in his cradle and Harrah was reading one of the Philadelphia papers that had arrived that morning, Cassandra tossed a note into his lap.

Putting the paper down, Harrah glanced up at Cassandra, then unravelled the note.

"I do love you," it said.

Harrah read the note over and over again, then put it in his pocket.

"A fine sentiment," he declared.

"Do you believe it?"

"Yes, Cassandra. I do."

"Despite my not marrying you?"

Harrah left his chair and took a long look at the child in his cradle.

"I have everything I want," he said.

"And so do I." Cassandra took hold of his arm and crushed it in her bosom. "A wedding band would change nothing, I tell myself. And maybe it would not. But my fear is that it would. This way when I love you it is of my own free will. And when I make love to you it is because I want to, not because I should."

"It would be no different if we were married," laughed Harrah. "It is not as if I'd force myself on you."

"I know that," she said. "Still, I would feel different. It's a little like smuggling, you see."

"Smuggling?"

"Yes, only in reverse. When the law says you can't do something, you naturally want to do it. When marriage says you must do something, you naturally oppose it."

"When I want you," said Harrah, "it will be as before. There will be no obligations in our marriage."

"Not on your part, I am sure. But I may feel an obligation. And that I don't want." She stopped suddenly. "Oh, I must be driving you mad with all this talk! Poor Nathaniel. What kind of a woman have you latched on to?"

"Cassandra Trescott," he replied teasingly. "And I hear the Trescotts are a bad lot."

"Let's go to church today," she said one Sunday morning.

"Pleasant Mills?"

"Yes."

"All right. But what about the stagecoach run?"

"Rachel can handle it. Everything's laid out. And there haven't been too many passengers this month."

Harrah hitched up his carriage, put on his best coat, and, helping Cassandra to her seat, rapped his horse into a trot. It was a splendid day, dry and sun-drenched. A sly, mischievous breeze whipped through the Pines, stirring up the bogs and running fingers through the winding streams that fed them.

Cassandra wore a dark coat over her lace dress to keep it free of sand. She was now twenty-five and more beautiful than he had ever known her. Slim still, she had a fuller bosom than in the old days. And where her femininity had once rested in pliant girlishness, it now peeped out of small mounds of white lace. Harrah wanted to stop the carriage and touch the girl-turned-woman, but he was afraid of being late and thought better of it.

They pulled up at the church just as the service had begun. Taking Cassandra by the arm, Harrah entered through the door on the right and found space in the next to last pew.

Reverend Peterson, a sallow man with dark hair which was sparse at the temples, was reading from Proverbs when they entered.

"Drink waters out of thine own cistern, and running waters out of thine own well.

"Let thy fountains be dispersed abroad, *and* rivers of waters in the streets.

"Let them be only thine own, and not strangers' with thee.

"Let thy fountain be blessed: and rejoice with the wife of thy youth.

"Let her be as the loving hind and pleasant roe: let her breasts satisfy thee at all times: and be thou ravished always with her love."

There was more, but that was all Harrah had heard and remembered.

When the services were over, the preacher came to greet them and to introduce himself.

"I'm Reverend Peterson. I'm told you're the tavern owner on Burnt Tavern Road."

"Yes, we normally find it difficult to get away on Sunday," said Harrah. "But Cassandra insisted we make church this day."

"You are most welcome."

"That was an interesting passage you read today," remarked Harrah.

"I often read from Proverbs. And in Pleasant Mills this particular passage seems most suitable. The waters in these parts are indeed pure. And we must keep them pure—if only to set a standard for the flow of the human stream. We must not muddy the waters of our daily lives—any more than the sweet water of Pleasant Mills."

This was not exactly the message that Harrah had got, but he let it pass. And then Cassandra spoke to the preacher.

"Will you be able to marry us two or three weeks hence?"

"But I thought—"

"No, we're not married—yet."

The preacher pulled out a little notebook.

"But, of course, my dear. This being the first Sunday of the month, I am sure we can arrange for a wedding on the fourth Sunday. Would that suit you?"

"Yes, it would suit us just fine."

The preacher closed his book and, offering his congratulations, moved on to his regular parishioners.

Harrah drew Cassandra aside.

"Well, that was a change of heart. What brought it about, may I ask?"

"Nothing in particular."

"But you were so adamant."

"That was last week."

"Last week?"

"Yes, this week things are different."

"How so?"

"This week I find that I'm pregnant."

"Is that true?"

"I am fairly certain."

"But—"

"But why marry with this one and not with Jonathan?"

"Yes, I suppose that's what I mean."

"Because this one will be a girl. It won't do for a girl to be born out of wedlock."

"I see."

"You still want to marry me, Nathaniel. Don't you?"

"I do."

"And how do you feel about a second child?"

"Much the same as the first. I'm delighted."

"Shall we tell Jesse Richards? He's over there with the preacher."

"Tell him about the child?" Harrah was not quite reconciled to the idea.

"No, silly, about the wedding. I'd like him to give me away—now that Bill's gone."

"Then, by all means, tell him."

Jesse Richards not only agreed to give Cassandra away, he offered to hold the wedding reception at the ironmaster's mansion.

"We couldn't do that, Jesse."

"Why not?"

"It's a different life I lead now. I'm not of Atsion anymore, or of the circle of people I once knew."

"Makes no difference."

"It does to me. But I thank you all the same."

"We'll hold the reception at the tavern," announced Harrah. "The few folks left at Burnt Tavern Road could do with a party."

"You will come, too. Won't you, Jesse?" asked Cassandra.

"I wouldn't miss it for all of Batsto."

On the way home Harrah drove his carriage off the road and onto a stretch of grass along the Batsto River. At a spot shielded by fragrant white cedars, he left the carriage and helped Cassandra down.

"Where are you taking me?"

"To the other side of the cedar swamp."

"Why?"

"I want to see if the wild turkey beard or the golden spike has sprouted yet."

"What do you know of plant life?"

"Nothing. But it gives me the excuse I need."

"For what?" she asked, holding his hand as he led her tripping over small brush and fallen branches.

"You'll see."

At a small clearing sheltered by a row of tall white cedars that all but obscured the river, Harrah sat her down.

"On this bed of green moss, with the cedars rubbing against each other in the breeze, I am going to celebrate our child and our oncoming marriage."

"But why here? Why not at home in a soft bed?"

"Because soon you will be telling me that we must wait till the child is born. And I have no intention of wasting the time that's left."

Cassandra's smile was warm but not yet maternal. Grateful for that, Harrah pulled the shoulders of her dress away and revealed her breasts to the forest. He did not touch her, content merely to look at the buds of her near-white bosom.

"What's that?" she said, covering up. "I heard a noise just

then.''

Harrah looked over his left shoulder. "It's only a couple of deer making their way through the brush. What did the preacher say? 'The loving hind and the pleasant roe.' Well, there they are."

With Cassandra reassured, he gently took hold of her. "And now it's time to be ravished with your love."

As Cassandra lay back for him, her breasts bare and sculptured in ivory, she could not resist saying, "If this is what church does to you, we'll spend Sundays at the tavern."

"With one exception," said Harrah, pressing toward her.

"And what's that?"

"The fourth Sunday of the month. The preacher himself marked it in his notebook."

MAKING IT LEGAL

A week before the wedding, Jesse Richards stopped at Burnt Tavern Road. He wanted to use a wagon as a raised platform and conduct a huge outdoor ceremony.

"The only way to handle the crowd."

But Cassandra and Harrah ruled against such grandiosity.

"Just a small, intimate gathering in the church itself," said Harrah. "That's all we want."

"How will I keep the crowd away?" asked the ironmaster. "Batsto loves a wedding and all of Batsto will be there. Not to mention Pleasant Mills. Do you have any idea what a turnout we have when one of our better known preachers visits these parts?"

"Arrange for an excursion to the shore that day," suggested Cassandra. "That will lure the crowd away."

"A splendid idea," said Richards. "It's certainly warm enough."

"But you will be there on Sunday, won't you, Jesse?"

"Of course. I wouldn't miss your wedding for the world."

Despite the excursion that day, there was a good crowd on hand for the wedding. Richards had his own carriage pick up Cassandra at Burnt Tavern Road, and Harrah followed at a distance on horseback. Rachel remained at home with Jonathan, Cassandra thinking it inappropriate that the child should be present at the ceremony.

When they arrived at Pleasant Mills, Richards helped Cassandra down and ushered her into the white clapboard church. He used the entrance at the right.

"Not that I'm superstitious," he whispered. "But the last couple to enter on the left had a short and stormy marriage."

Cassandra could not remember her own wedding to Edward. She recalled all the preparations leading up to the wedding but the ceremony itself was completely erased from her mind. She often wondered at this but could not explain it. It was as if her first marriage had been annihilated, not annulled. Now that she was taking Nathaniel as her husband, she felt that she was being married for the first time. And she knew she would remember everything about the wedding, the white altar, the sun-filled windows, the neat rows of pews. She believed devoutly that this marriage had been made in the eyes of God. The other was the victim of blind chance, sanctified only by self-deception, unholy and unwanted.

"I love you," she whispered to Harrah when the minister had

joined them in holy matrimony and put his bible down.

"And I you," he said, kissing her as if for the first time.

"There will be a reception at the manor house," said Richards, congratulating the couple. "Just the four of us. Mrs. Richards insists."

"She's a darling," said Cassandra, flushed with the heat of indoors. "But we must get back to the tavern. Rachel's all alone. You do understand, Jesse?"

"I never fully understand anything you do, my dear," replied the ironmaster. "But what does it matter? Everything bears your stamp, your imprint. A more intriguing young woman I've never known."

"How you go on!" exclaimed the bride.

"Promise me you'll visit us soon," called Richards as Harrah led Cassandra through the crowd.

"I promise!" She threw a kiss as she took her place in the bridal carriage festooned with yellow roses.

Tying his horse behind the vehicle, Harrah boarded the carriage at the driver's seat and waved goodbye to the happy throng. In wild response he and Cassandra were showered with flower petals and good wishes, an altogether sentimental out-pouring from relative strangers, and off they went.

Pleasant Mills had never known a prettier wedding or Batsto a prettier bride.

Six months after they were married, Cassandra had her "mustering out." Not a boy this time, but Cassandra in miniature. A fine featured little girl, very fair and very lean.

"I'm going to call her Willa, after Bill," Cassandra said when she held the baby in her arms. "Willa Harrah. I think that's a pretty name."

"Not pretty enough. I want her named for you. Cassie or Cassandra. She's so much like you, it's only right she take your name."

"Willa, Nathaniel. I insist. She may very well be my last. And I want Bill remembered."

Cassandra had a hard time giving birth, and it was the midwife, a Mrs. O'Brien, who opined that the child could be her last.

"From what I've seen you were lucky to have a musterin' out at all. She's a healthy lass. But you won't have it so good next time. Listen to me, my darlin'. I've delivered hundreds of babies in my time. I know what I'm talkin' about."

Cassandra did not have to be convinced. Her own body told

her the woman was right. Even now the memory of her pain was a piercing one.

"Is it Willa, then?" she asked.

Harrah sat down on the bed. "Let's compromise. Let's call her Willacassa."

"Willacassa. That's an odd name."

She played with it for a moment. "Willacassa? Yes, it is odd. But I like it. How clever of you, Nathaniel. Thank you. Willacassa she is."

And so Willacassa came into the world, and after a month or so made her presence known. Delicately molded but strong-willed, she sought the light wherever it shone and reached for her father whenever she saw him.

"She's definitely drawn to you," said Cassandra. "Even when I'm nursing her, it's you she wants. Wasn't that way at all with Jonathan. How does it feel to have a daughter who adores you?"

"I'll know better in sixteen years."

"Oh, she'll be a wild one, I'm afraid. I'm no match for her even now. As her father, you'll have to set things straight."

"How do you know all this?"

"It's in the eyes, Nathaniel. And in the earlobes. She has a gypsy's earlobes."

"Like yours?"

Cassandra laughed. "Like mine."

But Willacassa was soon turned over to Rachel while Cassandra resumed her duties in the tavern. For there was just enough activity these days for the two of them and not enough to afford taking on another girl.

"Why can't Rachel help out while you look after the little ones?" suggested Harrah.

"You know how Rachel is behind the bar or at tables."

"Not pretty enough, you mean?"

"Too slow, really."

"She is that," he acknowledged.

"But she seems just right with the children. That same slow pace has a soothing effect on them, particularly Willacassa. And though she is much too quiet for the tavern, she goes on and on with her stories and prattle when the children are about. Rachel may not be much outside the kitchen, but she is the perfect nursemaid."

"And you," said Harrah, "are the perfect tavern mistress."

"Well, let's just say I'm not the perfect mother."

Harrah wondered about that. As he attended the myriad tasks of tavern upkeep, he considered what nature of woman Cassandra truly was. No, she was not the perfect mother, if by mother one meant a sow with her sucklings. There were plenty of those in the workers' cottages at Batsto.

And yet there was no denying she was every inch a woman. Did a woman have to deny her own person once she bore children? Did she have to suspend her own life to nurture the new life she had brought into the world? For some indeed it seemed there was no other way. But for women like Cassandra, birth was only a way stop along the coach path of life. There were still other roads to travel and Cassandra meant to travel them.

Then, just as Harrah had painted her as the kind of person she was, Cassandra altered her image. She left the tavern after a full day's work and awoke in the wee hours of the morning to feed and fondle and fuss with her offspring.

"Well, Jonathan, what do you think of your little sister?"

"Wassa!" was all Jonathan could make of Willacassa.

"Do you love Wassa?"

He had not yet decided. A year and a half older than she, he had one moment nothing but regal disdain for the baby and the next a desire to stroke her flaxen hair.

"But you love your mommy, don't you?"

Oh, that he did. And he toddled toward her with open arms, pursing his lips for kisses.

"When will you get some rest?" asked Harrah, standing in the doorway of the children's room.

"This is all the rest I need."

"You're sure you're not pushing yourself? You haven't been all that strong since Willacassa."

"I'm fine. Rachel's the one that has her hands full."

But Rachel wasn't driven like Cassandra. Rachel rested when she had the notion, or she fixed herself a cup of tea or sliced herself a piece of whortleberry pie. She had the gift of knowing when she was tired. Even the children were used to her moments of respite.

Not Cassandra. Hardly a moment passed when she remembered a chore she had missed or a letter to be written. And at odd moments she found a new way to arrange the tables or the bottles behind the bar or the utensils hanging on the kitchen wall. She even dug some holes and planted flowers outside the tavern "to give it a little color."

"Why do you go on so?" asked Harrah.

"Why?" Cassandra brushed back the hair that had fallen over her eyes. "Because I'm thinking of selling the place."

BUYING TIME

Jesse Richards again stopped at the tavern. A huge stone of a man, he brought something of the ironmaster's mansion with him, a lordly elegance, a worldly extravagance. He found a chair next to Harrah who was settling accounts.

"What's this about Cassandra wanting to sell the tavern? I saw the advertisement in a Philadelphia newspaper."

"It's true," said Harrah. "In fact, she's already had a couple of offers."

"But why? I thought she liked it here."

"With Bill gone—you knew Bill Hostetler, didn't you?—she has no heart left for it."

Richards nodded. Yes, he had met Hostetler. Of course, he had been a shadow of the man Richards had once heard about. And he remembered too that Hostetler had made him a proposition many years ago, something about a paper mill at Pleasant Mills, that the ironmaster had turned down. But Richards made no mention of this to Harrah.

"What will you do if you sell?"

"I don't know."

"No idea at all?"

"Oh, a few thoughts have crossed my mind. The railroads, for example. A growing industry. There's money to be made in transportation. But Cassandra won't leave the Pines."

"Thought about a railroad myself," said Richards. "In fact, some business friends and I want to build a line through Quaker Bridge."

"Quaker Bridge?" mused Harrah. "That would kill the stage route through here."

"Yes, but a route from Philadelphia to the Jersey shore could go a long way to making bog iron cheaper. We've formed a company and we've been granted a charter. What's more, we hold over $200,000 in pledges. But the banks want specie, not paper. They say business is overextending itself."

"If you do go ahead with a railroad, I'd like a chance to buy into it," said Harrah. "I've got money to invest."

"All right. But it may be just as well we didn't build," said Richards. "We may find the railroad not to be the salvation of the Pines after all."

"What do you mean?"

"There would be big changes. The life we know would change. Besides, our competitors are building railroads. With trains to transport their pig iron, the Pennsylvania furnaces can put us out of business. They've got a good grade of iron. And plenty of it. Meanwhile we have to go deeper into the Pines to find new bogs and timber for charcoal-burning.''

"I see."

"But it's too soon to worry. We'll turn to glass if necessary and build new type furnaces. Cupolas."

"Cupolas?"

"A re-smelting furnace. Makes a higher quality pig iron. We'll keep the men working. Of course, we have a reputation for good workmanship. Our stoves, our pipes have the stamp of quality on them. Experience has kept us in good stead. Still, it's touch and go at Martha Furnace."

Martha Furnace. Harrah had heard of difficulties there. Labor in short supply. Poor management. Much drinking and fighting. It was no holiday running the place, he was sure.

"Would you be interested in working there?" asked Richards. "My older brother Samuel owns the works."

Harrah was astonished. At first he did not think Richards was serious. But when he read the man's face, his firm lips and jaw, Harrah was sure the man was not joking.

"Me? I know nothing about iron."

"You'll learn. I am not asking you to invest, at least not in Martha. Samuel himself may sell. But you can learn the business there. In a year or so you will know the ins and outs of iron. By then you may have some idea what you want to do with yourself."

Harrah put his account books away and rose to pace the floor.

"Now is a good time to sell the tavern," pursued Richards. "You can get a good price for it. When you're ready to invest, the money will still be there."

"But what will I do in Martha?"

"Assist the ironmaster."

"But why me? I am sure you can get a dozen men to do the job. Men who know the business."

"I've watched you run the tavern. You're a cool head and a sound businessman. You weren't always a tavern owner, were you?"

"No."

"Then you see what I'm getting at."

That night Harrah mentioned the offer to Cassandra.

She listened quietly. "It makes sense," she said, sitting back against her pillows.

Harrah shook his head. "I'm surprised to hear you say that. To me, it makes no sense at all."

"It will buy you time—until you decide what to do."

"I can decide now—if it comes to that."

"There's precious little to do in the Pines outside of iron."

So that was it. His options were open so long as they continued to live in the Pines. Try to go elsewhere and he would breach their relationship. Harrah bridled at the idea. Fact was, he had no option at all. There might be precious little to do in the Pines outside of iron, but he would do it. He glanced over at Cassandra to make this point. But he was stopped by her look of assurance. Devilishly confident she was, confident that he would not leave the Pines. Well, he couldn't blame her. That was part of their understanding when he returned to Cassandra, was it not? That it was left unspoken made it no less binding on him.

"You sound as if you knew Jesse was coming. Strange you weren't there to greet him," said Harrah.

"Yes, I knew he was coming. He wrote me. But it was strictly to see you."

"And you had no hand in it at all?"

Cassandra said nothing at first. When she did speak, it was with a crack in her voice.

"The decision is still yours to make."

Part Six

MARTHA

CALICO

No sooner did Harrah and Cassandra arrive at Martha Furnace than Mr. Evans, the manager, took Harrah to his office. Mr. Evans had been the manager and ironmaster of Martha for over thirty years. And a capable manager, too, according to Jesse Richards. But he looked tired as he invited Harrah to sit down in one of two captain's chairs.

"I'm weary, Mr. Harrah. I guess I've been in the business too long. Just as a furnace gets burnt out in time, so am I burnt out. But I'll teach you all I know. And then maybe you can spell me for a bit."

"I'll do what I can," said Harrah

"We've only just put the furnace in blast. So there's no reason for me to be so exhausted. But I am. And there's a pile of paperwork to be completed."

Mr. Evans leaned back and half shut his eyes.

"I'm sorry that you will be living in Calico," he said. "But the men need looking after. There are two basic problems at Martha Furnace. One is drinking, and much of it is done in Calico. We don't permit it in Martha. The second problem is turnover. The men come and go. The only ones that stay are the Blacks. No, they're not slaves. But they aren't exactly freemen either. Some are runaways, you see."

"We don't mind living in Calico. Cassandra will live anywhere so long as it's in the Pines."

"Good. But you must feel free to come and go at the ironmaster's house. We do not stand on formality there."

The structure that Cassandra and Harrah moved into was larger and better furnished than the workers' cottages in Calico. But it too was short on space and headroom. The first thing Harrah unloaded was Willacassa's cradle. A trundle bed upstairs would do for Jonathan. Cassandra shook her head as she stood at the center of the small living room.

"I must have been mad to give up Dorothea's house for this. Why did I do it, Nathaniel?"

"You wanted an end of Burnt Tavern Road."

"I know. But what have we now?"

"We have the best frame house in Calico. We could have done worse, my girl."

"Have you met any of our neighbors?"

"No, I haven't."

"We're surrounded on one side by a family of ore raisers. And on the other by a charcoal burner and his daughter.''

"Honest, hard-working people, I'm sure.''

"But not exactly aristocrats.''

"Neither are we.''

Cassandra laughed. "You do have a way of setting things straight,'' she declared.

"And you, a way of making a home out of a plain frame house. So go to it, my girl—while I unload the rest of our belongings.''

By evening the house was made comfortable enough to spend the night in. And by morning Cassandra had gotten over her prejudices and, with Rachel looking after the children, was ready to meet her neighbors.

She learned that the ore raisers were in the bogs and the charcoal burner was at his shed in Martha. The only one home was Peg Slaughter, the charcoal burner's daughter. She was no more than sixteen, with an unwashed face and soot all over her arms. She cooked for her younger brothers who attended the one-room schoolhouse at the other end of Calico, but in no way could it be said that she kept house.

"My poor mum died six years back. Since then I've been cook and laundress for the family. Don't see the old man 'cept as when the charcoal's finished. So when the kids are at school I take myself a cup of tea which you're welcome to pour yourself if you want.''

"No, thank you. I've just had some.''

"Joe Slaughter, I should warn you, likes his bottle. Don't matter that the ironmaster wants his men sober. He's a Quaker, you see. The ironmaster, that is. Not as strict as his wife but starchy just the same. No matter. Joe will drink when he's a mind, and hunt and fish. I told him I'm going to have my own home one day. Joe doesn't like to hear that. But I've got three or four men courtin' me already.''

"Is there work to be had?''

"Only at the tavern at the Landing or in the common kitchen at Martha's. And neither one much appeals to me.''

Cassandra wondered what did appeal to the girl. She found out later in the day when from her window she saw Peg Slaughter rolling in a hay wagon with one of her suitors. Dirty face and all, she was kissing and licking and finding herself squeezed and bitten.

When Mr. Evans likened himself to a burnt-out furnace, Harrah did not at first understand what he meant. At least not fully. But as the weeks passed and he spent more time with the man, the impact of the comparison was impressed upon him.

For Mr. Evans was burnt out. There was no fire in his eyes,

no color in his cheeks, no fever on his brow even when he was aroused. Instead an ashen pall was cast over his face and his brows hung like cinders over vacant sockets. His voice too had given out so that what once had been the bellows of an ironmaster's command was now little more than a raspy morning sound.

"The bills to Baltimore Pipe. Have you had a chance to reconcile them?"

"I have. The error was in the weight. Two numbers were transposed. I—"

"Good. Spare me the details, Mr. Harrah. Just see to it that corrected statements are sent."

"I've already sent them."

Later Mr. Evans was apologetic. "I didn't mean to cut you short, Mr. Harrah. It's just my nerves. Shall we share a pot of coffee?"

"Why not?"

Mr. Evans sank into a chair, rattling his cup in the saucer.

"I'm tired, Mr. Harrah. Need a change. Frankly I'd like to buy the works. But Samuel Richards isn't ready to sell. As owner, I could get a new manager and begin to live a more leisurely life."

"Maybe Mr. Richards will sell one day."

"I hope I'm not too old by then. Meanwhile it's no picnic running such a large establishment. You see, the men are restless. It's not an easy life at Martha—even though we try to make it as tolerable as possible."

"I understand."

"Do you? Perhaps. But I can see where it would be difficult for you to imagine that this tired old man sitting before you was the very heart of Martha Furnace for more than thirty-one years. There wasn't an event that took place here that I wasn't responsible for. I have been Justice of the Peace, Chosen Freeholder, Judge of Elections, even Town Assessor. I've built several of the bridges in these parts. And, of course, I've been Ironmaster."

Harrah had not known much of this and was genuinely impressed.

"I've even surveyed a good part of Martha and the surrounding areas. And I was as good a carpenter as any of the molders working at the furnace. If you're ever in the schoolhouse, you'll see the desk I made for the schoolmistress. Solid oak and finished smooth as glass.

"But I'm tired. I can't stay awake in the afternoons or at the Hicksite Meeting House near Wading River. Some, no doubt, say it's old age. Catches up with anyone. But I say it's more than that. The fire's gone out. And I'm not sure it will ever burn again."

"Have you considered a holiday?" asked Harrah.

"It'll have to be a long holiday," mused Mr. Evans. "And then only after I find someone to take my place."

Despite the ironmaster's almost ritualistic fatigue, the two men got on. Harrah arrived at the office adjoining the ironmaster's house early in the morning and lit the woodstove and wiped clear a few window panes. After setting a coffee pot on the stove top, he sat down to his table of ledgers. By nine o'clock Mr. Evans pushed through the door and laid his hat on his desk. He exchanged a few words with Harrah and then poured two cups of coffee which he mixed with sweet cream. Always he brought with him a half-dozen buns that Mrs. Evans had baked. Weather was discussed only in terms of the furnace.

"'Tis damp out. Might hurt the iron."

Or "Bit too windy. Hope it causes no puff."

Then to business.

"Now, Mr. Harrah. What think you of the new billing form?"

"It's easier to comprehend." Indeed, everything Mr. Evans did was a model of simplicity and efficiency.

"Good, then use it as a guide. By the way, I want you to accompany me on the rounds today. The last time we shall go together. Tomorrow you will fend for yourself. I have a few things I want you to do. In an administrative way, you might say. You don't mind responsibility, do you?"

"No."

Harrah's first administrative task was to fire Red Corcoran. Bill Hostetler's old crony had scalded a man with molten iron. Whiskey did not make for a steady hand.

"But I know the man," said Harrah. "He worked on Burnt Tavern Road."

"Makes no difference. He's got to go. Can't have anyone else scalded. Corcoran's always been one of the heaviest drinkers around here. But in recent weeks he's gotten worse. I told him to stay at home until he hears from you."

So Harrah had the dirty work again. Always the dirty work. First, Burnt Tavern Road and now Martha. Would he forever be going against the grain of his feelings? Why couldn't the distasteful jobs be left to others? Why was he invariably the anointed one?

The Widow Sizemore barely gave Harrah a greeting when he appeared at the weather-stained cottage door. The years had not treated her kindly. Her body had grown thinner and her face was spotted with crimson patches.

"Come for Red, have you?"

Harrah nodded.

At her call Corcoran came downstairs, slouching his wasted body to avoid banging his head on the ceiling of the narrow staircase.

"So it's you, is it? The bearer of ill tidings."

"We're going to have to let you go, Mr. Corcoran."

"Why?"

"The drinking."

"You always were bad luck, *Mr.* Harrah. Even on Burnt Tavern Road. What's a little drinking to you? So long as the job gets done."

"But it's more than a little drinking, Red. And the job isn't getting done."

"Wasn't that way at the tavern."

"The tavern was meant for drinking, but not the furnace. I can get you a job hauling timber. If you're tipsy, you'll hurt no one but yourself."

"Rather go to Weymouth or Hampton Furnace than do hauling."

"Suit yourself. Though I'd hate to see the Widow uprooted again."

"We were thinking of pushing on anyway."

"Were you?"

"Yes, they're much too strict here at Martha. And they pay only in scrip, as at Batsto."

"I'll see that you get two weeks' pay in specie—if you're set on leaving. A kind of going-away present," said Harrah.

"I don't want your money," growled Corcoran. "But—But I'll take it anyway. Not on my account—for the widow."

With Corcoran and the Widow Sizemore gone, Harrah visited Fred and Cora Botts only to discover that Cassandra had been there a week earlier.

"Yes, she did mention it," he said. "In the rush of things I must have forgotten."

But the fact was, Cassandra never said a word. Still protecting him from Burnt Tavern Road, no doubt. It was hard to live down the past, though Harrah had hurt Fred and Cora Botts in no way. Even on their wedding night, when the others were raucous and mischievous, he had taken no part in the shivaree.

Harrah produced gifts of candy for the twins and a bottle of wine for the young couple. Fred Botts showed no rancor towards Harrah, not even for the departure of Red Corcoran and his mother-in-law, the Widow Sizemore. He congratulated him on his new position and offered to show him about the small house.

"Cora has done a nice job with the place, hasn't she? Did

you see the quilts she made for the boys? Mrs. Evans was so impressed, she ordered one for the big house."

"And what's that?" asked Harrah.

"A model train."

"I can see. But how did you manage it? It's very skilled work. Highly precisioned."

The model Harrah was looking at was a copy of George and Robert Stephenson's *Northumbrian* with its muted incline of the cylinders, a horizontal boiler (with an internal firebox) and a proper tender tank instead of a water barrel over the coal. It was painted a light green, picked out in black, with a green-tinted silver chimney.

"I copied it from a drawing. And it's scaled to the inch," said Botts. "I study with Mr. Evans from time to time. He's an engineer, you know."

"I didn't know."

"He's taught me a good deal, Mr. Harrah. Though much of it has nothing to do with smithing."

Harrah came away impressed.

That night he got off a letter to Mr. Stevens of the Camden and Amboy railway. Two weeks later he received a reply.

"Send the young man to me. I will pay all expenses. If he is half as good as you say he is, he can begin working the day he arrives."

Cora had a kiss for him and Fred Botts a handshake.

"I'll never forget this, Mr. Harrah. Never as long as I live."

"Neither will Mr. Evans. Now he has to go looking for another blacksmith."

"I do feel guilty about that," said Fred.

"Never feel guilty. Mr. Evans will find another smith. And he'll be proud that he had a hand in this."

"Bless you," said Cora. And in a few moments they were gone.

STRIFE

The drinking had gotten so bad in Calico that even Harrah agreed something must be done.

"There's little else to do when their time is free," he acknowledged. "But it's getting out of hand."

"We cannot have two standards, one for Martha and one for Calico," said Mr. Evans. "We'll have to prohibit drinking in Calico as well."

"It won't work, Mr. Evans. I'd rather we fire the drunkards. We're going to have a serious accident one of these days."

"We've had a few already. But if I start firing the men who drink there'll be precious few left to work the furnace."

"On the other side, if you ban the sale of liquor, we'll have trouble on our hands. It's easier to take bread away than whiskey."

"There's no help for it, Mr. Harrah. What's the point of keeping Martha dry when Calico is wet as a swamp? I'm afraid we have no choice."

"I'm not so sure."

"What do you mean?"

"You were planning to lay some men off next week, weren't you?"

"Yes."

"Well, that's action the men understand. When orders fall off, we have to cut back. Why can't we let go of the heavy drinkers first—instead of those new on the job?"

"'Cause that's been the custom at Martha. When orders pick up, the men laid off come back. I don't even have to contact them. They know somehow. And they know who's been at Martha longest. I heard they even keep a list. So I keep a list too."

"Then it's a ban on drinking?" said Harrah.

"I'm afraid so."

"Whatever you say, Mr. Evans."

As Harrah feared, the ban spelled trouble from the start. The poster announcing the prohibition was torn from the wall. And half a dozen men broke into the general store to remove what bottles remained. In no time at all there was more tippling in the streets than Calico had ever known. And a few enterprising individuals promptly ran wagons to the Landing or Pleasant Mills to stock up on whiskey and to sell it at twice the going rate.

"They're bringing it in faster than we can confiscate it," said Harrah. "And those who confiscate it are selling the stuff themselves."

Mr. Evans nodded but said nothing. A Quaker, he did not have a passionate nature. He looked to the sky for an answer to his dilemma and it came with the rains.

For three days they fell. And the heavy downpour dampened the spirits of the whiskey rebellion. It made rivers of the roads and boats of the wagons. The sand turned not to mud but to an ooze that had the consistency and color of coffee.

Pat Taggart's coaling wagon, loaded with whiskey, was caught in a great freshet and sank like a rock. Taggart himself was in water up to his hatband but managed to swim to safety. The ore raisers in nearby Tranquillity were drowned out and had to pull up along the bank to wait out the rain. And James Gaskell, trying to raise a crate of whiskey bottles with pulleys, fell out of his stable loft and broke his arm. It went no better with the scowmen who were flooded out or beached.

"It appears the weather is your ally," noted Harrah, hiding under a slicker.

"Except that the furnace made bad iron," said Mr. Evans.

"But the flow of whiskey has virtually stopped."

"For the time being."

Peg Slaughter stopped by. She had taken the time to wash her face and arms but her neck was still streaked with soot.

"I'm getting married," she announced.

"That's good news," smiled Cassandra.

"Is it? My dad's none too happy."

"Why not?"

"I don't know who the father is."

"The father?"

"Yes, I'm going to have a baby."

Cassandra put her arm around the girl. "Oh, Peg, you've gotten yourself into a sorry mess."

"It could have been any one of four. I picked Wilfred Emlen because he'd make the best husband. Though I like Jack the best."

"Why not Jack, then?"

"'Cause he's already got a wife in Ireland."

"I see. What does Wilfred do?"

"He's a molder. Works nights in the carpenter's shed near the furnace. He doesn't drink half as much as Jack. And he won't beat me. And my dad won't have Jack."

"Will you stay for tea?"

"No, I've got to get back. School's out and the boys will be home soon."

"I'm leaving for a few days," said Mr. Evans, handing Harrah a sheet of paper. "These men are to receive notice."

"What shall I tell them?"

"That we don't know when we'll have work for them again."

Harrah was not too happy about having to break the news, but he took the list and stuffed it in his pocket.

Cassandra was distressed by the layoffs.

"It's bad enough the men get their pink slips. Why should you have to be the one to tell them?"

"Who else is there? It's part of the job, my girl."

"Let Mr. Evans do it."

"He has over the years, countless times. Now it's my turn."

"This is terrible," said Cassandra, reading the names. "The young man Peg Slaughter is going to marry is on the list. And one of the ore raiser's sons. They're our neighbors. Can't you do something about this?"

"Would it be any easier if they lived at the other end of Calico?"

"It might. This way I've got to pass them in the street and see the hurt in their eyes."

Harrah distributed the discharge slips on Friday.

"I'm sorry, men. The workload has fallen off. We've got to cut back."

Most of the men who received notices took the news quietly. But at least two were bitter.

"I've as much right to work as one of those blacks. How come you did not let any of them go?"

"Three of the blacks received notices, too. The others have been here a long time."

"They probably work for less. Slave wages, no doubt."

"They get the same as you."

"But we're free men."

"So are they."

"Free or not, how are we to eat?" one asked.

"You'll get credit in the store for a week or two. By then you'll know where you're going."

"Is there any work at Weymouth?"

"You might try Weymouth. Or Hampton Furnace."

"The hell with Jersey," said his friend. "Next job I take's in Pennsylvania."

And so it went until Mr. Evans returned.

"Can you use another charcoal burner?" asked Cassandra.

"Why?"

"Peg's father is willing to teach Wilfred the trade. He can always go back to being a molder when business picks up."

"A charcoal burner's no life."

"Why not?"

"Well, he's in that shed day and night. Until the coaling's done he dare not leave. He works with cones and charred wood and steady heat. There's nothing but smoke and fire to fill the nostrils. I'd sooner Wilfred looked for work in another furnace town."

"But Peg wants to remain here and look after her little brothers."

"Well, if she's set on it, I'll speak to Mr. Evans."

"That's what I wanted you to do in the first place." Cassandra's laugh was both a small triumph and a gesture of love.

Mr. Evans would not hear of it.

"What's the point of laying men off if we're going to put them to work at something else? It's the payroll must be cut. Will you remember that, Mr. Harrah?"

"I'm not likely to forget."

On Tuesday the molders stopped work and went hunting. These were followed by the fillermen and the hearthmen. The founder reported the action to Mr. Evans.

"First the ban on whiskey. Then the layoffs. The men are mightily displeased. So they quit work."

"Shut the furnace down," ordered Mr. Evans.

"Shut it down!"

"I don't mean for the day. I mean indefinitely."

"But the men will drift back by evening," predicted the founder.

"And then stop work again a few days from now? No, we'll shut the place down. I'll not be a wheel to their millrace."

The founder counted on his fingers. "We still have men enough to keep going—if we switch jobs around."

"What kind of iron will that make?"

"I can't say, Mr. Evans."

"An inferior grade at best. No, it's difficult enough competing with our best iron. Close the furnace down and take a holiday."

Harrah ventured no opinion when asked what he thought.

"Never mind," said Mr. Evans. "I can read your mind. But let me explain something to you. By shutting the furnace down, I put the burden on the men who walked off. They've got to eat. Without scrip, they haven't money enough to buy a bottle even if I permitted it. And those who want to work will blame them. In two weeks time they'll all forget their displeasure and go back to their jobs."

"Without settling their grievances?"

"What grievances do they have? A ban on drinking? All right, I can ease the ban. Fine those who frolic at Martha and fire those who frolic too much. They may go along with that. At least there's not total prohibition. But there is no way I can prevent layoffs."

"But all they want is a chance to work."

"I can't give them work when I have no orders."

"It doesn't have to be work at the furnace," said Harrah. "Let them log and saw timber when things slow down. Then bring them in again when orders pick up. There are always men running off and we end up looking for replacements. This way we have a reserve and we can assure each man a full season of work."

Mr. Evans leaned back and rested his head on his hands. "To do that," he said, "I'd have to cut the number of lumbermen hired at the beginning of the season. How do I ensure a sufficient supply of timber?"

"You build up a reserve from the year before."

"It might work," said Mr. Evans. "The plan's worth trying. But it will be more palatable if the men go hungry for a while."

"I don't understand."

Mr. Evans leaned forward and spoke almost in a whisper. "If I offer this plan now while the men are still high with common purpose, they'll find fault with it. You can't talk to a man who's just been liberated. All he knows is that he's free. No boss, no toil, the day is his. But if you wait until the raw fruit grows ripe and his belly begins to growl, he might just be willing to listen."

"But it's not only his belly goes hungry. His wife and kids go hungry, too."

"Be grateful for that. Because of the wife and children, the men will only fast two weeks. Without them, they could go on for months."

Harrah found himself staring at the ironmaster.

"I'm not a hard man," said Mr. Evans. "The cruel fact is Martha will have to shut down if the men don't go back to work soon—with all problems resolved. And if Martha goes under, the fate of these men—and their families—will be far worse than a two-week fast."

Mr. Evans knew his men. For the first few days there was a good deal of frolicking and whooping things up. With the furnace out of blast, several families went down to the shore to gather clams and run along the beach, though it was cold for April. Others went hunting and brought back bags full of small game and wild turkey. At night all hands got hilariously drunk, chased stray dogs that roamed through the town, and played hide-and-seek in the saw mill. Still others got into a grand fight and tumbled into the creek, breaking at least one nose and one leg.

By the end of the week there was some sobering up and a good deal of quarreling about the wisdom of their action. This led to some bickering about foodstuffs that were smuggled out of the general store. There was no real leadership among the men; anyone who assumed authority was looked upon as one would an ironmaster at this time.

"How long will this go on?" asked Cassandra. "I feel guilty going to the store with money in my purse. I've given food to Peg Slaughter and the ore raisers. But we haven't enough to feed the whole town."

"Mr. Evans gives it another week."

"And then?"

"And then they'll go back."

"On whose terms?"

"His. But he'll be fair about it."

"I hope so. I don't like seeing men at one another's throats. And that's what it's coming to."

In a week the men were back. Evans made no concessions. The layoffs stood. The ban on drinking stood, but the manager agreed to consider a small allowance for each man after working hours. If the privilege were abused, he would go back to a complete prohibition. The men glumly accepted the terms and reported to the common kitchen for a meal. And food was distributed by wagon to their needy families.

"I trust you learned something," said Mr. Evans when they were alone.

Harrah did not comprehend.

"Time is always on the owner's side—if he's willing to sweat it out."

Maybe, thought Harrah.

"But there has to be some give," added Evans, "if only to take the sting out of defeat. They're still men, you know."

IN PLACE OF MR. EVANS

"I can't get out of bed, Mr. Harrah. Aches and pains all over."

"What about the tubs? The seal is broken and the inner tub has shifted to a side."

"You will have to resolve the matter. I can't move."

The founder explained the problem to Harrah.

"Without the leather washer, no seal is made. The inner tub moves up and down inside the outer tub. But no air is sucked in on the upswing and no air is forced out on the downswing. With no air going through the pipes to the tuyère, we can't whip enough heat for the smelting."

"So let's get another seal."

"We'll have to go to Batsto or Atsion for one."

"Don't you have any in reserve?"

"No."

"Then let's make one. It will take less time than going to Batsto. There are leather hides in the tannery."

Mr. Evans had not recovered when one of the flood gates threatened to give way. Harrah put a team of men to work repairing it, men from the second shift who normally would be asleep. The hands were so tired for the next few nights that they could hardly man the furnace.

Meanwhile the saw mill was stopped by back water. Harrah told the men to hand-saw the needed planks. As soon as the floodgate was repaired and the water began to flow again, a belt on the saw mill broke. That same morning a new belt was fitted.

Harrah had his "breakfast" at noontime.

"It's as if the place waited for Mr. Evans to get sick before things began breaking down."

"Waited for you, you mean."

Harrah looked at Cassandra whose cool composure was in sharp contrast to his own gnawing anger.

"Yes, I suppose that was what I meant. What bothers me is that I've had no time for you or the children. I might just as well be the ironmaster for all the work I'm called on to do."

He had scarcely finished his eggs when the founder appeared at the door to advise Harrah that a wagon was going to Batsto. Was there anything he wanted brought back?"

"Another leather seal for the tubs. We should have at least one in reserve."

"Very good, Mr. Harrah."

Harrah nodded and gulped down his coffee.

When Mr. Evans was up and about again, there was no respite. Having filled in so well for the ironmaster in his absence, Harrah was called upon to straighten out other snags.

"Something's wrong with the coaling," said Mr. Evans. "See what Joe Slaughter is up to."

Harrah rode up to the charcoal burner's shed and found the place full of smoke, more smoke than was proper. Inside he found Slaughter sprawled on the floor, very drunk or very dead. He was joined by Wilfred Emlen.

"What's the matter with Joe?"

Harrah put his head to his chest. "I think he's dead."

"Dead?"

"Dead or drunk."

Wilfred looked for the man's pulse but found no beat.

"He must have been very drunk. The smoke got him but he never let go of the bottle. Poor Peg. What'll I tell her?"

"Tell her about the smoke, but forget about the whiskey."

"She'll know anyway."

"Makes no difference. He's still her dad."

"Just as you say, Mr. Harrah."

"And Wilfred—"

"Yes?"

"The company will pay for the burial." If Harrah was going to have the responsibilities of an ironmaster, he would damn sure exert his authority.

"Thank you, Mr. Harrah. At least that will be a comfort to Peg."

When the coffin of Joe Slaughter was lowered into the ground and the burial ceremony completed, Mr. Evans caught up with Harrah who was leaving the cemetery.

"It appears you were right, Mr. Harrah."

"About what?"

"About holding men in reserve. Mr. Slaughter ran off in a way, didn't he? And now Wilfred Emlen is ready to take over."

"Yes," acknowledged Harrah, "Wilfred is ready." What Harrah wanted to know was whether he himself was ready to take over. By word and by deed Mr. Evans was preparing him for some kind of succession.

"How does the job sit with you now?"

"Now?"

"Now that you know what you're doing?"

"It sits heavy," said Harrah.

"Why is that?"

"Because I want to please you, Mr. Evans." Harrah paused a moment. "And at the same time I want to please myself."

"How does it feel to be ironmaster?" teased Cassandra.

"I'll know when there's a bulge in my pay envelope."

"What do a few dollars matter? Think of the prestige and authority. They say 'Mr. Harrah' now the way they used to say 'Mr. Evans.' There's talk Mr. Evans has bought Martha Furnace from Samuel Richards and will play the absentee owner."

"It's only talk. He's not the owner yet."

"Still," said Cassandra, "it's something to think about."

"I've given it some thought."

"And you'll accept the position?"

"It's what you want, isn't it?"

"I don't know," said Cassandra.

"You don't? Well, then you'd better think about it. We've been invited to the ironmaster's house for dinner."

"Tonight? Why didn't you tell me? I'll never be ready in time."

"I only just learned myself."

They arrived but a few minutes late and were greeted at the door by Mr. and Mrs. Evans. Relieved of their coats, they were ushered into the living room which was dominated by a large walnut table and six straightbacked chairs. A mahogany desk, a bookcase, and a corner cupboard filled with China graced one wall. And a fireplace, a clock, and six pairs of candlesticks decorated another. But the magnificent table was the centerpiece, overwhelming the decanter of wine and the two glasses that sat on it.

"Mrs. Evans and I do not drink," said the ironmaster. "But I understand this is very good wine. Will you have a glass?"

"Thank you," said Harrah.

Cassandra replied with a nod.

"I'm afraid," said the ironmaster, "that Mrs. Evans and I are unregenerate Quakers. In '25, after the break with the Conservatives, Lucy joined the Hicksite Meeting House that was built at Bridgeport. Over the years the Quakers have moved away. But Lucy still attends regularly. In fact, there are times when she is the sole member of the congregation. What with the furnace and all, I have little time for such matters."

"With a seven-day week, it is no wonder," said Harrah.

"We've got to take everything in sevens," added Mr. Evans. "We've had our lean years. Now I'm looking forward to seven good ones at Martha."

Mrs. Evans agreed that times would get better.

"My husband has always been an honest, industrious man. Martha Furnace will flourish under his ownership."

"Then you have bought the place?"

"Not exactly. I have option to buy," said Mr. Evans.

At dinner the conversation turned to the past.

"You have no idea how different Martha was when we first arrived here. What you saw this year, Mr. Harrah, was bitterness over spirits and hard times. In years past the mood was carefree."

"Carefree, yes," remarked Lucy. "But there has always been a struggle over temperance."

"The difference, then, was that iron was king. And Jersey was the king of iron. And the men knew it. Oh, there was no lack of frolicking. Some of the men slept the afternoon away on their shop benches. Others made a clandestine retreat from chopping or ore-raising. But by and large they got the work done. I remember one stout fellow bending a hand bar out of shape. We fired him. The next day he bent the bar back and we rehired him."

Harrah laughed, but Cassandra and Mrs. Evans found no hilarity in the story.

"When Solomon Truax was married, the hands had a great time eating, drinking, and kissing the bride. Later the men took the gates off the hinges of the bride's house and hid them in the woods."

Still no response from Cassandra and the ironmaster's wife. But Mr. Evans was undaunted.

"On all fools day—"

"My dear," said Mrs. Evans, "why don't you and Mr. Harrah repair to the living room while Mrs. Harrah and I look at some of my quilting? I believe you have some serious business to discuss."

Mr. Evans took his wife's criticism good-naturedly. And though Harrah was sure Cassandra wanted to be a party to the discussion he knew that in this instance she would yield to Mrs. Evans.

"This has been a good year for you, Mr. Harrah," began Mr. Evans as he drew up his favorite chair. "You've had a successful apprenticeship, and I have no doubt you would make an outstanding ironmaster."

"Thank you," said Harrah.

"Of course, there is still much to learn. But I will be on hand to teach you. Contrary to speculation, I do not expect to become the absentee owner of Martha Furnace."

"I see." Harrah understood that Mr. and Mrs. Evans would continue to live in the ironmaster's house while he and Cassandra remained at Calico.

"You're still interested in the job?"

"I am. But, of course, I would want to discuss it with my wife."

"A splendid-looking woman, Mrs. Harrah. She would be a decided asset to your position as ironmaster."

"Would there be an increase in salary?" Harrah asked.

"Something in line with what an ironmaster could expect?"

"Yes," said Mr. Evans. "But much would depend on the company's earnings for the next few years—assuming, of course, that I do buy. All things considered, I have reason to believe that you will be satisfied with your compensation."

Later that night Harrah discussed the offer with Cassandra. "He never put forth a specific figure. Much, I think, depends on how well the furnace thrives. And should Mr. Evans buy, it might be a year or two before we move into the ironmaster's house."

"Makes no difference," said his wife.

"Then you want me to take it?"

"No," said Cassandra.

Would she ever run out of surprises?

"Why not?" asked Harrah, still somewhat bewildered.

"I would rather we started our own ironworks."

She said no more than that. But it was enough. Harrah was taken completely unawares. As well as he knew Cassandra, it seemed he never knew what to expect from her. But, more important, Harrah could see that the lines were drawn for battle. The truth was Harrah wanted no more of iron. He was fed up with fighting the elements and playing master to the hired hands. He wanted no more of prohibition or layoffs. He wanted to withdraw from the din of daily battle to the hilltop of prospect and speculation. Cassandra understood none of this. How could she? What experience had she had with the fickleness of machinery or the drudgery of detail? And so they were at odds.

There would be a heated exchange. Not at the moment perhaps, but sometime soon. He had no idea what shape the war would take, but he had no doubt the clash would come. And the fight over their future course might be a bitter one.

COLLISION COURSE

Jonathan had midnight terrors. Now two years old, he was an odd combination of inchoate infant and perceptive child. Talking freely and deliriously, he saw in every shadow, in every flicker of light, shapes and shadows that beggared Rachel's descriptions of goblins and Jersey devils.

Cassandra held the little body close to her and tight, talking softly, reinterpreting what the boy saw, and soothing his fears.

"Ah, your head is not so warm now. Little Jonathan's head is cooler to the touch. Does my baby want a little water?"

"Wa wa," he said, though he was perfectly able to say water.

Cassandra signalled to Harrah. "Get me some water, Nathaniel."

Harrah poured a cupful from the pitcher on the nightstand and Jonathan sipped it slowly, letting a few drops slip down his chin. In a few moments the child was asleep again, but Cassandra continued to walk back and forth, carrying him close.

"The motion comforts him," she said.

"Here, I'll carry the lad," volunteered Harrah.

"No, the shift may disturb him."

Harrah gave ground. He saw that in holding the boy close and tight Cassandra was also embracing his future. And there was no way she would relinquish her hold.

"When will you speak to Mr. Evans?" she asked after a while.

"When I've decided what to do."

"But I thought you were going to build a new ironworks?"

"I didn't think you were serious about that."

"But I am."

It was late, and Harrah did not want to argue the matter. But he knew Cassandra well enough not to forestall discussion.

"There's no more future for a new ironworks in the Pines than there is for Martha Furnace. At Martha at least, I have no money at stake. If the place closes down, I will only have lost a job."

"Jesse sees hope for iron."

"In Pennsylvania maybe, but not in South Jersey. Besides, Jesse will branch out into other things. Glass, maybe. Or paper. McCartyville has had some success with paper."

"Martha is in trouble because the bogs are giving out. And the timber. A new ironworks in virgin territory would have these things at hand." Cassandra continued to walk back and forth with the sleeping boy in her arms.

"Martha is in trouble because she can't compete with Pennsylvania. Even Jesse is importing ore for his furnaces—wherever he can get it. Morris County, Staten Island, Rancocas. And then there's shortages of good hands. Even when drinking is not a problem, inexperience is.''

"Jesse will find the men for you," said Cassandra. "He's always had a better breed of laborer than Mr. Evans.''

"And I suppose you've talked all this over with Jesse?"

Cassandra stopped short. "Yes, we've talked.''

"Does he know how I feel about iron?"

"Meaning?''

"Does Jesse know I don't like it? I don't mean the iron itself. Though the touch of it leaves me cold. The whole blame process of manufacturing it, I'm talking about.''

"I don't believe I know either," said Cassandra quietly.

"Well, its difficult to describe. There are the bogs, no more than mud holes. And the charcoal, nothing but lampblack for the lungs. And the fishy stench of the clam shells. And the furnace itself, forever breaking down and needing tending to. And the men with their drinking and their horseplay, with no more responsibility than schoolboys on a holiday. What it all boils down to is that the process is too dependent on too many things. Before you produce a ton of iron or a boatload of hollow ware, you're pretty well wrung out. And it's all in a losing battle—either with the elements or with pig iron from Pennsylvania.''

"But as ironmaster you are above all that. At least the bogs and the charcoal and the shells. It is other men who have to do the dirty work. All you have to worry about are the men themselves and the furnace.''

"Is the work any less dirty, Cassandra, when other men have to do it?"

"I don't understand you, Nathaniel.''

"What I am saying is, I'm not Jesse Richards. I don't enjoy running a feudal fiefdom. I'll do it if I have to—so long as someone else owns it and I see a way out one day.''

"But with your own furnace you can operate any way you want. Jesse hardly conducts himself as lord of the manor!''

"And how do you propose I finance such a furnace? Do you have any idea how big an operation a new ironworks is?"

"We have some money. Jesse will get backing for the rest. There are banks in New York and Philadelphia where Jesse's name is magic. Even in the Panic of '37 Jesse was able to get credit.''

Harrah was overwhelmed by her confidence.

"Why are you willing to risk such a venture? Isn't it enough that I will be ironmaster? Why must you gamble your life's savings when we can live in comfort without taking wild chances?''

"Yes, my dear, you will be ironmaster. And I am not unimpressed with your achievement. I won't deny that being an ironmaster's wife appeals to me. For someone born a bastard this would be a big step up. But I want to be more than an ironmaster's wife. I want independence.''

"Independence?''

"Yes, even an ironmaster is not his own master when he works for someone else. I have no quarrel with Mr. Evans. He knows better than any man how important it is to own the works. Wasn't he an ironmaster for more than thirty years? Well, Nathaniel, I don't want to see you wait that length of time. I want you to build your own works now—while you're still young enough to enjoy the fruits of it.''

Harrah watched as Cassandra set the boy down in his bed. He marvelled at the strength underneath all that tenderness. Cassandra was not a strong woman as her sex went. Some might even think her delicate, thin as she was. But her will was tempered iron. And what made things worse was that he loved her. If he had not loved her, he would not be rushing headlong to his ruin. For that was how he viewed the course he was on, though he would no more switch it than he would lose Cassandra.

"I'm still young enough to try other things," he countered. "For years I've thought of the railroads. If I'm to start out anew, I'd just as soon go with the iron horse than with iron works. If Jesse wants to back me, let him back me in that.''

"I'm afraid of the railroads.''

"What's there to be afraid of?''

"They will change the Pines. They will bring too many people in and out. They will put an end to the coach stops and the taverns. They will make us nothing but Philadelphia and Tuckerton way stations. And my husband will always be off somewhere to build a new road.''

"I'll take you with me, Cassandra." Even as he said this, Harrah knew that his wife would refuse to accompany him.

"My place is here," she said. "You know that by now.''

Yes, he knew. And he accepted it as fact. But he could not accept the notion of building a new ironworks.

"It's doomed, I tell you. Iron in the Pines is doomed. How many furnaces must shut down before you admit they're a thing of the past?''

THIRD PARTY

Jesse Richards played the role of mediator.

"So Mr. Evans offered you the ironmaster's post?"

"Yes."

"Well, that's interesting."

"Why?"

"My brother Samuel isn't selling just yet. He's changed his mind. Maybe in a couple of years he'll offer Martha for sale again. Meanwhile Mr. Evans will stay on as ironmaster."

"That changes things, doesn't it?" observed Cassandra.

"I suppose it does. Not that it matters. I wasn't thrilled at the prospect of remaining at Martha either."

"Nathaniel has his mind set on the railroads," advised Cassandra.

"So I've heard."

"Did anything come of that plan to build a railroad through Quaker Bridge?" asked Harrah.

"No, the Panic pretty well ruled that out. Those of my friends who speculated in paper suffered badly. A route through the Pines is out of the question at this time."

"It would have made all the difference," said Harrah.

"Possibly. But there are other places to build railroads, I would think."

"For my wife there are the Pines and only the Pines."

"I'm of the same mind," said Jesse Richards, watching Cassandra leave the room to see Rachel for a moment.

"But you at least spend part of the year in Philadelphia. Cassandra never leaves the place."

"What's wrong with that?"

Harrah tried to explain. "I'm sure the people of the lost city felt the same way about Atlantis. Had they a chance to leave before the debacle, they probably would have stayed on."

"But the Pines face no such debacle."

"Don't they?"

Richards fathomed his meaning. "You mean that iron is doomed here."

"Isn't it?"

"Very likely. But there are things we can do to keep the place above water. The men have to be kept working."

"It's not just iron," said Harrah. "The whole way of life here is doomed. The taverns, the stagecoach routes, the traffic in smuggling—it's all part of the past. Even the mansions will give way to abandonment and decay one day. And the forges will be nothing but ruins.''

"You're a cheerful soul, aren't you?" gibed Richards.

"I'm trying to look ahead," said Harrah. "For my children's sake as well as Cassandra's."

"There's time yet," pronounced Richards, noticing that Cassandra had returned with some wine. "There's still time."

Jesse Richards had been putting on weight. Always a massive man, he now stood near three hundred pounds. He tried to cut down on his consumption of food, but his taste for drink was unabated.

"I tell you, Harrah, that we'll turn the tide. What Cassandra says is true. You'll not only have a new furnace, you'll have new bogs and uncut forest. It will be twenty years before you run out of iron. And then, if you're careful, the bogs will replenish themselves. Don't bury South Jersey yet."

"What about our neighbor, Pennsylvania?"

"What about it? We'll keep apace. We'll install cupolas. We'll introduce the latest improvements. We'll smelt with the best of them. We'll produce a better quality of pig iron than Pennsylvania ever saw!"

Harrah was not convinced.

"Besides," said Richards, glancing over at Cassandra, "I know just the site. There are large tracts of land in the area, for sale at rock-bottom prices. If all else fails, we'll make money on the land."

"Where is this El Dorado?"

"On the North Branch of the Wading River. Only a few miles from Leeks Landing. Want to take a look at it?"

"Do that at least," said Cassandra.

"All right, Jesse. We'll take a look."

"I love that wife of yours," said Richards when on horseback they had reached the Wading River. "I would no more let her leave the Pines than I would leave them myself. You don't understand how strong she is for the place and how lost she'd be out of it."

"I have no plans to leave," said Harrah.

"But if you stay, you must become part of the place. The surest way is to own some of the land—and to work it. Between you and me, Martha is not long for this world. Being ironmaster there would be like overseeing a wake. Evans knows this. He's too wise not to know. But he won't admit it to himself."

"Martha was not my idea either. I took the job only because you and Cassandra thought the experience would be valuable."

"And it was! Look at what you've learned." Though a heavy

man, Richards sat lightly on his horse.

Harrah reined in his mount.

"Jesse, you're a good friend. I've never doubted that. But let's understand one thing. I'm here—in the Pines—because of Cassandra. I don't see any other reason to stay. I'm not sanguine about the prospects of the place. Beautiful it is. Unspoiled it is. But it will not sustain life for long. Or industry. The Pines are a fool's paradise. Or maybe a haven for runaways. It has a certain lure—even for me. But I'll not close my eyes to its faults."

"Then you won't build?"

"Let's see the site first."

After a short ride they brought their horses to a grassy terrace fringed with coarse tufts of sedge. They moved on to higher, drier ground past clumps of inkberry and ilex and a couple of bayberry bushes. There among the sheep laurel they stopped. What they saw up ahead was an immense stretch of forest fringing the shore of a branch of the Wading River. Neither Harrah nor Richards spoke. They simply surveyed and studied. As they proceeded along their side of the river's edge, they came upon a flat, grassy plain dotted with clumps of white cedars and solitary pitch pines on dry knolls.

"This is where I would build the works," said Richards.

"Why here?"

"Because there are few trees to fell."

"But the savanna is wet and grassy."

"I would build on high ground. The wet areas are covered with white-cedar swamps. And, of course, bog iron. Notice the iron-stained pools of water."

Harrah made a mental note of what he saw.

"Now," continued Richards, "if you look toward the south, you can spot trees again. Tall trees that stretch as far as the eye can see. Trees enough for building and for charcoal burning."

"And, of course, there is the river."

"Exactly. For transporting ore in and bringing the pig iron out."

"And for the mill race."

"Right again! You see what a splendid site this is!"

Harrah found Richards's enthusiasm to be contagious, and soon he was finding things to get excited about.

"See those majestic white cedars?" He pointed north.

"Yes."

"How tall they are, and straight! Like giant Druids wending their way to an outdoor cathedral."

Richards laughed. "You sound like my Irish workers. They see chapels in every turn of the woods."

This sobered Harrah. From then on he controlled his enthusiasm, content to listen to the screams of the circling herons or quietly to savor the fragrance of the swamps and the cedars.

"Well?" asked Richards at last, resting his case.

Harrah shifted in his saddle, patting his horse on the flank.

"There are still some questions. Money, for one."

"I told Cassandra I would raise some for you—enough to get the project under way."

"What do you want for collateral?"

"The land. Nothing more."

"Nothing?"

"Nothing," said Richards.

It was a subdued and thoughtful Harrah who turned his horse about and pointed it home.

"Well, what do you think?" asked Cassandra when the men had returned, tired and hungry from their ride.

"I think it's worth looking into," said Harrah.

Richards sighed with cavernous relief. And what reservations Harrah had were dispelled by Cassandra's embrace and unashamed squeal of delight.

Part Seven

TRESCOTT

THE BIRTH OF AN IRONWORKS

Harrah did not want to build a second Martha but as he drew plans for Trescott he found that he was using Martha Furnace as a model. Even the idea of calling the place Trescott after Cassandra was an echo of the other irontown. Some fifty years earlier Isaac Potts had named his furnace after his wife, Martha. And now Harrah had done much the same.

In its heyday Martha had about four hundred inhabitants, fifty houses, a general store, a saw mill, a grist mill, a hospital of sorts, and a school—if one counted nearby Calico where the workers lived.

Harrah projected a smaller village. He figured on about one hundred fifty inhabitants with some thirty cottages on the style of the workers' houses at Batsto. These were far superior to the crude frame structures at Martha and would attract a better worker. In fact, it was Cassandra who designed the cottages. And she designed them well, with small bright kitchens and each sitting room around a hearth. Harrah planned to employ the men who built the cottages as woodsmen or molders.

The heart of Trescott, of course, would be the furnace. In operation twenty-four hours a day, seven days a week—all the time it was in blast—the furnace required great skill in its construction. So Harrah went to work on it before he completed his plans for the rest of the town. He did reserve a spot for a forge about a mile away, but he did not plan to build one at this time.

Hauling in brick by oxcart, his men built a double-walled brick chimney that was faced with stone on the outside. This chimney was about twenty feet high and looked like a sturdy, sawed-off pyramid. The square base of the furnace had four squat arches on each side, which gave the workers access to the inner chamber. About three-quarters of the way down the chimney was the "bosh" or widest part. The "hearth" below the bosh was really no hearth at all. The fire was above it. But the hearth held the huge crucible into which the molten iron ran.

As in Batsto the furnace was built in a depression so that a bridge of sighs could span the chimney top and the higher ground at the edge of the bank. It was on this bridge that Harrah inspected the construction of the furnace.

"How is it going?" he asked of the foreman.

"Right well, Mr. Harrah. And right on schedule."

"Good. I want it in blast by May. The men can live in tents till the cottages are constructed. It should be warm enough by then."

"It's almost warm enough now."

Trescott was built on a stream to provide a spillway for the furnace. The stream, a branch of the Wading River, was dammed up and a water-wheel was placed in the spillway to power the two large leather bellows which gave the furnace its draft. The stream also made it possible for the ore to be carried in by flatboats, and the pig iron and hollow ware to be transported out of town in scows to Leeks Landing where ships and schooners from Philadelphia and New York were anchored and ready for loading.

Cassandra was anxious to inspect the place.

"I'd rather you see it when it's all finished," said Harrah. "Or at least when it goes into blast."

"No," she said. "It's my town. At least it's named for me. So I want to see it now."

Harrah laughed. "You're worse than a filly at the starting line. You have no patience." But he took her along.

When he showed the furnace to her, she merely acknowledged that it was big. She was not so agreeable when they supervised construction of the ironmaster's house.

"I admit I don't know much about furnaces," she said. "But I do know houses. And I don't like what they're doing with the kitchen."

"What's wrong?"

"It's too small. Have them bring it out a bit."

"Then we'll have no room for storage downstairs."

"Bring it all out—the whole structure."

Harrah took her hand and led her away. "This is the last time I take you with me. I know you want it to be a big house, like the one in Batsto. But we can only afford what you see. It will have to do, Cassandra. And once it's built you'll agree that it will do very nicely."

"Still, let them pull out the kitchen."

"Only if you promise—"

"To stay away?"

"Yes."

Cassandra allowed him to help her to the carriage. "All right. I promise. But the drawing room could be a little bigger, too."

Harrah sighed. "You drive a hard bargain. But we'll see what can be done."

When Cassandra returned in May, Trescott was completed. The furnace still dominated the place, but other structures had sprung up around it. There was a casting shed and a carpenter's shop where the patterns or molds were made. And a blacksmith's shop and a low-lying warehouse. Beyond the furnace she could see the dam, the wind rippling its water. And she could make out a saw mill, a stamping mill, and a grist mill. Trescott had come into being. And the idea made her giddy.

GETTING STARTED

Harrah had placed advertisements in Philadelphia newspapers and in *The Camden Mail and General Advertiser*. He had also distributed handbills in Tuckerton and Barnegat for men to work the new bog-iron furnace at Trescott. When he had checked *The Camden Mail* to see how his advertisement read, he was distressed to read in an editorial that "more and more in the State of Pennsylvania anthracite fuel is being used in the smelting of iron ore. This refinement in the production of iron ore can be very injurious, if not fatal, to the iron works of South Jersey." But he did not let this impede his search for experienced fillermen, hearthmen, guttermen, molders, ore-raisers, charcoal burners, teamsters, and lumbermen.

When applicants began to trickle in, having some difficulty finding Trescott, Harrah interviewed them just outside the warehouse. He had some pointed questions for the ironworkers and selected those who seemed to know their trade and who looked sober enough to stand the toil and the heat. The lumbermen he addressed in general terms:

"I need men who can chop two-sixths of a cord of wood a day and who can do this without breaking the ax handle."

And then Harrah wrote down the names of all the men hired, marvelling at how, apart from the Irish names beginning with *Mc*, there were so many men whose surname began with S: Sheil, Stegman, Strook, and Sweeney.

He wasted no time putting the lumbermen to work. While they felled timber for the workers' cottages, the others erected tents for themselves until the cottages were ready. And he appointed Venable, a man who had "bossed" in Hampton and Weymouth furnaces, as his foreman.

"When shall we go into blast?" the new foreman asked.

"As soon as we bring in sufficient loads of ore and flux. Now that we have teamsters on hand, commence hauling coal and sand to the furnace. If there aren't enough oxen, wheel the ore and shells in with barrows. I'd like to go into blast on the 3rd."

"How are we going to feed the men?"

"Until the cottages are built, we'll use the warehouse as a common kitchen. But when the weather's right we'll eat out of doors. McCauley's wife, Mary, will do the cooking. A quantity of fresh pork and a wagon of corn are due any moment."

Venable seemed satisfied that Harrah knew what he was talking about. It wasn't until later, however, that he learned

Harrah had been ironmaster at Martha.

"There's one cabin has to be built before the others," said Harrah.

"Which one's that?"

"The one for the ore-raisers at Magnolia bog. It's dank enough out there. When it rains, it is one soggy mess."

"We'll get some logs there straightway."

"Good."

The next day all the men were at work. The furnace men acted in other capacities, and there was no grumbling. The only mishap occurred when one of the teams fell into a swamp coming back from Magnolia bog.

"What happend?"

"They tried to make way for John Towner's cart and left the road."

"Anyone injured?"

"A few bruises, no more. The wagon's still whole."

"Then have it pulled out of the swamp. There's a scow load of hay has to be transported."

"Very good, Mr. Harrah."

"And Venable—"

"Yes, Sir."

"If you find some tobacco, I'd be much obliged. I haven't had a pipe in days."

"As a matter of fact," said Venable. "Teams just brought up sundries from Leeks Landing. There's flour, soap, sugar, and tobacco among them."

"That's what I call fortuitous happenstance."

Cassandra was on hand for the blast, as were all the hired men and the few families that had moved in. It was the 5th of May, not the 3rd, but close enough to Harrah's target date. Earlier the furnace had been filled with charcoal, and a fire had been put in at the top of the chimney to heat and dry it out. After the fire burned down to the hearth, the furnace was again filled with charcoal which burned its way back to the top again. At a signal from Venable the men began to fill the furnace. Wheelbarrows of ore, flux, and charcoal were rolled over the bridge of sighs and dumped into the furnace stack. Then the men went back across the bridge for additional loads. This pattern—dumping ore, then flux, then charcoal—was repeated until the furnace was filled. At last a mighty roar signalled that the furnace was in blast. The men cheered and some tossed hats. It would be some eight months before the furnace would go out of blast—if all went well. And Harrah and Cassandra, looking up at the huge sign of six-foot letters that spelled

"Trescott," drank a toast to its success.

"To Trescott Furnace," said Harrah. "Long may it roar!"

"To you, my Dear," said Cassandra. "For making it all possible."

The next step was to fill the orders Jesse Richards had thrown their way and to develop new outlets for their iron. Harrah's idea had been to make rails for the growing ironroad industry; pipes, stopcocks, and stuffing boxes for a projected new water works in Baltimore; and fireplug tops for New York and Philadelphia water systems. His aim for the furnace at Trescott was 800 to 900 tons of castings a year with approximately one hundred men directly employed in one aspect or another of the ironworks.

But Cassandra's passion was for stoves and firebacks and some hollow ware. "Glorious firebacks!" she said.

"We can't compete with Atsion," protested Harrah. "They make stoves to order and they've got New York and the Hudson River towns pretty well tied up. And, Lord Knows, everyone gets orders from Philadelphia—Batsto, Hampton Furnace, Weymouth."

"We can make them to order, too. Church stoves and box stoves and open tops in different sizes. How they're decorated can make a big difference in sales. I'll do some sketches and mail them to Albany and Troy and Poughkeepsie and New York. We'll get a fine response. You'll see."

"But there's little competition in rails. And the demand is growing."

"But I don't like rails," insisted Cassandra. "I get no more satisfaction out of looking at them than I do water pipes. Wouldn't you rather see Trescott stamped on a cozy woodstove than on a stretch of pipe?"

"Of course. But I don't want to see Trescott stamped on a foreclosure notice either. We've got some pretty heavy debts to pay."

Fiscal matters did not interest Cassandra. One could see that at a glance. She was mindful that Harrah had borrowed heavily to make Trescott a reality. And she had put all the money that Hostetler had left her in the enterprise. But she knew that Jesse Richards stood behind them. In fact, Jesse had arranged for a number of the loans and held some notes himself. With his support she need not worry about such trifles as meeting mortgage payments or workers' salaries. Besides, Richards had thrown some of his orders their way just to get them started.

"I'm overloaded now anyway," he had said. "With Martha going under, orders have shifted to Batsto. Besides, I'm thinking of building a glass factory."

Moreover, in recent years Batsto had been making its own brick and was shipping it to Weymouth and other furnaces. Richards had it in mind to reduce his dependence on the ironworks. And he was ever mindful that if Trescott could not make a go of it, his own notes would prove worthless. The one thing that put the venture in good stead was the large tract of acreage, woodlands and bogs, that the Trescott Company had bought, and that for a pittance. If push came to shove, Richards could recoup his losses with the sale of this land.

In the end Harrah compromised—or was compromised, as he divined it. He divided production between rails, pipes, etc., and stoves. And for days and into evenings Cassandra drew designs for these stoves and firebacks. She was partial to the box stoves because the large rectangular spaces lent themselves to ornamentation. And she modified the design of the Franklin cook stove so that this too could be more easily decorated in its various sizes. In the end she had some two dozen designs and had difficulty choosing among the best of them.

"What do you think?" she asked.

"I have no real preference."

"Do you like this one?" She held up a design with a deer and some trees in it.

"Yes."

"What about this, a cornucopia of fruit?"

"That's handsome, too."

"Are you being honest with me?"

"Why should I be dishonest? They're all well done—as becomes an artist."

"You're trifling with me."

"That's the trouble," said Harrah. "I'm not trifling with you. You've been too busy for that kind of thing."

"But we must have sketches to mail."

"We have a sufficient number now, wouldn't you say?"

"You're annoyed with me?"

"No."

"Yes, you are. You're feeling neglect, aren't you?"

"On the contrary, it's I who have been neglecting you."

"True enough. You've been busy, Nathaniel. You sit over those account books as though they were a sick child."

"Well, they could be healthier."

"I don't want to hear about it."

"Then I'll spare you."

He kissed her on the forehead and made for bed.

An hour later she climbed in beside him.

"I'm happy now," she said.

"You've decided which ones you like?"

"Yes. The cornucopia was too commonplace—I did one of a pretty girl instead."

"Does she favor you?"

"Should she?"

He pulled her gown back. "With bare breast?"

"Of course not!" Cassandra covered herself once more.

"Let me have your breast," said Harrah.

"What are you going to do with it?"

"Hold it till Sunday. We're good friends, you see."

"But why Sunday?"

"It will not do to hold it in church."

"It won't do to hold it at all," said Cassandra. "I'll get all excited and be too tired to work in the morning. And the designs will never get mailed." With that she turned her back on him and rolled over on her side.

MEETING AT QUAKER BRIDGE

"You're still interested in railroads?" asked Jesse Richards one day.

"Yes."

"At the next ironmasters' meeting, a spokesman for a Camden to Tuckerton line will present a proposal. Why don't you come? I know you're busy, but a railway could be a vital link in these parts. A benefit to all concerned."

Jesse Richards was beginning to sound like Harrah himself. Did he know it? Harrah wondered. Probably not. People have a way of embracing other men's ideas as their own.

The ironmasters met at Thompson's in Quaker Bridge. The hotelkeeper reserved the dining room for the occasion and screened off his regular patrons with lacquered panels painted in Oriental scenes.

Among those present were Jesse Richards, his brother Samuel, looking old and ill, Mr. Evans of Martha Furnace, and ironmasters from Hampton Furnace, Gloucester, Weymouth, and Atsion. As always, Jesse was the driving force at such meetings and he regaled his fellow ironmasters with stories about some exotic furnace or ill-fated land schemes.

The spokesman had not yet arrived. Harrah took the opportunity to order a shot of rye at the bar.

Thompson's bar was unlike any in the Pines. It had a huge mirror behind it, crenelated with the tops of bottles, which lent the hotel a grandeur that Harrah had seen only in Philadelphia. There was even a small chandelier in the room whose candles reflected fiery jewels in the tinted glass of the mirror. A luxurious setting in all, made more luxurious when the white-gowned figure of a lady appeared in the mirror, just below the chandelier. Harrah took immediate note of it. And then he discovered that it belonged to Georgina Pierot!

Georgina had put on a little weight but she was still a gorgeous presence, especially in a room full of prosperous men whose bodies and jowls plumped out in direct proportion to their pocketbooks. With Georgina, of course, was her everpresent brother. George Brookens looked no worse for the passage of time. But, then again, he had little to lose. And in his drab way he made Georgina appear all the lovelier.

The couple made their way to the dining room and the speaker's table where they were greeted with customary cordiality by Jesse Richards. They sat down to a meal of chicken and dumplings, after which George Brookens stood and made a fine presentation. He reviewed the remarkable progress that the railroads had made in the past decade. He described some of the advances made in boiler and engine design, and took note of the cow catcher, now a familiar sight on engines. He quoted figures on the dollar volume of freight that had been carried by the Camden and Amboy Railway last year alone. He declared that the coming of railroads to the Pines was inevitable. It was just a matter of who got there first and who would reap the rewards. And then he discussed the financing of his proposed railway.

Everything Brookens said was true. It was what he did not say that bothered Harrah. How was one to know that shareholders would be getting a fair shake? Just how many shares were there and who owned them? Had a right of way been secured by the proposed railway? What guarantee was there that the money invested would in fact be spent on the railroad and not drained off? Which banks were putting up money for the first leg of the road? And was there any assurance they would go the whole route?

What bothered Harrah even more was that Georgina gave a glossy patina to what he regarded at best as a shabby operation. Merely by sitting in her chair, looking ladylike and angelic, she single-handedly disposed of any objections, any doubts one might have.

With the presentation over, George Brookens smilingly made himself available for individual questioning. Immediately he was surrounded by the ironmasters whose chief concern was tying in the railroads with the shipment of ironware. Georgina meanwhile drifted over to where Harrah was sitting.

"May I join you?"

"By all means," said Harrah, rising and offering her a chair.

"I heard you sold the tavern at Cooper's Point. But I had no idea I'd find you here."

"Yes, I'm ironmaster at Trescott now." He did not bother to explain where Trescott was or how it got its name.

"Ironmaster? Sounds impressive. You have really come up in the world."

"At least I'm no longer doing portraits for my supper."

"A pity. I so like your work."

"Do you still?"

"More than ever."

"I'm glad."

"I'd love so much to see you," she said, clasping his hand.

"Not here," he replied softly, fathoming her meaning. "I know these people."

"Where then?"

"Let me think. I'll hire a carriage and take you for a ride. And then we'll see."

She shook her head. "No, George will suspect."

"What do you suggest?"

"My room. While George is downstairs with the others. It's time we became reacquainted."

"Then I'll rent a room, too, so I have a pretext for going upstairs. In fact, we could meet in my room."

"I couldn't do that," she said. "Don't ask me why. In my room it would seem proper. In your room I'd feel like a hussy."

And so it was her room, half the size of the chamber in Elfreth's Alley, but without the clutter of furniture, that they became reacquainted.

"I know you're an ironmaster now," she said, sitting down on the bed. "And that's all to the good. But I do wish you had gone into railroads."

"With your brother?"

"On your own."

"Why?"

"Apart from the money—and there's a great deal to be made— I'd be able to see more of you."

"It's good of you to say that."

"Just as you are seeing more of me now." She smiled as she undid the top of her gown.

"Actually I've never lost interest in the railroads," said Harrah, enjoying this immediate renewal of intimacy with Georgina. It was as if they had never gone their separate ways.

"Then why not pursue it?"

"I've other irons in the fire."

Georgina smiled at his choice of words as she struggled to divest herself of her gown.

"You could help me," she said, not without annoyance.

Harrah took hold of her sleeves as she pulled free of them.

"These other irons? Are they a wife and child?"

"Two children," said Harrah.

"How fortunate you are! I so wish the children were mine." She removed the last impediment and was now naked to the waist. "Do you think I've put on too much weight?" she asked, placing his hand on her breast.

"You are fuller than before. But you're still lovely."

"Then I'm not too full?"

"No."

"Squeeze me again."

He did.

"And again."

She closed her eyes. "Ah," she said. "That's better." And he saw that her lashes were moist.

The next morning Harrah had breakfast downstairs and waited for Georgina to appear. He knew she was not an early riser. But he wanted to say goodbye before leaving. The other ironmasters had departed the night before. By eleven o'clock there was as yet no sign of her.

"She's still in her room," said the clerk, a surly young man who also helped at the bar. "She and her husband have not come down yet."

"Mr. Brookens is not her husband. He's her brother."

The clerk looked surprised. "You could have fooled me."

Despite the comment, Harrah waited for Georgina. And when at last he caught sight of her coming down the stairs, he did not so much greet her as accost her.

"The clerk thinks George is your husband."

"Does he?"

"Is there any reason to think so?"

A flush crossed Georgina's face. She even looked dowdy for a moment.

"There is."

It was no use. She would never live up to her portrait.

"But—"

"You're thinking he's my brother? Well, there's no resemblance that I can see."

That was true. "Then—"

"Yes, he's my brother, my step-brother. We'll be married as soon as Gerald gives me a divorce—or dies from malnutrition, whichever comes sooner."

"Your step-brother?"

"My mother married again. A much older man. I took the name of Brookens. My original name was Bradley. It's all terribly confusing, I know. But my whole life has been one turmoil. That's why I love your portrait so much. It's a picture of serenity."

Harrah supposed it was. But he could not help thinking, as she broke into her lovely smile, that even in the midst of all her travails, Georgina Brookens even now emerged unscathed, unruffled. She had a placidity that was unscratched by adversity. This was her particular charm, her special appeal. And he admired her for it.

"Then you no longer live at Elfreth's Alley?"

"No, Gerald's creditors took everything, including the house.

I live on Germantown Avenue with George.''

She took Harrah's hand. "Don't be disappointed in me. I'm doing the best I can. I know that George's business practices are questionable. I know that he's using me. But I'm using him too. And I knew that you were finished with me that last time I saw you at Cooper's Point. A woman knows these things.''

"But it's such a waste. You're so beautiful and he's so—''

"Plain? But he's good to me. Never raises his voice. Looks after my comfort and my welfare. Just as his father did.''

"So you're happy?''

"I'm never unhappy. I'd be happier with you. But that's neither here nor there.''

Harrah put on his hat and made ready to leave.

"Goodbye, Georgina.'' He kissed her on the cheek, that lovely cheek. "May that face of yours never change.''

"It never will, Nathaniel, thanks to you.''

AFTERMATH

Harrah's ride back to Trescott was the longest ride of his life. At first he allowed his mount to saunter, then as the events of the past two days crowded his mind, he began to drive his horse into a gallop. But however hard he rode he seemed to make little progress.

He had always harbored some guilt about Georgina Brookens. She was another card to play in life when things with Cassandra were not going well. From the time he had done his portrait of her, Georgina Brookens lay in his pocket to be pulled out when the moment was right. Of course, he did not in the beginning seriously believe the moment would ever be right. He never seriously believed he would meet Georgina Brookens again. And with Cassandra filling his heart and desire he did not really mind. Georgina Brookens, the young woman of the portrait, was just someone passing through Burnt Tavern Road. An apparition, a vision, no more. When she had materialized at the Germantown and Norristown Railway Depot exhibition, he could not believe his good fortune. Despite her complaints and lamentations, he reached into his pocket for his card.

But having played it at Elfreth's Alley and Cooper's Point, he realized he had no card at all. Physically Georgina was as fine a woman as any he had ever known. Emotionally she was wounded, wounded beyond repair. And this last meeting at Quaker Bridge more than confirmed his suspicions. Only a John Witt, with powders and elixirs of the mind, could see her through her sentimental convalescence.

But what about his own emotional wounds? If a slight by Cassandra, a slight she didn't even suspect was a slight, was enough to cause him to stray, what would a serious rift bring about? No, there was something more than a mere slight in his relationship with Cassandra that troubled him. Because of Cassandra he was in the Pines instead of into railroads. Because of Cassandra he was ironmaster.

Still, he loved her and longed to be with her. Like a man who had traveled without his talisman, he was desperate to see her again. But he did not want to watch her pit her strength against her fate, however doubtful it might be. He did not want to know that in a matter of wills she would never surrender. He admired her aspiration, but he did not want to be ironmaster. That was the heart of the problem. He did not want to be ironmaster any more than he had wanted to be a government agent once he arrived in the

Pines or a tavernkeeper on Burnt Tavern Road. He wanted simply to be Nathaniel Harrah. Nothing more.

As far as he knew, only Cassandra was always Cassandra. Barmaid, artist, tavern mistress, ironmaster's wife, mother, she never departed from the essential Cassandra he had met on Burnt Tavern Road. There was always a vein of iron that ran through her body and her mind, a vein whose bog would never give out. Her station in life had changed, her dress had altered; she had even grown more attractive with the years. But her spirit was as fresh and unpredictable as on that first day.

At last Harrah came within the hammer-sound of Trescott. Moments later Cassandra came down the stairs of their house to greet him. Harrah found her welcome unrestrained.

"I missed you," she exclaimed. "How I missed you! If you ever go off again without me, I'll create an infernal row. Your place is here, Nathaniel, beside me. Here in Trescott. Do you understand, my man!"

Harrah understood all too well. But he was so pleased by the reception he got that he suffered, in fact enjoyed, all of Cassandra's embraces.

She was so excited he might have thought she had been drinking. But Cassandra rarely touched wine and she almost never drank whiskey. Harrah finally attributed her exhilaration to his homecoming, plain and simple.

"When you were gone, Nathaniel, I felt not only like the ironmaster's wife, but the ironmaster himself! Of course, I'm relieved that you're here. I don't know a gudgeon from a bellows. Fortunately Mr. Venable does."

She passionately embraced him again. "Oh, Nathaniel, this has been the happiest year of my life. Imagine, our own ironworks in our very own town! What more could we ask of the Pines? Of life, really? And you! You made it all possible." She stepped back the better to see him.

"It was Jesse made it possible."

Yes, if he were twenty years younger and seventy-five pounds lighter, Jesse Richards would have made the ideal husband for Cassandra.

"No, no other man would have been able to put up with me. I know that. And no other man could have kept me in harness."

But was he keeping her in harness? Or was Cassandra driving him down the long road from Burnt Tavern to Trescott, letting him think he was in the driver's seat when in reality he was little more than a lead horse?

She kissed him smack on the lips once more. "Come upstairs," she said, "and let's get acquainted again."

"But I'm tired and need a bath—"

"No matter. I'll take you as you are."

So he followed her upstairs and before he could take his clothes off he was pulled down on the bed. A half hour later Harrah took his bath.

Lying back in the warm water, he wondered how Cassandra would feel if she knew he had been with Georgina Pierot. Was his reception such a warm one because he had been unfaithful? Did Cassandra somehow sense that another woman was attracted to him and she was attracted in kind? He had heard some women had an instinct about these things.

But Harrah's welcome was shortlived. It was Jesse Richards who spoiled things. Not a deliberate act on his part. Pure circumstance. On one of his visits to Trescott, Jesse related how the ironmasters had been briefed at their meeting on a railway to Quaker Bridge and later to Tuckerton.

"Nothing really came of it. Too much money called for, and some of my friends have not yet recovered from the Panic. The spokesman, a Mr. Brookens, was willing to take paper money. Still, the project had its pitfalls. Didn't you think so, Nathaniel?"

Harrah was only half listening.

"Yes, too many pitfalls."

"But the lady Mr. Brookens traveled with showed him to good advantage. Didn't she?"

"The lady?"

"Yes, she was quite taken with you, I noticed."

Cassandra put her teacup down.

"You didn't tell me about her, Nathaniel."

"What's there to tell?" laughed Jesse. "It's not as if Nathaniel had a tryst with her."

"I knew the lady in Philadelphia," explained Harrah, "when I owned a tavern at Cooper's Point. I met her and her brother at the Germantown and Norristown Railway Depot exhibition. She's married to a Mr. Pierot, also in the railroad business."

"That perhaps accounts for Nathaniel's interest in railroads," was Cassandra's icy comment to Jesse Richards.

"Rather the other way round," said Harrah. "Her brother—"

"Never mind," said Cassandra. "I'm not in the least interested in the lady or her brother."

When Richards left, he took Harrah aside and apologized for his lack of discretion.

"I'm sorry, Nathaniel. I didn't mean to cause any trouble. I was just—"

"Don't worry about it, Jesse."

"I do hope Cassandra understands. I was only joshing."

"I'm sure she understands."

Cassandra, it appeared, understood only too well. Harrah knew Cassandra was livid. But he knew too that she did not know the extent of his involvement with Mrs. Pierot, and he counted this as his salvation.

Still, he would have to pay for his indiscretion, even if the indiscretion was no more than looking at another woman. Cassandra would see to that. In the next few days his nights proved to be nothing more than darkness. No candles, no closeness, no coming together. He could scarcely complain. He didn't have a leg to stand on.

RETRIBUTION

With an estranged Cassandra to contend with, there was nothing for Harrah to do but throw himself into his work. And there was opportunity aplenty here. One day, owing to bad weather, the furnace made a puff.

"Nothing much can be done," said Mr. Venable. "Let's hope it doesn't hurt the iron."

"Where's the scow?" asked Harrah. "Anderson was to bring in a load of ore."

"Might be stuck in the mud. They've had trouble with that spit in the stream. The scow got caught one day and McGahen fell overboard."

"I'll have a look," said Harrah.

"You'll get soaked, sir. It's raining pretty heavy."

"Can't be helped."

Harrah rode out about a mile and found the scow beached in mud and the boatmen drenched from the rain. He dismounted and went into the water up to his waist. He was shocked at how cold the stream was.

"You'll catch your death, Mr. Harrah," shouted one of the scowmen. "We pulled and pulled. But the son-of-a-bitch wouldn't budge."

"Tie the scow to my horse and then give a pull." Harrah could barely finish the sentence for the chill.

The men did as they were bid.

"Come on! You pull too!" shouted Harrah, pushing at his end.

The men strained to the utmost, red with exertion. Still no movement.

"Once more, men. The bastard's got to give. And this time shove back a little before you pull!"

The men pushed, then pulled back. The scow squeezed mud and this time was dragged free.

Harrah climbed out of the water but could not prevent his teeth from rattling. His hands were numb and his fingers a ghastly blue.

"How do you stand it?" he asked.

"We don't go into the water, Mr. Harrah. Not if we can avoid it." They did not mention the half bottle of whiskey they had consumed. "You'd best get home and into a hot tub. We'll bring the scow in."

"Good enough."

The next morning Harrah was down with a fever. And then a cough developed, which shook him like a bellows.

"I'd best get you a doctor," said Cassandra.

"I need no doctor. Only some rest and a hot drink or two."

She did not press the point. But after a few days the cough was no better and Harrah felt a stitch in his side.

"I've sent for John Witt."

"Did you?"

"Your own ministrations did no good."

"I suppose not."

Harrah turned over on his back, but not without pain.

"You're annoyed with me, aren't you?"

"Of course I am. It was a foolish thing you did."

"Someone had to do it. Or we would have lost two days at the furnace."

"And how many days will you yourself be losing?" she asked.

The black doctor appeared with his black bag. John Witt had prospered in recent years. No crude medicine chest this time; no cigar box, except for cigars, with restoratives in them. John Witt had a carriage this time, not an old gray wagon. And reports had it that he had enlarged his land holdings, having attached an office to his old house, an herb shed, and a barn. The house itself had been renovated. "Made presentable," was the way the doctor put it. And he had paid off his not inconsiderable debts.

"Where is the patient?" he asked, putting down his cigar.

"Upstairs, in the bedroom."

When the black doctor finished examining Harrah, he told Cassandra that her husband would brief her on his findings. And then he left to visit a patient at Leeks Landing.

"Well?" asked Cassandra. "What did he say?"

"He said I need a change of air. Sea air is what he recommends."

Cassandra showed annoyance. "Sea air? And where are you supposed to get that?"

"At Joseph Horner's Guest House near Barnegat Light or in Cape May. Cape May has much the better places for convalescence."

"Don't you think you'd better get another doctor to look at you?"

"There's no mystery about what's wrong, Cassandra. It's the lungs. No real danger. But sea air for a month or so will speed recovery. The Pines this time of year will do me no good."

"Nonsense. The Pines are especially good for throat and lung. Sea air is dank." Cassandra was almost contemptuous of him. "I didn't know you were so frail, Nathaniel. Other men get sick and don't have to go away."

"Other men have been known to die." Harrah was surprised

at his own bitterness. But he had not expected Cassandra to be so pitiless.

"You needn't come along," said Harrah. "In fact, it's best you stay here. Traveling will do the kids no good. Rachel can accompany me and do the cooking. We'll be back before you know it."

Harrah was aware of his wife's unwritten law. Cassandra never leaves the Pines! And he was not about to put it to the test. He sat up in his bed and put the best face on things though he was still quite uncomfortable. He wanted desperately to cough but did his best to suppress the urge.

"I see other men in town," remarked Cassandra. "Ironworkers. They put in a full day at the forge and carouse at night. And they're none the worse for it."

Harrah gave her a tolerant smile.

"All right. Maybe their heads hurt the next day. Or their stomachs. Much of what they drink is the dregs of the still. But they have no trouble with their lungs."

"That's not what the doctor says."

Cassandra rose and walked to the window to the right of the bed. "When will you be leaving?" She parted the curtains and looked out into the street.

"As soon as I get out of bed."

"And when will that be?"

"In a day or two. The doctor said to take a week. But I'll be out of bed before then."

"Who's the Irishman named Muir?"

"He's not an Irishman. He's a Scot. One of the carters that Berryman brought in."

"There he is, working in the rain. But I wager he never gets sick."

"Let's hope you're right."

"I know I'm right." With that, Cassandra went to see about packing his clothes.

CAPE MAY

A carter was hired by Cassandra to convey Harrah and Rachel to Tuckahoe Bridge at Beesley's Point. Harrah's carriage was then driven back to Trescott by way of Mays Landing.

At Tuckahoe Bridge Harrah and his nurse boarded the Cape May stage. It was a long, rough journey to Cape Island. The roads were bumpy and uneven and often lost themselves in the woods or twisted in and out of cedar swamps. An occasional clearing revealed small, but not prosperous farms and yellow meadows where sheep and cattle and horses pantomimed winter grazing.

Rachel was quiet but solicitous, rearranging Harrah's blanket and providing him with sweet tea which she carried in a whiskey jug. Towards evening Harrah drifted off into sleep and when he awoke, the coach had rolled to a jerky stop. Unable to find rooms in The Atlantic, a small inn on Cape Island Road, Rachel took lodging in an undistinguished dwelling called the Kimball House.

The Kimball House slept ten to twelve guests, and Harrah's room faced the ocean. At first Rachel proved to be an invaluable aid. She brought him a blanket when he sat on the wide verandah, a Philadelphia newspaper—usually a week old—and cups of cocoa. But as Harrah grew stronger he sent her off to a church sewing circle and dined by himself on "potluck."

But he got tired of Kimball's fare and decided instead to lunch in the dining room of Congress Hall. Congress Hall was a large unpainted and unplastered barn of a structure that had been built to house summer tourists. Board and lodging could be had for ten dollars a week. The rooms upstairs were no more than cubicles, however, and Harrah preferred his lodgings at Kimball's. But the dining room, which occupied the whole first floor, was open to all. Here the prosperous and powerful from Philadelphia, Delaware, Baltimore, and Richmond met in comparative luxury and dined on oysters, crabs, drumfish, bluefish, or lamb in season. And the cellar was stocked with fine liquors. Even in January a good crowd was on hand during the noon hour. Bankers, sea captains, ship builders, glass manufacturers, plantation owners, gentlemen and a few ladies filled the immense dining room with chatter. Waiters darted back and forth, catering to their needs.

One patron, a regular, who did not introduce himself but who was served Napolean brandy no matter what he dined on for lunch, took a liking to Harrah.

"You're not very good at quoits, I see. But you have an excellent eye with a pistol. I've watched you on the beach."

"It helps pass the time," said Harrah.

"I prefer cards. Do you play?"

"Not anymore. I had a falling out with a friend once. And I haven't played since."

"What do you do when you're not on holiday on Cape Island?"

"I'm an ironmaster."

"In Pennsylvania?"

"No, in the Pines. And you?"

The paunchy dinner guest, a man in his fifties, turned red, pulled out a handkerchief, and blew his nose.

"This brandy is better than snuff!" He shook his head to clear it. "I'm in iron, too. The iron horse."

"Rail carriages?"

"Exactly."

"Is it profitable?"

"Everything is profitable, son, if you manage it properly. But railroads, they are the tide of the times. A good choice of words, don't you think? For a visitor to Cape Island, I mean."

Harrah nodded acknowledgment.

"You look skeptical."

"Not at all," said Harrah. "The railroad holds a particular fascination for me."

"And why not! What we have in this country is a revolution. Not of men but machinery. Do you have any idea what steam power is going to do to the States? The railroads alone will tie the nation together more than the rivers or the paddlewheel ever did. Our dependence on England is over. And it wasn't the Revolution that did this. Or '12. That was only the first turn of the wheel. It's the steam engine that will set us free.

"I'm fifty years and six," he added. "And I feel as if I were just starting out. If I were a young man like you, I'd beg, borrow, and steal whatever money I could get my hands on and invest it. Not in iron, not in ships, but in the railroads. And not here in South Jersey—not yet. And not in Baltimore or Philadelphia where others have got a foothold. But in Delaware and Richmond, and New York and New England. That's where the race will be won. And whoever gets there first will be sitting on a throne of gold."

Harrah did not know what to make of his tablemate who grew redder and paunchier with each swallow. Was he blowing hard, like the whales that once spouted in these waters? Or was he indeed a prophet of new times?

Harrah returned to Kimball House with his head rocking. The railroads. Had he missed his golden opportunity? Hadn't he told Cassandra of his desire to invest in the new industry? But he had been dissuaded and now he was into iron—iron which in the Pines would one day go puff, like a blast furnace that gasps its last.

Harrah realized that to some extent he was playing for time with Cassandra. When he had returned to the Pines, he was sounding the fiddle of courtship with her bow. He could ill afford a sour note or a broken string. Though he had taken a firm stand on the house at Atsion—Edward's house—he could not push Cassandra too far. There was a line she drew and beyond it he could not step. He had not really savored the idea of building another tavern on Burnt Tavern Road. And much as he respected Cassandra's wish to provide a new life for Hostetler, he was not entirely in favor of bringing the old smuggler in as a silent partner. He wanted in no way for "The Crossroads" to remind patrons of Burnt Tavern Road's illicit past.

What Harrah had hoped for was that one day he and Cassandra would find a way of life and a way of livelihood that suited them both. It might be in a tavern or an inn but not on Burnt Tavern Road. It might be in a manor house but not an ironmaster's mansion. For he saw the role of ironmaster as a thankless job, if not an impossible one. Even Jesse Richards, who was the epitome of an ironmaster, had to do a juggling act with Batsto's finances and with alternative forms of manufacture to maintain a viable present and some hope for the future. And Harrah, though he prided himself on his competence, was not Richards. He was not, like Jesse, to iron born. And he had none of the access to the centers of trade and money that Richards had developed over the years, and his father before him.

Harrah had harbored these thoughts before. But always he was too close to the situation, in the midst of the life at the tavern or in the middle of a welter of problems at the furnace. He had no time to act, only to react; much less, time to think. On Kimball's porch he could look out at the sea, in sight of the lighthouse and the ships that crossed the ocean into Delaware Bay. Or he could watch an isolated carriage of some sea captain drive back and forth along the edge of the ocean on roads of hard white sand. And the stiff breeze would blow his mind free of clutter and endless detail. And he would find not only the time he was looking for but the ability to think fresh, deep thoughts and unfettered concepts. And Cassandra would loom anew, not as the arbiter of choice, his ransomed wife, but as one whose headlong search for fulfillment implied no restrictions on his own pursuit of life.

But when he left Kimball's the next morning in a hired farmer's wagon to see the portable dock at the Point of Cape May, and marked cowpaths and wagonroads along the way, he was no longer agitated. In fact, like his father's son, he wondered what kind of crops the sandy soil would grow. And when he reached Lily Lake and rode around it until a path spun off toward the ocean, he knew that he would not invest in the railroads after all. He was an ironmaster by chance, not design. By design he would never win the race for the throne of gold.

At the Point he discovered that the portable dock had been taken down for the winter, a fact that the farmer whose services he had hired never bothered to mention. And so he stood for hours as other farmers in whaleboats tried to bring passengers and luggage ashore from an anchored three-master. But the waters were so rough and the shoals so shifting that the men gave up the attempt for another day. Harrah spied well-dressed women and men at the ship's rail, eager to disembark. And he sympathized with their frustration as gulls circled and mocked them. After all, his own waves of frustration were rolling on the beach. It was one thing to arrive at an anchorage; it was another to tame the last few yards of surging sea.

He drifted on in this way at Cape Island for some time. Over and over again he reviewed his past actions and weighed his choices for the future. When he did not consider Cassandra, he could see clearly what he wanted to do. But without Cassandra he knew that he was only play acting. Cassandra was at the center of his reality. To deny her was to deny life itself.

But his convalescence dragged on, and Harrah began to wonder whether his progress was not all it should be. Was he still on the mend or was he putting off his return to Trescott? He knew only that he did not feel up to the demands of his task at the furnace. While he saw himself hale enough, he clearly did not have the reserves of strength he knew he would have to draw on. At the same time he missed Cassandra. He missed her not as one misses a friend or an old acquaintance. He missed her as he might have missed his arms or legs. In the middle of a bowl of chowder at Kimball's "potluck," he decided he would cut short his convalescence and return to Trescott at once.

Part Eight

STRESSES AND STRAINS

MR. MUIR

He found a subdued Cassandra.

"Are you stronger now?" she asked.

"Much stronger."

"No trace of the cough left?"

"It's gone."

Cassandra did not help him with his coat. "Rachel returned only a week after you arrived at the Cape."

"I didn't need her anymore and sent her home."

"If you were that well, you might have come home, too."

"Are you going to kiss me or scold me?" Harrah felt weak after the long journey but was determined not to show it.

She reached up and embraced him, but there was no passion in her kiss. Harrah had known better homecomings.

"I have a present for you," he said after a time.

"A present?"

"In that sack." He pointed to a muslim bag which he had dropped in the hallway.

Cassandra untied the bag and looked in.

"Stones?"

"Diamonds," corrected Harrah. "Cape May Diamonds. They wash up on the beach at Cape May Point."

"They are pretty," said Cassandra, somewhat disapponted. "For stones, that is."

"Semi-precious stones," said Harrah. He pulled a necklace from his coat pocket. "This is what they look like when they've been tumbled."

Cassandra held the necklace in her hand. She smiled in spite of herself. "They do look like real diamonds."

"A kind of quartz they are. If they weren't so plentiful, people would be breaking their necks to gather them in. I understand that even the Indians wore them to advantage. And, of course, anything *you* wear will be to advantage, too, Cassandra."

"That's precious, Nathaniel—even if the stones aren't."

Cassandra retreated to the kitchen where she helped Rachel prepare supper while Harrah went upstairs to see his son who was not yet asleep. When he appeared at the dining table, Cassandra brought him up to date on the doings at Trescott.

"With the furnace out of blast, there isn't much to tell. The men are out gathering in wood—before the sap begins to flow. That is, all but Asa Hedgecombe who made a clandestine retreat from chopping."

"Will we ever see him again?"

"I doubt it. He left everything behind—ax, saw, blankets."

She continued. "Andrew Prine was in to repair the bellows tubs. One of the missing cows was found dead in a mire. I settled with the moulders and they left for Philadelphia. And, oh yes, Mr. Muir has been bringing us fresh fish out of the pond. Rachel's delighted with it."

"Muir, the carter?"

She nodded. "The Scotsman."

Harrah questioned her no further, but he thought it strange that she addressed him as *Mr.* Muir. And he found it strange, too, that when he made ready for bed Cassandra had a whole pile of accounts to sort out.

"I'll get to them in the morning," said Harrah.

"Yes, but they need to be put in order. I was not sure when you'd be coming home. You only wrote but one letter."

"I wrote four," said Harrah. "But the mail is uncertain. The others will no doubt arrive in a day or so."

The next morning he caught a glimpse of Muir from his window. He was a dark-haired man with good if not remarkable features and a medium build. He impressed one with being on the quiet side, well-mannered but with brooding brown eyes. Though he talked little, those eyes seemed to say a great deal. When Harrah had first hired him, Muir had introduced himself not as a carter or ironworker but as a Presbyterian.

"My family is still in the old country," he said. "And one day soon I'll be joining them and work my own croft. Too many Catholics, Methodists and Episcopalians in this neck o' the woods."

"They're all ironworkers here," Harrah had remarked. "Their religion is their own business."

"Aye," said Muir. "But with me it's fundamental."

And now the man had somehow ingratiated himself with Rachel—or was it Cassandra?

"Everyone's been down with catarrh," observed Cassandra. "But not Mr. Muir. He smokes his pipe and goes fishing in all weather. And never comes back with so much as a sniffle."

"Must have his share of luck, then," said Harrah.

"It's more than luck. It's his fine constitution. And a certain manliness."

This surprised Harrah. He did not find Muir particularly manly. He thought him studied in his manner and not without a certain awareness of the impression he made on people, particularly women. Muir apparently thought better of himself than he deserved. And this was a luxury no working man could afford.

There was little time for airs or posturing in Trescott even during the off season. If on his own time the man wanted to go fishing, that was one thing. To go fishing on company time was another—no matter how pleased Cassandra was with his catch.

"I understand you're a fisherman," noted Harrah when he encountered him one day sitting atop his empty wagon.

"Aye," said Muir.

"We're grateful for that."

Muir nodded, raising a supercilious brow.

"But do you see yourself as a carter?" asked Harrah.

"A carter?"

"That's what we pay you for, isn't it?"

Muir did not reply; he simply dropped his eyebrow.

"There are logs to be hauled," said Harrah. "Please see to it."

Another time Harrah saw Muir leaning on an ax while three other men were furiously chopping wood. Harrah waited several minutes to give the man time to rest, if that was what he needed. But the rest period dragged on and even after thirty minutes there was no indication by Muir that he was ready to join in.

"Mr. Muir!"

"Aye."

"I thought you were to be cutting wood today."

"I am."

"With your axhead on the ground and you leaning on the handle?"

"I'm resting a spell."

"Let's not overdo it. I've been watching you the past half hour. The other men don't look like woodsmen but they're working up a sweat. Not once did you lift the ax to strike a blow."

"I'm a carter, not a woodsman."

"Then why did you volunteer for the job?"

"I needed the money."

"You'll see no money if you don't start swinging."

This time Muir glowered at him with his big brown eyes. And Harrah realized that it was not his eyes so much that caught one's attention as the way the man raised and lowered his brows.

"You see, Mr. Muir," added Harrah. "With me it's *work* that's fundamental."

"You don't like Mr. Muir, do you?" asked Cassandra at dinner.

"How do you know?"

"He told me so."

"When did you see him? It wasn't at work I'm sure."

"He brought us some fish. Cut a whole in the ice to get them."

"Most enterprising."

Cassandra seemed mystified.

"Then what he says is true?"

"I don't like shirkers. That's true enough. He was paid to cut wood and he leaned on his ax all day." With that, Harrah went on eating.

Cassandra did not broach the subject again. It was clear she did not share Harrah's opinion of the carter. Nor did she want to hear any derogation of the man.

Harrah found all this mildly disconcerting. He was not a jealous man. And he did not suspect any relationship between his wife and the carter. But he did acknowledge that Cassandra had a romantic picture of the man. It all stemmed from what she supposed was the man's strength or endurance. For his part, Harrah could not imagine where she got this idea from. To his mind, Muir was rather chunky, even soft. The only strength he saw in the man was a kind of defiance that kept people at a distance from him. Muir was definitely different, even unorthodox in his attitude. But it was an unorthodoxy Harrah found in men who were hostile to work, men who regarded work as something beneath them even though there was little else they could do.

He would have dismissed Muir straightway if he did not think Cassandra would take him to task for doing this. So he allowed Cassandra her flirtation, or at least tolerated it, confident that in time it would pass. Maybe it was motherhood made his wife question herself. Was she still attractive to men? Could she still turn a man's head? Not that Muir's head was turned—except from work. Women were uncertain creatures especially as they grew older, and Cassandra was now in her thirtieth year.

"Morale is low," observed Cassandra a few days later. "The men are finding February too much to contend with."

"It has been cold," agreed Harrah.

"Why don't we hold a dance?"

"A dance? We're not grand people here even if we live in an ironmaster's house."

"No, a square dance. Something the men and their wives can stamp to."

It was interesting she mentioned the wives, thought Harrah, as there were only three or four families living in Trescott. The rest were single men, like Muir, who left their wives behind.

"All right," he said. "But you take care of the arrangements. I've got my hands full with other things."

When Harrah saw how thrilled Cassandra was at the prospect, Harrah began to wonder how the idea had come about. His wife was going to great length to see Muir socially, he thought. A dance, a square dance, required a good deal of preparation. And what if Muir couldn't dance? The notion amused him. Oh well, what harm could it do?

Cassandra made it her business to greet new arrivals. On her way to the Dowds, who hailed from Weymouth, she passed the gristmill. Noticing a carter's wagon outside the high platform leading to the door, she pulled up her box buggy and climbed the steep steps to the mill door.

Once inside she saw there was no grain in the hopper and no millstones turning. But the dust and smell of cornmeal and rye were still in the air, and several bushels of grain were lined in rows away from the grinding floor. She looked for the miller, but he was nowhere to be seen. Stepping up to the grinding floor, she examined the stone casing of the millstones, the shoe, and the hopper. But she did not understand what the vertical rod with the square cross-section was supposed to do.

"The rod you're touching is the 'damsel,'" a voice informed her. And when she turned round she saw the carter, Mr. Muir, emerge from behind the posts that separated the grinding floor from the rest of the mill.

"It's the damsel that shakes things up and gets the grain to trickle into the 'eye' of the millstone. Without the damsel we'd be hard pressed for flour to bake our bread."

Cassandra realized that Muir took delight in pronouncing the word 'damsel,' raising his brows each time he uttered the word.

"Were you a miller once?" asked Cassandra, trying to hide her embarrassment.

"No, but I've carted enough bushels out of mills to know how they came about."

"I'm sure you did, Mr. Muir."

Muir returned to the lean-to section of the mill to blow out the lantern, then returned to the dividing posts.

"Are you here to see me?" he asked, not with suddenness but with a desire to jostle her equanimity. "Or to sample the flour?"

"Neither," said Cassandra. "But I must be keeping you from your work."

"You needna worry," said Muir. "The bushels will sit on the floor till I move them."

He left the post he was standing behind and stepped forward.

"Is there anything I can do for Mrs. Harrah?" he asked. A mischievous smile all but cornered his lips.

Muir's proximity disturbed Cassandra and instinctively she

stepped back, away from the grinding floor. There was nothing servile about the man. He was not awed by her station. If anything, he was too self-assured and Cassandra meant to stand her ground.

"You can bring up more fish—when you get the chance."

"Ah, you like my fish?"

"It makes for a good table."

"Then you would like my kippers."

"Kippers?"

"Smoked sea trout or salmon. But the fish don't run in these streams. In the old country they are plentiful."

Cassandra pretended to understand, but she was concerned more that with each comment Muir took a step closer to her.

"I could put together a fish fry for you," he said. "Not quite as tasty or as salty as kippers, but fine eatin' all the same."

"How would you bring it to the house?"

Muir hesitated. "I wasn't thinking of bringing it there. I thought you might want to eat it where it's caught."

"Out of doors?"

"Aye."

"I think not," she said.

"Why not?" He drew closer and for moment Cassandra thought he had pursed his lips, but she dismissed the idea.

"It will not do, that's all."

She made a move to go, but Muir took hold of both posts, almost casually blocking her way.

"Will you excuse me, Mr. Muir?"

"There's some flour on your coat," he said, reaching forward and brushing it off her sleeve.

"So there is."

As he stepped back, Muir turned his face and leaned forward to kiss her. It was a tentative attempt, for bold as he was Muir was mindful that he was dealing with the ironmaster's wife.

Cassandra pulled away. Flushed by the impudence of the action but flattered by the idea of it, she crimsoned from neck to ears. At the same time she detected an awkwardness in Muir she had not seen before. In taking a step back, Muir shifted the weight of his body to his haunches and just for a moment he cut the figure of a middle-aged farmer. But this quickly passed before her eyes, and all she could think about was the aborted kiss.

"It's time you carried those bushels out of here, don't you think?" Cassandra tried to gain control over her composure and to restore her advantage over him.

Muir was puzzled by the tone she assumed. He would have preferred being scolded by Cassandra. He did not like being reminded of his task or her station. Without a word, he stepped aside and occupied himself with the bushels. When he finally secured one of them and hoisted it upon his shoulders, he carried it outside to his wagon. He made a great show of swinging the bushel onto the floorboard and dusted his hands free of the flour. He was certain Cassandra had taken notice of the skill with which he handled his burden. And he swallowed a deep breath to indicate he was ready for the next bushel. But when he turned back towards the mill and looked to her for approval, he found that Cassandra and her box buggy were gone.

THE SQUARE DANCE

The announcement of Cassandra's square dance was good medicine. Though the normal complement of men and their families at Trescott numbered some one hundred, this figure fell to forty during the winter. And only half of these were employed by the Trescott Company. These men felled trees, hauled logs, butchered hogs and smoked the meat, repaired the stables and the grist mill, and when the weather was right hauled ore by ox-team from nearby beds. The others decided to stay on at Trescott until the furnace went back in blast early in May. They passed the time fishing or hunting or mended things in their workers' cottages or brought in wood for the schoolhouse. But mainly they got drunk. It was this group Cassandra had in mind when she said morale was low.

But with a dance in prospect everyone scurried about to help. Cassandra selected the general store as the dance site. It was the only place with floor enough to accommodate forty people. Though Cassandra and Harrah lived in the ironmaster's house, it was small compared to the ironmaster's mansion in Batsto or Atsion. And Cassandra was not about to turn her drawing room into a dance hall.

Cassandra was in high spirits. She supervised the removal of the barrels that had been placed about the store and had them shoved up against the counter. The same with the boxes and harness racks. She even thought of dismantling the stove until she was reminded that it was the only source of heat in the room. She then had the men carry tables into the store, which they pushed up against the walls. Punchbowls, silverware, and other party paraphernalia were carted in and put in a safe place. Even an old fiddle was commandeered and set on the counter, and a sign was placed between the strings: "Do not touch. Reserved for the dance."

The only problem was a paucity of women in town, a problem compounded when Strook, an idle carpenter, threw his common-law wife out and told her to seek "lodgins."

"Can't we take her in?" asked Cassandra. "Strook will get over it as soon as he sobers up. And we'll need her for the dance. A pretty young thing, too. You'd think he'd have better sense."

"I suppose we can. But Strook won't like it. He wants her to go begging."

"I don't care what Strook likes," said Cassandra. And so the girl was brought into the house.

Cassandra put her to work in the kitchen where Rachel was pickling beets and baking pies.

At night Suzie Strook was invited to dine with Cassandra and Harrah. She apologized for any inconvenience she caused.

"What did you quarrel about?" asked Cassandra.

Suzie shrugged her spindly shoulders and promptly put her knife and fork down.

"You can go on eating," said Harrah. "My wife was only asking. You needn't tell us."

"We didn't quarrel," she said. "At least I didn't. He's always throwing me out when he's into the bottle."

"But why?" asked Cassandra.

"'Cause I won't marry him."

"But you're living together."

"I can't help that. I've no one to look after me but Rob. But I'm not obliged to marry him."

"How old are you?" asked Harrah.

"Seventeen. We've been together for three years now."

Harrah went back to his soup. A mere child she was. And bedding down with a man twice her age. What kind of a hold did he have on her? He threw her out regularly, it appeared, just as regularly as he took to drink. Not much of an existence for one so young. And not much hope for a better life in the future.

"A man's here to see you," announced Rachel.

"Who?"

"He says his name is Strook."

Harrah looked at Suzie. "He's come for you, I imagine. Are you ready to go back?"

"She'll not go back!" Cassandra rose from the table. "Tell him to go away, Rachel."

"One moment," said Harrah, putting his napkin down and rising, too. "The girl's got to decide that."

"You'll stay here, won't you, Suzie?" Cassandra was adamant.

"No, Ma'am. I think I'd best go."

"But he'll only throw you out again."

"I know. But what am I to do?"

"You can stay here—until we find a place for you."

"I thank you. Really I do. But I'd best go." She left the table and followed Rachel out.

"Do you understand her?" asked Cassandra, pouring herself some water.

"No," said Harrah. "But the girl had little choice."

"She could have stayed here. I offered her that."

"But for how long? And then what?"

"Do you have any idea, Nathaniel, what her life with Strook is like?"

"Not really."

"He beats her regularly. He's almost never sober. I'm sure he forces himself on her when she's ill or in blood."

Harrah cut Cassandra short. "She knows that. But she went back anyway. Life is hard, Cassandra. And people make it no easier for themselves."

Cassandra could see that her husband was upset about the girl and changed the subject.

"Is Mr. Muir still hauling?" she asked.

"Muir?"

"Yes, he brought us no fish lately."

"No, he's down with a cough. A bad one, I'm told."

Cassandra expressed surprise. "I didn't know that."

"It's true nonetheless. I don't think he'll make your square dance."

But Cassandra went ahead with her plans anyway. She had Rachel roast some hams, pickle beets, and bake several loaves of bread. She sent to Quaker Bridge for oysters and mixed the punch herself. She had no reason to think that Mr. Muir was not sick, but she had no doubt that he would be up and around in time for the dance. What did disturb her was the fact of Mr. Muir's indisposition. With all of her taunting Harrah with the Scotsman's invulnerability to illness, this reversal of form made her look foolish. Only an appearance by Mr. Muir at the square dance would enable her to save face. Only an appearance by Mr. Muir would assure her of her sway over him. And while she would not admit this, it was important to Cassandra that Mr. Muir pay her homage.

The square dance began as a staid affair. The men of Trescott appeared with their coats brushed, their hands scrubbed, and their necks washed. The half-dozen women of the town brought platters of food with them as their contribution to the festivities. Both groups had taken great pains with their boots and shoes, bringing them to a high polish so as not to be shamed on the dance floor.

There was an awareness that Mr. Burdette, the store manager, was on hand. Normally a pleasant man with wide jowls and an ample forehead, he had put on a stern face. If the general store was being turned into a dance hall, he was going to protect his goods and property. Not that he was unduly concerned. With the ironmaster's wife present and in charge of things, a certain amount of decorum was expected.

But once the dancing got under way things loosened up a bit.

The stamping of feet took place in earnest now, putting the structure of the room to test. The punch bowl was repeatedly spiked and "intensified." More than a few plates of food had been spilled over. And while the fiddler scratched his tunes, the men who had no women to dance with took to feminizing their partners.

"Now, let me see your pretty smile, Sweeney. And swing them hips when your turn comes!"

"Your petticoats are showing, Stegman!"

"Those have got be the thickest ankles a girl ever kicked with!"

As the tempo increased, so did the temperature. Though it was late February, bodies were hot and brows broke into sweat. And then a table was overturned and a punchbowl fell to the floor. Mr. Burdette, who tried to intervene, finally gave up in despair.

When Harrah appeared, he gathered that the dance was a crashing success. But he could not tell this from the expression on Cassandra's face.

"What boors!" she exclaimed, breaking away from her partner. She left the place as though she had been on watch and Harrah had come to relieve her. Harrah tried to follow after his wife, but Suzie Strook caught his arm and brought him into the square. A dour look by Rob Strook did not prevent Harrah from dancing with her.

"It wasn't my idea to hold the dance," said Harrah later that night. "It was yours. Sometimes it's best to let things stand as they are."

"I thought it would pick up spirits."

"Well, it did. But not your spirits, I see."

Cassandra cut Harrah with her gaze.

"Why do they act that way?"

"It's their idea of a good time."

"Well, it's not mine."

Harrah carried some wood to the fireplace. "I told you Muir wouldn't make it," he said without looking back at her.

"So you did."

"His cough's worse. We sent for a doctor."

"I'm sure it's not as bad as all that."

The next morning Cassandra slipped out of the house. She did not return until noon. When she did reappear she wore a sullen look of contempt.

"I've been to see Muir," she said.

Harrah wondered what happened to the *Mr.*

"There's nothing improper in it," she added. "As the ironmaster's wife I visit all the sick and injured."

"You needn't explain," said Harrah.

"But I want you to hear this."

"You'll tell me later," he said.

"But—"

"Later, Cassandra."

"No, I'll tell you now!" She strongly resented being put off. "He was lying when I got there as if on his death bed."

"I told you he was ill."

"But he's not as ill as he makes out. Even you put the best face on things. Men are such infants!"

"They get sick, that's all."

"No. It's more than that. They like being babied. They never grow up." She shook her head in disgust. "And he looked so soft in his bed, like a bread pudding. I don't know where I got the idea he was manly."

Harrah took her arm. "Before you go any further," he said. "You should know we have company." He called gently into the next room. "Would you come here, please."

Cassandra looked across the room and saw Suzie Strook emerge with a black and blue bruise beneath her left eye.

"Yes, Suzie's been thrown out again."

"And Rob wasn't even drunk," whimpered the girl.

SUZIE STROOK

This time Strook did not come for Suzie. Instead he bellowed about town that he had no use for the slut, that if she ever returned to his cottage he would knock her eye out, not blacken it. He intimated that he knew things about her that made it impossible for him to take her back.

Apart from the fact that he was twice her age, Strook had nothing about him that Harrah felt would appeal to the girl. His hair was nondescript. He was neither shaven nor unshaven. He was neither tall nor short. He was neither handsome nor charming. Sour when sober, he was downright vicious when drunk. The only thing he was good at was his work. As a carpenter, he knew no peers. He made precise, durable patterns and kept his shop as orderly as he was disorganized.

Cassandra asked her husband why he didn't fire the man. "Good carpenters are hard to find," replied Harrah.

But it was not Strook that troubled him; it was Suzie. He simply did not want her in the house. As ironmaster, he would have a hard time justifying his wife's interference in the personal affairs of his men. And Harrah was not sure they believed Suzie's staying at the house was all his wife's doing. Black eye and all, she was well molded and shaped; her nose was particularly well-turned. And though deprived physically by Strook, she was not without womanly attributes. And so it was not hard to assume that Harrah had an interest in her.

"She'll stay as long as necessary," said Cassandra when Harrah suggested they find lodging for her elsewhere.

"But she's a distraction. And Strook will take it amiss."

"What kind of distraction?"

"The men will find excuses to pass the house. There are few enough women about to leave one unattended."

"Nonsense," said Cassandra. "There's not one of them worthy of her, black eye and all."

"Makes no difference. They're no worse than Strook, the way they see it."

"Well, they'll not pass this house."

Harrah cut short his argument. He suspected that Cassandra was simply contrary. Had he been arguing for the girl to stay, she would have insisted on her leaving.

Meanwhile Rachel raised some questions.

"How am I to treat the girl? Is she a servant here or a guest? If she's a servant, I can find work for her to do." Rachel displayed

171

no malice toward the girl; she merely wanted to know her standing.

"She's a guest," said Cassandra. "But she can do her share—just as we did at the tavern in the old days."

Rachel nodded and went on her way.

"I still think you're making a mistake," said Harrah, sitting down to his desk and pulling out his ledger.

"And here I thought you like the girl."

"I don't like or dislike her. I'm partial to women in their thirties, remember?"

This was true. To Harrah a woman in her thirties was in her prime. Still youthful, she had none of the awkwardness or naivité of a younger woman. She understood the nature of her sex and was mature enough to dismiss the qualities that did not become her. She had also learned to know herself and to enhance what charms she had. And in this Cassandra was no exception.

"I believe you mean what you say," said Cassandra coquettishly. It was the first time in weeks she was receptive to his compliments.

She approached his desk and hovered over him as he pored over his accounts. "Can't this wait until tomorrow?" she asked.

"You mean you've forgiven me for getting sick?"

Cassandra put her hand on his shoulder.

"I'm the one that needs forgiveness. I was wrong, terribly wrong. I don't know what came over me. I imagine it frightened me to see you anything less than sound. Will you forgive me?"

"Depends on how nice you are to me tonight."

"Why wait until tonight?"

"Because our son's in the next room. He may be talking to himself, but he's old enough to hear what's going on."

She leaned on her husband.

"Then I'll torment you every minute until he's asleep."

And torment him she did. With the slightest shift of her body she made him see her with new eyes. This was Cassandra Trescott. Mother of his children, yes. Wife, yes. But her breast lay in wait for him, not for a sucking babe. She was finished with that. She was a seductress once more, not a mere slip of a girl with a lean dancer's figure. She was a woman, lean still, but with a fullness that was the gift of the years. She never looked more desirable.

He took her in the early hours of the morning when the house was asleep and the bedroom doors locked. And he clasped her to him, her nakedness glowing in the dark. And he wondered how she could be so yielding and so pliant when only a day or two ago Cassandra held herself aloof from passion, in anger almost if not contempt.

But Harrah did not dwell on this. It was enough that he was suitor once more. The only thing that disturbed him was that they were not entirely alone. In the next room slept his son. And Rachel slept in the room adjoining Jonathan's, with Willacassa in her crib. And now in a room off the hall downstairs still another slept, Rob Strook's common-law wife, Suzie.

A DELEGATION

A delegation of men wanted to see Harrah. The ironmaster met with them in the drawing room. He recognized Sweeney, the hearthman; Stegman, the gutterman; an ore-raiser whose name he could not recall; and Sheil who evidently was the spokesman.

"What's on your mind?" asked Harrah.

Now that they had met with him, the men were reluctant to speak.

"It can't be wages," said Harrah. "I pay you the going rate. What the men get at Batsto and Hampton Furnace you get here."

"It isn't wages," faltered Sheil. "Though a man could always use more."

"What then?"

"You see, Mr. Harrah," said Sheil, leaning forward and speaking almost in a whisper. "We're most of us single men. Only half a dozen of us have wives here. And there are those whose wives still dwell in Philadelphia or the old country."

"Why don't you send for them?"

"It's not as simple as that."

Sweeney and Stegman wore sheepish grins, and the ore-raiser broke into a broad smile.

"Well, I'll admit," said Harrah, "that an irontown is not the best place for domestic bliss. Iron and whiskey don't mix too well. But they mix better than iron and women."

He realized as he said this that the men envied him his own situation. They didn't know him when he was shoveling horse manure. All they knew was that Harrah had a fine house and a pretty woman in it. And she did not have to be a drudge to the stove or her offspring. This was a far different state of affairs from what other familes knew in Trescott.

"We recognize this," said Sheil. "And we were thinking—"

"Go on."

"We had in mind to ask you—No, to suggest that maybe women could be provided from time to time."

"On a regular basis," added Sweeney becoming deadly serious.

Harrah put his pipe down. "A whorehouse?"

"If we may be so blunt."

"Out of the question."

"But it would solve a lot of problems—"

"On the contrary," said Harrah. "It would create a few. In the first place, I make iron. I don't peddle flesh—"

"You needn't have the worry of it. We'll get someone to

handle the business.''

"What's more," said Harrah, "it's degrading. Not only for the women you'd bring here—"

"They're paid well—"

"But for the men themselves. There's plenty of women in Philadelphia who would be only too happy to marry and live in an irontown. And Trescott is better than some.''

"That's not what we have in mind.''

"Then turn your mind to other things. I won't allow it here.''

Sweeney was crestfallen. "It's not natural for men to do without.''

"I'm not telling you what to do. That's your business. There are men who put to sea for a year or two without ever touching land—or a woman. They survive. I haven't heard of floating whorehouses, have you?''

"No," said Sheil.

"And the men here are free to leave when the furnace is out. Those who stay on do so voluntarily.''

"We know that, Sir.''

"I repeat. No one is preventing you from taking a wife—with or without benefit of clergy.''

"But—"

"But whores are out! Is that clear?''

"Yes, Mr. Harrah.''

"Then let's get back to other matters. Good day, gentlemen.''

"What did they want?" asked Cassandra when the men had gone.

"They were complaining about their diet.''

"Their diet?''

"Yes, they want more meat.''

"But there's plenty of pork. Let them go hunting if they want something better.''

"They are," said Harrah.

WOMAN OF THE HOUSE

More and more Cassandra played the part of the ironmaster's wife. One or two days a week were set aside for visiting the sick and the needy of Trescott, and the new arrivals. She brought medicine for the sick, baskets of food for those who could not make ends meet, and hollow ware for the new worker's families: pots and pans; stoves and firebacks with the Trescott imprint on them.

"It's a good thing the furnace is out and we don't have a rapid turnover," remarked Harrah. "Or you'd put us out of business. When will you be back?"

"Before dinner."

"Rachel seems to be ailing. What shall I do if she can't get out of bed?"

"Have Suzie prepare lunch and dinner. Jonathan will play by himself. Just put him in the kitchen with the pots and pans and he'll fancy them knights in armor."

"All the same. I wish you'd stay home today. There's a bitter March wind out there."

"The more reason why I'm needed."

"Cassandra—"

"Yes?"

"You've become quite the lady. I don't know whether I'm pleased or annoyed by it."

"Annoyed?"

Harrah half-smiled. "I thought I'd do your portrait today. Just a sketch for something bigger later on."

"My portrait? What a silly idea."

"I know I'm out of practice. Or maybe you think I'm not good enough."

"Oh, you can do fine work when you're inspired. I remember a young woman that sat for you on Burnt Tavern Road. I was so jealous I could spit."

"Well, I feel inspired now. You look absolutely ravishing—especially with your hair up."

"Then I will sit for you," she laughed. "But another time." Cassandra left all aglow.

Rachel was indeed unable to get out of bed. She half rose, then sank back into her pillow. Harrah let her sleep, and rather than bother Suzie, he found something for himself in the cupboard. But when Jonathan announced that he was hungry, Harrah decided he had better get the girl.

He looked for Suzie on the main floor. No one there. And

only Jonathan was in the kitchen downstairs. So he climbed to the second floor, heading for the sewing room. In passing he found the bathroom door open. Through the doorway he saw Suzie sitting quietly in the big iron tub. Her hair was tied behind her; her shoulders were wet; and her breasts rested on the water. The girl had the biggest and reddest nipples he had ever seen on a woman. They covered almost a third of her breasts. But Suzie made no move to cover them. She continued to lean back against the tub with arms extended, allowing the water to lap against her body. And she looked straight at Harrah with brown speckled eyes and a fine-turned nose. Harrah had not wanted to stare at the girl or meet her gaze. But he found himself unable to turn away. After a while he managed to say, "Rachel is ill. Can you prepare lunch for Jonathan?"

"Why, yes, Mr. Harrah. I'm about done anyway."

Harrah returned downstairs. When he realized he could not shake what he had seen from his mind, he opened the entrance door for air and took a deep breath.

The girl would have to go. That was clear. But how would he justify this to Cassandra? He was not about to tell her what had happened. Not that anything had taken place in any real sense. But the girl's presence from now on would be unsettling—to say the least.

Dressed now, Suzie fixed lunch for Jonathan who ate and ran. She then made some lentil soup for Harrah.

"I've already eaten," he said. "Maybe Rachel will want some, or Willacassa."

Suzie nodded and carried the bowl upstairs. There was nothing in her manner that suggested anything untoward had happened.

It was not a delegation of men this time. Just Mr. Venable.

"What's on your mind, Mr. Venable?"

"It's a personal matter."

"Come inside," said Harrah, closing the door against the wind. "Would you like a cup of tea?"

"No, Sir. Thank you just the same."

Venable kept shifting his hat in his hands.

"The men are upset, you know."

"What is it this time?"

"It's the proposal they made to you, Sheil and the others."

"The whorehouse?"

"Yes."

"I thought that was settled."

"There's still some grumbling."

"About what?"

"Can I be frank?"

Harrah sat back in his chair. "I thought we were being frank."

Venable acknowledged this. "They're grumbling over your decision. They think you're being unfair."

"Unfair?"

"Well, you've got a wife—"

"No one's stopping them from marrying."

"And that girl in the house. Bob Strook's woman."

"Strook threw her out."

"We know. But the men are saying—"

"Saying what, man?"

"I don't know how to put it."

"Put it straight."

"Then I will, Sir. If you will forgive me for using their very words, they're saying the girl is Harrah's whore!"

Harrah shot a scathing glance at the man. "I don't get angry very easily, Mr. Venable. But if I hear anybody say that again, I'll run him straight out of Trescott. That girl is my wife's house guest—"

Mr. Venable rose. "I know you're angry, Mr. Harrah. And I understand why. But I should warn you. The girl is bad business. If there's nothing between you now, there will be if you let her stay. And it'll be no fault to yourself. She's a slut, as Rob says. That's why he threw her out."

"And what is he?" asked Harrah. "A candidate for sainthood?"

"Is there any truth to it?" asked Cassandra, removing her coat and gloves.

"To what?"

"To what they're saying about you and Suzie Strook."

"You mean 'Harrah's whore'?"

"Yes." Cassandra took her bonnet off and lay it on the hall table.

"Of course not."

"Are you telling me the truth? I know you love me. But men are such weaklings. All a girl has to do is rustle her skirts and the fools are ready to frolic."

"I'm telling you the truth, Cassandra. There's nothing between us, absolutely nothing. But having her in the household is not a good idea. It can only lead to talk."

"I see. But what will happen to her? What will she do?"

"I might be able to get her work at Quaker Bridge."

"Thompson's Hotel?"

"It's worth looking into."

"Then look into it, my good fellow. I'll not have any talk of a whore in my household."

HARRAH'S WHORE

Harrah rolled out his carriage and put Suzie aboard. Cassandra had already bid goodbye to her in the house. Rachel, however, who never took an open dislike to anyone, pretended to be busy in the kitchen.

They were a mile or two on the road to Quaker Bridge when Suzie questioned the action.

"Why are you taking me away? Don't I please you?"

"That's not the problem."

"Then what?"

"It's no good having two women in the same house. People talk."

"But I want nothing from you—just to stay." She did not look to advantage as she said this, all bundled up in Rachel's coat.

"You should have a place of your own," said Harrah, urging his horse on.

"But no one wants me."

"Rob Strook is not the world."

"You don't want me either." She began to shed tears. Not the tears of a grown woman, but uninhibited, petulant, whining tears which threatened to unleash a flash flood. And Harrah realized what a child she was.

"I want a peaceful household," said Harrah abruptly. "And I don't want it noised about town that you are more to me than you actually are."

Wiping away her tears, she enveloped his arm and leaned against Harrah. She wanted to remind him no doubt of what was underneath her coat. "But I could be more."

Yes, he thought, she could be more. "Harrah's whore," the men had called her.

Harrah turned to face the girl.

"Cassandra—my wife—is all the woman I need. You'd do well to remember that." Then pulling his arm free of her, he turned his attention to the road.

Cassandra had no rest since Suzie Strook left the house and went to Quaker Bridge. Disturbed as she was by the reckless rumors, she was not without a deep sense of guilt for sending the girl away. She had taken Suzie under her wing. Like a big sister, she had given her refuge from the wretchedness of a life with Rob Strook or, worse still, a life in the streets. And now she had turned the girl out.

Cassandra was still young enough to appreciate the perils that would befall Suzie. As youthful as she was, as pretty, she was fair game for any lecher who would take advantage of her. Suzie did not even have the instinct for self-protection that most girls come by as a matter of course. Suzie, it appeared, was destined for trouble—unless someone like Cassandra guided her and sheltered her.

But Cassandra also saw the peril of keeping her close to home. An extra hand in the household she could welcome. But "Harrah's whore" she could do without. Still, she wanted in some way to know that the girl was all right.

"Can I trust you to go to Quaker Bridge and find out how she's doing?"

"Suzie?"

"Yes, I'm worried about her."

"Then come with me."

"No, you go alone. If I go, I will only take her back with us."

Harrah did not relish his task. He had work to do at the furnace—problems were piling up—and here he had to take time off to go to Quaker Bridge. Besides, he found the girl a distraction. She had that waif-like quality that both appealed to a man and turned him away. On the one hand, he wanted to protect the girl, to shelter her from all the troubles that she seemed to invite. On the other, he found that he was repelled by her inability to discriminate. The first one to come along would be the first one she would respond to.

At Quaker Bridge he sought out the hotelkeeper.

"How is the girl doing? The one called Suzie Strook."

"I wouldn't know. She's up and left."

"What happened to her?" asked Harrah.

"She worked hard for a few days. Then got tangled up with a stagecoach driver. She wanted to go to Tuckerton with him. But he wouldn't have it. Probably has a wife and kids there. So she fetched a ride with a peddler to see for herself. And now I'm told she's whoring there. She'll be sick and old by the time she's twenty."

Harrah could not hide his concern.

"There's nothing can be done for her," said the hotelkeeper.

"There must be something."

The hotelkeeper shook his head. "There are only two kinds of girls go in for whoring. Those that have known men since they were thirteen or fourteen. And those that are feeble-minded. This one started young. There's no hope for her, believe me."

But Harrah felt responsible. Had he kept her at Trescott, had he not talked Cassandra into getting rid of her, Suzie might have gone a different path. He had bowed to public pressure. He had eased her out to ease his own predicament. Wasn't that the truth of it? Then he was as culpable as she was. On the other hand, he could not persuade himself that the hotelkeeper was wrong. Apparently Rob Strook saw this flaw in her. And the men of Trescott. Why else would they call her Harrah's whore? Harrah's woman would have been enough. But Harrah's whore? Whore she was, even if they were mistaken about Harrah.

TUCKERTON HUSSY

In September Harrah travelled to Tuckerton to see a T. Crowley, skipper of the *Ida*. He had it in mind to hire the schooner to ship pipe and stoves to Albany, Poughkeepsie, and Troy. By hiring the schooner at Tuckerton, Harrah calculated he would be able to get the jump on the "Landing" vessels which charged fees according to the backlog of goods left standing on the wharf.

He met Crowley at the Customs House and then accompanied him to a waterfront tavern frequented by seamen and prostitutes.

"There's nothing like a Tuckerton hussy," said Crowley, downing a "stiff one" to clinch the deal. "None of that shy, maidenly fluff. They get right to the point and to the rooms upstairs. It'll cost you a pretty penny, but it's worth it."

"I see what you mean," said Harrah as he watched a red-haired girl and her seaman make their way upstairs.

"She'll be back again at eight bells, ready for another go-round. Are you interested?"

"Not this trip." Harrah had no wish to offend the man, but having accomplished what he had set out to do, he saw no need to humor him.

"What are you drinking?" asked a young slip of a girl with hair down past her shoulders.

"I've already had half a bottle of rum," said Harrah.

"Then let's share the other half."

Harrah did not know what was more familiar, the girl's voice or her figure. And then through the long hair he recognized Suzie Strook.

She recognized him at the same time.

"Why, it's Mr. Harrah. I never expected to find you here." She was genuinely surprised, even embarrassed.

"I'm looking for a ship to hire," said Harrah, almost apologetically. "Mr. Crowley has agreed to charter the *Ida*. And now I'm planning to return to Trescott. Captain Crowley, this is—"

"Never mind, Mr. Harrah. I can see you're old acquaintances. I've got to return to the *Ida*. We're setting sail with the tide. See you at the Landing." Tipping his hat, he gracefully excused himself and made off as Suzie stayed Harrah's hand.

"You won't be leaving just yet," she implored him. "I want to tell you what happened at Thompson's."

"You owe me no explanation," said Harrah.

"Oh, but I do. You and Mrs. Harrah were as kind to me as kin." Harrah gently removed her hand but allowed Suzie Strook to go on.

"I fell in love with a stagecoach driver. In fact, I'm always falling in love. It's my juices, I suppose. But he was married and wanted no part of me in Tuckerton. His wife's a pretty woman, and his children the spittin' image. I guess Albert doesn't want to lose them. The peddler who brought me here set me up in business. It's not so bad really. The men are no worse than Rob Strook and they don't beat me. The only one I can't stand is the tavernkeeper. He looks like a wharf rat. And if I'm not working all the time, he threatens to toss me out into the street."

She was halfway there already, thought Harrah. Then ashamed of his lack of charity, he berated himself. He could not deny that one reason he went to Tuckerton to hire a ship was on the slim chance he might run into the girl. But he now found Suzie sadly unappealing. Slatternly and brazen, she wore a cheap fragrance that all but stifled him. She could arouse neither his pity nor his passion. He decided to make quick work of her.

"Here," he said, pulling some gold coins out of his pocket and laying them down before her. "This is for you. I want nothing in return."

Suzie Strook put the coins in her pocket.

"I thank you for the money, Mr. Harrah. But I wish you wouldn't leave just yet."

"Why not?"

"The tavernkeeper will think there's something wrong."

"Just tell him—"

"He'll think I'm not fetching the men. Please take me upstairs."

"But—"

"Nothing will happen, but he will think you want me. Otherwise, I'll lose my place here."

"I should think you'd want to lose it."

"You sound like one of those Quakers. They're always urging me to leave Tuckerton. They don't understand that a girl needs to eat and keep clothes on her back."

Harrah doubted that she always kept clothes on her back in the room upstairs, but he said nothing.

"Won't you come with me?"

Harrah looked at the tavernkeeper. A curious blend of seacook and ship's rat, he was. And Harrah detected a look of displeasure in the man. He then took Suzie Strook by the arm.

"The Quakers are right, you know," he remarked as they climbed the stairs.

"Then why do they come here?"

"It's a meeting house of sorts—for some of them."

"That it is."

In the room upstairs, no bigger than a ship's cabin, she began to undress and pull her hair back.

"I thought we were here for appearances' sake?"

"You refused me once. You're not going to refuse me again?" she asked, baring her breasts and her magnificent red nipples.

"I didn't refuse you," said Harrah, finding the offensive fragrance gone now that her dress fell to the floor. "I had no right to take you. And I have no right now."

"But you do want me, don't you?"

"Be a good girl and cover up. I'm not made of iron, you know."

Suzie Strook stared at Harrah a long time. She thought it would be a handsome feather in her hat to seduce Harrah. She had no conventional regard for herself. She did not understand the mores and morals of "proper" girls. She knew only that she was improper. But, allowing for that, she did take pride in her conquests. A religious man, a Quaker, she counted above and beyond normal patronage. A gentleman, likewise. But at the top of the ladder were sea captains, senators, and ironmasters. And Suzie had never had an ironmaster.

But Harrah was not just an ironmaster. He was the employer of Rob Strook. He was the husband of the woman who had shown her great kindness. He was the man who had given her shelter when Rob Strook threw her out. It would be asking a lot to make him bed down with her.

After a while she slipped her dress back on and slipped it over her bosom.

"I'm sorry," she said at last. "I thought I would shame you. I'm not only a whore, you see, but a bitch. I've come to a pretty pass, haven't I?"

"A pretty pass, yes. But you're only a child."

She pulled her hair back once more. "Give Mrs. Harrah my— Or, better still, say nothing of me at all. Just tell Rob Strook to go to hell! That's all I ask."

"Rob Strook?" Harrah smiled as he pulled open the door. "I think I can manage that."

As he headed for the staircase, Harrah saw the back of another man leaving one of the rooms on the floor. The departing figure was dressed like a gentleman, hat and all, and as far as Harrah could make out he had been visiting one of the other girls of the establishment. A smile began to form on Harrah's lips—until the man turned round. When he recognized Edward Blount, the smile faded. So this was how he passed his time since the divorce! A pretty comedown for an ironmaster's son.

At the same time, he was aware that Blount had recognized him. Neither of the two men acknowledged the other. They simply stared back in surprise and wonder. And then it occurred to Harrah that Blount knew nothing of what had really transpired with Suzie Strook. He would suspect the worst, of course. He would regard Harrah as no different from himself. He would see his presence in Tuckerton as a call to the flesh, much as his own presence had been. Well, there was no help for it. At least what Harrah had seen would silence the other. Just as Harrah himself was silenced as he made his way downstairs.

Part Nine

A WORLD'S END

AT SEA

Jesse Richards and Nathaniel Harrah were holding a two-man wake in the ironmaster's house at Trescott. Piles of bank notes were spread across the table.

"That's the lot of them," said Jesse. "They come at different times, but the banks will be wanting the money."

"I haven't got it just now."

"Don't you think I know that? I'd pitch in myself, Nathaniel. But Batsto is not doing that well either."

"Maybe things will pick up," said Harrah wearily, realizing he sounded like Cassandra.

"With winter coming?"

"I guess it's too much to expect."

"The only way, Nathaniel, is to close the place down. If we close Trescott down, we can sell the land. And you at least will come out of it alive."

"What about you?"

"My losses will be small, much smaller than I had a right to expect. And come spring, Batsto will pick up the orders Trescott could not fill."

"That's not the problem," said Harrah.

Jesse Richards pulled up a chair and sat himself down. "You're thinking of Cassandra?"

Harrah nodded. "I won't be able to close down, Jesse. Not while she's around."

"Then she'll have to go on holiday."

"Easier said than done."

"What about Cape Island? You were there. I understand it's quite beautiful this time of year."

"Cape Island's a long, tiresome journey, and Cassandra hasn't been too well."

"Then go by boat," said Richards. "I have a schooner sails that way from time to time. I'll have it dock at the Landing. And you can board her there."

The ironmaster of Batsto seemed satisfied with his plan, but Harrah poked it for weaknesses.

"Who will close Trescott down? It will take more than a day's work, you know."

"I will," said Richards with authority, though he did not often assume the baronial manner.

"And what will happen when Cassandra returns? The shock may be too much for her."

"You'll have to prepare her for that."

Harrah wearily fell into a chair.

"I suppose you're right. There aren't too many options, are there?"

"I'm afraid not."

Although steamboats sailed from Philadelphia, Chester, and New Castle during the bathing season, there were none from Tuckerton or Barnegat to Cape May at any time. Harrah considered himself fortunate that Richards placed a schooner at their disposal. But Cassandra opposed the plan.

"I need no vacation. I've work enough to keep me busy through winter."

"But this is a splendid opportunity. How often is a boat made available to us? We may never get the chance again."

"What about the children?"

"Rachel will look after them, as always. And Jesse will look after the ironworks. He assured me he'd do whatever had to be done."

"Jesse said that?"

Harrah nodded.

"What a fine man he is," volunteered Cassandra.

"Then you'll go?"

"Only because you need a holiday. You haven't looked well at all these past few weeks."

Harrah was surprised at the ease with which Cassandra agreed. Thank Heaven for Jesse Richards! The mere mention of his name had cleared the way of obstacles. To Cassandra, Jesse Richards was authority and good sense, all in one. If Jesse Richards thought they should go, then go they would.

On Tuesday morning they met the schooner at the Landing. Its cargo had already been hauled aboard, and its captain, a Mr. Eliot from Boston, introduced himself. Within minutes they set sail and within the hour they plunged into the deep waters of the broad Atlantic.

It struck Harrah that Cassandra did not look well as she stood at the rail, staring at the sandy beaches and the pine and oak forests beyond. Harrah attributed Cassandra's pale color to what he believed was her first sea voyage. But his wife showed no sign of seasickness or discomfort.

It seemed to Harrah that Cassandra could not help but know that Trescott was failing. She had access to the company books and had been witness to declining orders. But either she pretended not to know of this or she had somehow deceived herself that things were better than they stood.

Yevish

As he took her cold hand to warm it, he recalled that his wife had not really been herself since the birth of Willacassa. Since then she had lost much of her color and was able to mount only spurts of energy, although she appeared tireless to outsiders in her role as wife of the ironmaster. It was as if in giving birth to Willacassa she had lost something of herself, something essential and irreplaceable. And yet it was not so much lost as transferred, for the child had energy and health in abundance. She had no need to husband her strength or store up enthusiasm. She was a self-powered mill wheel.

"I never knew a sea voyage could be so peaceful," said Cassandra, ending a long silence.

"Nor I," said Harrah.

"And yet I feel wanting."

"Why?"

"For leaving the children behind. And Trescott. I sometimes feel I'll be punished."

"The children are in good hands. Rachel is family by now."

"I know. But it doesn't seem right just the same. If it weren't for more than a few weeks, I don't think I would have gone."

Content that she did not mention Trescott again, Harrah drew his wife away from the rail and led her to the officers' dining room where good bread, hard Philadelphia butter, and boiling hot coffee were the midday fare.

After lunch, warmed by the coffee, Cassandra again ventured out on deck. Standing with Harrah by the rail, she was witnesss to a glorious sight. Laced with clouds, the sky made a prism for the sun's rays, scattering them in strong shoots of color to the ocean's crest. And the ocean in turn reflected the light off the water into glistening shafts of silver and gold. It was a spectacle of shifting colors and it all but dazzled the eye.

"You do regret not going into railroads," Cassandra said quietly, as though she had been thinking about this and not nature's extravagant display.

"At times," said Harrah.

"Tell the truth."

"I am."

"Wouldn't you give up Trescott for a voting share in the Camden and Amboy?"

"I wouldn't give up a Trescott for anything, particularly if her name was Cassandra."

"You know what I'm saying."

"And you know what I mean, Cassandra." But then Harrah

reconsidered. "Yes, I do have regrets sometimes. But I suspect I wasn't cut out for the railroads. Maybe I'm not aggressive enough. Maybe I lack the drive that railroad men need. I've had my chances and did nothing with them. Besides, I wanted to be with you."

By late afternoon, passing several ships in full canvas and an occasional steamboat, the schooner approached Cape May Point. With dark clouds threatening overhead, Captain Eliot was anxious to drop sail and lower the ship's anchor.

"Higbee's Landing, sir," announced his mate.

"Did you signal for a boat, Mr. Crawford?"

"Aye, sir."

The captain turned to Harrah. "I'm afraid you'll have to go in by whaleboat. The wharf has been put away for the season."

"I understand," said Harrah.

"I'll be back here Tuesday next," said Captain Eliot. "Wait for us on the beach." He turned to Cassandra. "I trust you will enjoy your stay here. If I didn't have business to attend to, I'd take a week myself."

Cassandra did not relish going ashore by whaleboat. Until now she held up rather well aboard ship, thanks to a calm sea. But the rolling black clouds above and the increasingly rough waters began to undermine her stamina. As Harrah helped her into the boat, he could not help but notice the change in his wife. Fire, forest, bog, and furnace did not phase her. But the rocking of a boat amid the swelling roll of waves took their toll.

"I should never have left the Pines," she said, her voice becoming husky in the afternoon chill.

Sitting down on the gunwhale, she closed her eyes as the boat dipped and surged its way towards shore. She opened them from time to time as the oars creaked in their locks, only to find there was still a good deal of water between the sharp bow of the boat and the shore. When with the aid of the oarsmen she finally put her shoe down on the wet sand, Cassandra was all but exhausted.

"Never again," she said. "From now on it will be dry white sand and pine needles."

A farmer's wagon was seen on what passed for a road.

"Will you be wantin' a ride to Cape Island?" asked the bent figure on the driver's seat.

"Yes," said Harrah.

"Then this is all the conveyance available."

Harrah tossed their bags onto the wagon and helped Cassandra aboard.

"One dollar, if you please," said the farmer.

"You sound more like a New Englander than a Jerseyman,"

said Harrah.

"Strange you should say that."

"Why?"

"My family come from Massachusetts. Off the Mayflower they were. A whole bunch of us settled in South Jersey."

"I come from Connecticut myself," said Harrah. "They drive a hard bargain up there. But you can out-Yankee them anytime." He tossed the man a dollar.

"That's two dollars, sir. One for your wife and one for yourself."

"Two dollars!"

"'Less you'd rather go by foot."

Thinking of his weary Cassandra, Harrah paid the man and thereafter spoke no word between them.

CAPE ISLAND

Harrah at first regretted that the summer crowds had left. On his last visit to Cape Island he had heard of carriages racing on the sand, theatrical presentations, open air concerts, and fishing in Cape Island Sound, and had seen none of these things. But with the departure of the summer patrons, lodging proved to be no problem and he opted for the Mansion House which fronted on the north side of Washington Avenue between Jackson and Perry Streets. Signing the hotel register, he was given Room 24 which he quickly found for Cassandra who was eager to rest.

From the first Cassandra was displeased with the place. She bridled at the three-footlong sign which bore the regulations of the Mansion House.

"I will not breakfast at 7½ o'clock. Nor will I eat dinner at 2. And I don't care if they ring the bell one-half hour ahead of time. I'll eat when I very well please."

Though he tried to mollify his wife, Harrah was happy to see her spirit restored.

"This is very inferior fare," Cassandra said at supper. "The fish is tolerably cooked. But the potatoes are water-logged and the vegetables non-existent. For the money we're paying I expected considerably more."

"We can switch to another house if you wish," said Harrah, none too pleased himself with the laggard service or the barn-like dimensions of the dining room.

"Good. Let's get a place facing the ocean."

Well, this was progress. A critical Cassandra was a healthy Cassandra.

Early next morning they walked along the beachfront look-ing at houses. The rooms at the Kimball House where Harrah had stayed were too small. And there were not too many places to choose from this time of year. But Cassandra found a white three-story structure with a widow's walk that caught her fancy and they inquired within.

"Yes, we have a room facing the sea, several in fact. Take your pick of them."

Cassandra chose the room with the biggest window.

"This will do fine," she said to Harrah and they quickly returned to the Mansion House to fetch their bags.

"See, there is no list of regulations in the dining room. In fact, it's hardly a dining room. More like a breakfast cove. And I'll wager the food is not only well-cooked but plentiful."

Yevish

Cassandra was right. They lunched on chowder and steamed crabs and succulent oysters, and washed it all down with a pint of ale. Then they walked the beach which had a derelict boat on it with "373 feet" painted on its side.

"What does that mean?"

"373 feet to the water, I would say. The proprietor of the house tells me they're losing beach every year. Was 400 feet once. See where it's crossed out."

"Just like the Pines," remarked Cassandra. "They're losing sand the way we're losing bogs."

This was the first recognition by Cassandra that the Pines were losing ground in the struggle to produce iron. Harrah welcomed the admission but did not say what was on his mind.

That afternoon, as the wind was up, they watched the ocean from wing chairs in their room. It was a wind-swept beach they saw, with waves spuming white foam and a reckless surf pounding the shore. Overhead thunder clouds gathered and sea gulls circled, making ready to dive. And the gray light of the sky cast a pearly, luminescent wash upon the sea, with its distant sails, and the pale sand.

"It's a beautiful scene, isn't it?" said Cassandra.

Harrah nodded. "Stretching as far as the eye can see."

"But there's one thing wrong."

"What's that?"

"It's like an oil painting. You think you're there. But you're not. Only your eyes are satisfied. Your body is quite still—if not asleep, at least not completely awake. I never feel that way in the Pines. The ocean is too overwhelming."

"You'd feel different after a time."

"I think not. If it's a new life your planning for us, put it out of your mind."

"How did you know what I was thinking?"

"I know you, Nathaniel Harrah. You have it in mind to go into the hotel business, don't you? Or is it a tavern you're contemplating?"

"Is that so poor an idea?"

"It is for me. We have Trescott now and that's all I want. It's all I ever wanted really."

"But—"

"It's my doll house, my ironmaster's mansion, my world all wrapped in one. I wouldn't exchange it for all the castles in Scotland."

Harrah did not pursue the matter. But he was inclined to think that setting up a business in Cape Island, a business that catered to summer guests, was an idea worth looking into. There were, he knew, regularly scheduled steamboat trips for vacationers, and a stage between Philadelphia and Cape May had been in operation for years. "Tommy's Folly," as Congress Hall had once been known—even the Mansion House—was making money hand over fist. Cape Island loomed as a viable escape route from the Pines. But first he had to deal with the irontown. Until Trescott was disposed of, any talk of Cape Island would be sheer folly.

Harrah thought it best that he tell Cassandra about Trescott before returning home. But he never found the right moment for the telling. It was one thing to declare that their business venture had failed. It was quite another to inform Cassandra that her whole world had collapsed. And yet he knew that if he waited until they returned it would be too late to soften the blow.

On their last day at Cape Island he made an effort to break the news.

"Cassandra, about Trescott—"

"Let's not talk about Trescott now. We've got to be at Higbee's Landing by 9:00 o'clock."

"I've got a carriage waiting."

"Then let's be gone. I saw the schooner sailing by from our window."

The carriage ride was a jolting one and not conducive to conversation. Harrah sat back and prepared himself for the inevitable while Cassandra took in the flat, scratchy landscape of Cape May Point. At Higbee's Landing a whaleboat was waiting to take them to the anchored ship. Harrah helped Cassandra into the boat and watched as the oarsmen skillfully pushed their way into the bay. In moments they were aboard ship again.

"Did you enjoy your holiday?" asked Captain Eliot.

"Immensely," said Cassandra. "But I'll be happy to see Trescott again."

THE TRUTH IS HARD

When the schooner reached the Landing, Cassandra could see that something was amiss. There were no other vessels tied up and very little cargo was piled on the wharf. It was as if a general holiday had been declared. Only the tavern was bustling.

"Things must be slow at Martha these days," she said disembarking.

"It's not only at Martha. We've gone out of blast," said Harrah, leaving for a moment to inquire at the tavern for a carriage.

"But it's scarcely October," remarked Cassandra when Harrah returned. "Why should we go out of blast so soon?"

"Listen, my dear," said Harrah, taking her arm. "Trescott'll be well-nigh deserted when we get back. I've had to let the men go."

"You're not keeping some on through the winter?"

"No," said Harrah. "There seemed no point."

"No point? No point! There's all kinds of work to be done. Hauling timber. Laying in supplies. Repairing the cupola."

"We've run out of funds," said Harrah. "The orders are not coming in. I asked Jesse to close the place down."

"Jesse! Closed down!" A cloud of disbelief hung over her eyes. "That's not true! Jesse would never close Trescott down. Not without telling me first."

"It was my idea, not his."

"Still, he wouldn't do it." She looked scathingly at him. "You lied to me once before, Nathaniel Harrah. On Burnt Tavern Road. I've almost forgotten that. Now you're lying to me again."

So strange was the cast on her face as she said this that Harrah feared to go on.

"You will see for yourself," he said at last. Stung by her reproach, he managed to quiet his personal feelings and helped her aboard the carriage.

They approached Trescott from the east. As soon as they left the river road, they were met with an awful stillness. No sound of giant hammer blows, no roar from the furnace, no grinding of wagon or mill wheels to greet them. The wind was gone out of the massive bellows. The air was empty of shrill human voices. As Harrah slowly rode past the silent furnace and the empty sheds that surrounded it, Harrah could see that Trescott was already a ghost town.

But Cassandra grasped at straws. Half leaning out of the carriage, she motioned.

"Isn't that Venable sitting on a chair? There, near the carpenter's shop."

It was Venable, fast asleep in his new capacity as watchman.

"Mr. Venable, where is everyone?" called Cassandra. "Are we on holiday?"

Venable stirred and roused himself from his nap, Venable who never knew an idle day at the furnace. "I'm sorry, Ma'am," he said, getting to his feet. "If it's a holiday we're on, it's threatening to become permanent. Mr. Harrah, I'm glad to see you, sir. I'll be taking a look around if you need me."

With that, he scratched his head and stretched his back and shuffled in the direction of the saw mill.

Harrah continued along the road to the ironmaster's house. Cassandra saw no sign of life in the sprawling barn, the general store, or any of the cedar-framed worker's cottages.

"No," she reiterated. "Jesse would never have permitted this."

At the ironmaster's house she stood for a while, looking at the empty streets and would have remained standing had not Harrah taken her by the arm and led her into the house.

"Now tell me what's going on," she said when she had removed her shawl and had taken stock of their living room once more.

"It's all over," said Harrah. "We're closing down."

"It can't be all over," cried Cassandra. "Not Trescott. Not everything we worked so hard for."

"But it is. The banks are calling in their notes. No one will extend us credit. The workers will not accept scrip. Even Jesse has gone as far as he can stretch himself."

"What about the money the Mohawk Pipe Company owes us?"

"The Mohawk Pipe Company is bankrupt. I have a letter from their solicitors."

"Bankrupt?" Cassandra grew vague. Then she drew out a box. "But I still have some money. There's Bill's legacy and—"

"No," said Harrah.

"But if it will save Trescott—"

"Nothing will save Trescott, Cassandra. Don't you understand? It's not the banks killed us. Or the Mohawk Pipe Company. Or any of the half-dozen other things that have been destroying us. It's our competitors. Iron is finished in the Pines. The whole industry is tumbling down. In a few years the furnaces will be a pile of rubble."

Cassandra stood immobile.

"You said this all along, didn't you?"

"Yes."

197

"You predicted this would happen."

"It was inevitable. All the signs were there."

"Then why did you let us build Trescott? Why didn't you invest in the railroads?"

"Why? Trescott was what you wanted."

"But if you knew—"

"I would have rebuilt Troy for you, Cassandra. Even if it fell a second time. Being with you was all that mattered."

"But you might have persuaded me Trescott was a mistake."

"There was no persuading you. Your mind was made up. And Jesse was there to give you encouragement."

"Jesse has always been generous. But how does he manage to stay afloat? How does Batsto keep going on?" Cassandra sank into a chair, unable to grasp the complexity of the situation.

"Jesse's been in this business a long time. And Jesse's prepared for an end to iron. Didn't he just complete a glass factory in Batsto? Hasn't he turned to brick making? And there's a schooner or two he's built at Batsto and launched. The *Frelinghuysen*, for one. He ships pipes and kettles and brings back supplies for the general stores in the towns throughout the area. So he'll survive for a while. But even Jesse is living on borrowed time. And don't think he doesn't know it."

"Then why does he go on?"

"Because his heart's in the Pines, like yours. And as ironmaster of Batsto, he feels a deep sense of obligation. A kind of *noblesse oblige*. Besides, Jesse's the one professional in these parts. Even Mr. Evans can't touch him as a business man. All the rest of us are amateurs."

Cassandra reached for Harrah's hand.

"Then let's try again, Nathaniel. Just one more time. Let's try to keep Trescott alive."

Harrah had never seen his wife in tears before, not even at Hostetler's burial. And he was shaken by the experience. Gently he dried her eyes with his hankerchief.

"Trescott is gone, my dear. There is no 'one more time.' Let her rest in peace."

"She's not gone." Cassandra rose and peered out the window. "She's still there, Nathaniel. The houses are there. The furnace still stands. The sheds. The mill. How can you say she's gone?"

"What you're looking at is a hollow corpse," said Harrah. "Nothing real remains."

"Well, then I'll remain! I'll remain here until smoke belches out of the furnace once more, and men and women crowd these streets. I'll never leave!"

"Cassandra—"

"I mean that, Nathaniel. I'll never leave Trescott again! So you will have to bring her back."

Harrah could see that she was still in shock. He took Cassandra's hand and led her away from the window. Then all at once her face turned white and she slowly crumpled to the floor.

Though he was afraid the news would take its toll, Harrah was not prepared for what had happened. Helping his wife up, he carried her to the bedroom. There he brought her a cup of brandy and tried to get Cassandra to take some. When after a few hours it appeared she was making little recovery, he bundled her into a blanket and helped her into his carriage. That afternoon he abandoned a deserted Trescott for Lower Bank.

LOWER BANK

Harrah took a cottage in Lower Bank not too far from the black doctor's place. As soon as he had installed Rachel in the house to look after Cassandra and the children, he sent for John Witt again.

"I don't know what's ailin' her," confessed the black man who had seen her the day before. "You had better send for one of those white doctors in Mount Holly or Philadelphia, who specializes in these things. Or, better still, bring her there yourself."

"She won't go. She insists she's all right. And there are moments when she seems to be well again. Isn't there anything you can do?"

"I have potions and mixtures and elixirs. But that's for ailin' bodies. It seems to me what's troubling your wife is something more than that."

"A brain fever?"

"No. No fever. It's something that her mind is fixed on. Could be all she needs is rest. Could be something's vexin' her. Could be a lot of things. Whatever it is, I haven't the medicine to make things better. Or the experience to know what to do. Get a doctor from Mount Holly, Mr. Harrah."

"Do you know of anyone?"

"There's Dr. Fowler. Arthur Fowler on Branch Street. He deals with afflictions of the soul. Just as I deal with afflictions of the body. I can send a messenger for him, if you wish."

Harrah nodded. "Whatever you think."

But Dr. Fowler, a portly white-haired man with a watch fob on his stomach, was no nearer finding the cause of Cassandra's illness than the black doctor.

"It's a kind of depression she's in. The shock of Trescott closing down must have caused it. But I am at a loss how to treat her. I would suggest a change of scene but she's already had that."

"It may be the change of scene contributed to her illness," said Harrah.

"Then I don't know what to prescribe. I do know one thing, though. Her condition is not good. And the pity of it is the poor girl doesn't know she's sick. She admits to being tired. But she acts as though she has a monumental task to perform and that what she is experiencing now is a kind of respite. It would surprise me very much if she should make a rapid recovery. If anything, I see a deepening decline."

"She wants to go back to Trescott," said Harrah. "She knows it's deserted but she wants to go back anyway."

Dr. Fowler looked at the black doctor. "What do you think, John? Shall we risk it? Weak as she is, I hate to see her just wasting away."

"Let her go," said John Witt. "It may be the one chance she has."

SENTIMENTAL JOURNEY

The next morning Harrah prepared to set out for Trescott, but Cassandra said she wanted to stop at Batsto before returning home.

"But Batsto's in the other direction. We'll lose a lot of time and add miles to our journey," said Harrah.

"I know. But I want to see Jesse again. We can always stay for the night."

Harrah did not argue with her. Cassandra was too weak to offer resistance, to weak to sustain any pain, body or mind. So he climbed up beside her and nudged his horse into moving the carriage. He tried going slow at first but the ride was no easier than when the horse picked up speed. Harrah glanced at Cassandra to see how she was bearing up and he winced every time the carriage hit a rock or was jolted by a gully.

When they reached Batsto, Cassandra was pretty well tuckered out. To make matters worse, Jesse Richards was not at home, having gone to Mount Holly on business.

Cassandra rested for a while at the mansion, then insisted on returning to the carriage. Though it was an effort for her, she climbed back on.

"Pleasant Mills next," she said, mustering a smile for Harrah.

"Why Pleasant Mills?"

"I'd like to stop at the church."

"All right, Cassandra."

"I was happy that day."

"And I," said Harrah.

"Not only because we were married—but because you seemed so content with me."

"I was. And I am still."

He drove up to the twin doors of the church and helped Cassandra down. She was so weak that her ankle gave way even before it touched the ground.

"Easy, girl," said Harrah, supporting her at the waist. "Wait till you're on your feet before you start walking."

Hers was a gentle smile, turning wan as he helped her onto the right portico. Harrah tried to open the door but found it locked.

"That's all right," said Cassandra. "I can see through the window." Again with his assistance she stepped down onto the flower bed and peered through the small glass panes.

"There's the altar. Such a pure white it was. And the pews. We had a goodly crowd, didn't we?"

"That we did."

"Did you think that day we would come to this?"

"To what, my dear?"

"To Trescott. And the life of an ironmaster and his wife?"

"I had no thought of anything that day but you."

"There's that silver tongue again. How you do go on! All the same, I'm glad we married in a church—in this church. It's such an elegant place—for all its simplicity."

When they left the white clapboard structure, Cassandra stopped for a moment to look at the grave markers in the tall grass of the cemetery nearby. She noted the names, and the dates of birth and death. "So young," she moaned.

Harrah agreed.

"Nathaniel, I'd like to be buried here when I die. Not at Trescott."

"But I thought Trescott was to be our resting place."

"No. It's Trescott for me while I live. But when I die, I think I'd prefer Pleasant Mills. It's so peaceful here and so everlasting. And I'd like a stone to mark my grave, not iron."

"Cassandra—"

"Promise me."

"All right, my dear. But it will be our son who'll have to keep the promise. Not I."

"You're wrong, Nathaniel. You will be there at the end. I want it that way."

She squeezed his hand, and he gently squeezed it in return.

"We'll never make Trescott today," said Harrah. "It's best we return to Lower Bank and try again tomorrow or the next day."

Cassandra, utterly fatigued, did not oppose the plan.

"Let's take the road back to Lower Bank. It's a prettier ride anyway. I do love looking at the Mullica. If by the time we reach Green Bank I'm too tired to make the trip north, we'll stay the night."

Harrah knew that if Cassandra was that agreeable it was from lack of strength rather than purpose.

"That sounds reasonable." He clicked his tongue and the carriage moved forward again, making its way through the Pines. At times they rode in shade and enjoyed the cool of it. At other times bursts of sun broke through the trees, casting florid patterns on their backs and on the shifting haunches of their horse.

Cassandra reached for Harrah's hand; her fingers were cold to the touch.

"I do love your patience," she said. "Don't you ever tire of my prodding?"

"Is that what you call it?" he said. "I thought of it as striving, as wanting to make more of life."

"You always put the best face on things. If that's what it was, I've neglected you in doing it."

Harrah put his arm round his wife and let her rest against him.

"There was never any question of neglect. Do we neglect the sun and the sky even when we don't take particular note of them? No, we know they are there. That is enough for us."

"And it was enough you knew I loved you?"

"More than enough."

"You're so good to say that. But you could have done the things you wanted. Built railroads or opened a great guest house on Cape Island. That's what you really wanted, wasn't it?"

"Only if you did it with me. Without you, they mean nothing."

"And without you, Trescott means nothing to me. With my husband at my side it means everything. Do you understand, Nathaniel?"

Harrah turned towards her, but he was suddenly alarmed at what he saw. Cassandra bore no resemblance to the vital woman he knew. Her eyes were glazed and her lips drained of all color. She had sunk into a kind of languor.

"What is it, Cassandra? What's wrong?"

"I don't know. I feel faint. Better stop the carriage."

Harrah halted his horse and, sustaining his wife with his arm, gave Cassandra some brandy which he carried under his seat for just such an event.

"Feel better?"

She nodded and half opened her eyes. Once she was able to sit up without him, he jumped down and came round her side of the carriage.

"Here, lean on me. We're going to stop for a bit."

He was astonished at how light she seemed, putting no weight on him at all. She tried to take a step but despaired of keeping her feet. Holding to a tree for support, she leaned back against it. "I'm all right now. Just had to catch my breath."

Harrah returned to the carriage for a blanket. He kept talking, looking for a response from Cassandra that assured him she was all right.

"I'll send for the children first thing. Rachel's taken them to Tuckerton where her parents have a home. They'll be missing us by now, I'm sure."

"Yes, do that. I want so much to be near them!"

"And when we get to Trescott we'll see what we can do to get things going again. You were right, we never should have closed the place down. We'll find the money somehow. You'll be the ironmaster's wife once more—with all the duties attendant to such a station. I promise you.''

The change in Cassandra was quick as a shot. It was as if with his words Harrah had poured life into the dying woman. No magic elixir, no doctor's potion could have had so immediate and positive an effect.

''Do you mean that?''

''Of course I do.''

''Then let's not waste time. Let's go to Trescott directly.''

''But it will be dark when we get there.''

''So much the better. I'll imagine it alive and filled with people. Not deserted as it is and desolate. Then in the morning we can take stock of things.''

Cassandra looked so much stronger, so determined as she said this that Harrah knew it was futile to argue with her.

''All right. But do try to sleep while we're journeying there.''

''I'll not sleep till we arrive,'' said Cassandra as he helped her into the carriage. ''But I will rest.''

Harrah looked down at her as she lay her head against his arm. How grateful he was to have known her. He had said he would start things up again at Trescott, and she was content. How he loved her for trusting him. And now she was in quiet repose. Like the once-picked lady's slipper, her head tilted slightly to a side.

TRESCOTT ONCE MORE

Harrah allowed her to sleep late the next morning although Cassandra had expressed the wish to rise early. She wanted to see the town again, not the shadowy forms of the night before. She wanted to take stock of things, much as a duchess surveys her realm. Harrah secured some eggs and coffee from the watchman, Venable, and prepared breakfast.

"You meant what you said yesterday, that you will start things up again?"

"I did, my girl."

"And Trescott will succeed this time?"

"What choice does it have? You wouldn't let it go under."

"Even if Jesse can't help us this time?"

"Even without Jesse."

"I'm so glad!" she cried, almost ecstatic at the prospect. She stood up, putting her cup aside. "Here, help me with my shawl. I want to walk down Furnace Street."

Harrah was pleased with what she found. The casting shed was as tight as a ship, without one loose board. The blacksmith's forge had all its tools hanging neatly on its walls. And the only dark spot on the low-lying warehouse was a weather-stained stretch of wood above the entranceway where rainwater had seeped in from the roof. Near the livery stable Harrah found her a chair and she sat down.

Cassandra rested for a while, husbanding her strength. When she had caught her breath, she permitted herself the luxury of sitting back and becoming a passive observer of the place she and Harrah had built out of a wilderness. Until now her gaze had been cast downwards, resting on the white sand of the road and the desolate doorways of the buildings and structures that opened on Furnace Street. The late afternoon sun was too bright for her. As she looked up at the sky, it almost blinded her with its glare. But she persisted, shading her eyes in order to make out the shapes of the roofs and the chimneys.

"It's broken loose!" she exclaimed suddenly.

"What?" asked Harrah, alarmed by the pitch of her voice.

"The T in Trescott has broken loose. It's hanging by a thread!"

Harrah looked up at the sign that in six-foot wooden letters identified the town. The letter was loose but it was not "hanging by a thread."

"It's in no immediate danger of falling," he said after squinting a brief inspection. "I'll get Mr. Venable to help me slide it back in place."

"Please do. It's bad enough the town is falling apart. I can't have my name a shambles, too," sighed Cassandra.

Harrah went in search of Mr. Venable and found him in the carpenter's shed. Venable was cutting slats for boarding up windows.

"The letter T in Trescott is hanging loose," announced Harrah. "I'd like you to give me a hand with it."

"No trouble at all," said Venable with his pipe in his teeth. "It slides into a groove. The wind must have whipped it loose. Wasn't cut right to begin with. But at the time Rob Strook did not want to cut me another one."

"Come then," said Harrah. "Let's put it right."

Venable laid his saw down and followed Harrah into the street.

"I was going to work on it this afternoon."

"Yes," said Harrah, "I saw the ladder there."

"Not that it matters anymore," continued Venable, shuffling behind. "With the town going down as it is, it doesn't really need a sign."

"But it's important to my wife," said Harrah. "She—

He stopped suddenly. "My God!"

As he looked toward the sign, he saw Cassandra halfway up the long ladder Venable had left behind. Rung by rung, slowly but doggedly, she had managed to climb upward. And now, thinking she could manage it, she was stretching to touch the bottom of the dislodged letter but was unable to reach it.

Harrah broke into a run.

"Cassandra!"

But so intent was she on the sign that either Cassandra did not hear him or she chose to ignore his call. Clinging close to the ladder, she climbed still another rung.

"Cassandra, come down! We'll fix it! You'll only—"

He could not finish. In utter desolation he watched her struggle one rung higher. This time, stretching beyond herself, she appeared to touch the six-foot letter. And he could see that in the touch there was an instant of triumph. Harrah knew that for Cassandra, high above the town she had created, this was the moment supreme. Her ultimate striving could now be denied by neither man nor God.

Though still tentative about her hold on the ladder, Cassandra straightened up. Slowly she allowed her left arm to let go of the ladder, and for a moment she stood free and unencumbered. Once more she reached for the letter. But this time she faltered. For an instant she could not maintain her balance nor make contact with the letter. With her arms uplifted as though in prayer, she seemed suspended in mid-air. Then suddenly she toppled backward. Not a scream, not a sound accompanied her fall. Hers was a long, arching, silent, graceful descent—until her body hit the ground. Then she bounced an inch or two and fell back again with a final, shattering thud.

"Oh, Mr. Harrah," moaned Venable. "Why didn't she wait?"

But for Harrah there was no thought, only devastation.

PLEASANT MILLS

And at the end he was there. With his son Jonathan in hand, he visited the grave. Harrah had planted four young cedars to stand as silent sentinels at the corners of the ground where she was buried. Though the sun was warm, she lay in a cool spot with a stone marker as she had requested.

He thought for a time to move Bill Hostetler beside her. But as Harrah thought about it, it seemed proper for Bill to remain buried near the inn at Burnt Tavern Road.

"What does it say, Father?"

"The stone, Son?"

"Yes, the gravestone."

"It says, 'Cassandra Trescott Harrah
        1810-1841
        Beloved Mother, Beloved Wife
        Daughter of the Pines'"

"What does that mean, Father?"

"What it says. Your mother loved the Pines. Oh, she loved you, Jonathan, and Willacassa. And she loved me. But the Pines were home to her. Just as you will have a place to call your own some day."

Harrah turned toward the gravestone.

"We'll try Cape Island after all, Cassandra. At least for a time. I've been to the farm at Ten Mile River, but it has no hold for me without you. Yes, we'll settle in Cape May and open a small inn. It's not the Pines. But it's on the sea. And it will be a good life for the children. Jonathan will become a man there and Willacassa the image of her mother. And each summer we'll be back to see you."

He wondered how such a plan would sit with Cassandra. In life she would have fiercely opposed it. In death he looked for a softening of attitude. So long as she was in the bosom of her habitat, she had no compelling argument. And when it was his day to lay his head down, Harrah would be buried beside her.

No, he did not think she would oppose him. Batsto was still limping along, as was Hampton Furnace. But Trescott was gone and Speedwell, and Martha Furnace was on the way out. Even Atsion's days were numbered, Atsion where Harrah had reclaimed her. And now that railroads were being built, competing with the stagecoach and the stagecoach stops, it was only a matter of time before Burnt Tavern Road would come to an end. All that remained—or would remain—were the Pines, the sand roads, the bogs, and the sweet water.

Not that it mattered to Cassandra. She would have settled for the Pines alone. Harrah closed his eyes. And he fought the rush of images that flooded his mind, images of a crowded past and of moments eternally lost.

Yes, he hoped Cassandra had found her final resting place, but in truth he doubted it. A stone marked her grave and a casket held her body, but nothing could contain that restless spirit. Cassandra was not so much a daughter of the Pines as its very essence. That was the truth of it. And as such she would forever have her way.

Squeezing the hand of his son, Harrah led the boy from the grave site. But Harrah was in no hurry to board the wagon. For him this was a leave taking. Where was the roar of the Pines now? Where were the coach stops and the taverns? Where the wild, outcast world? He looked once more at the straw-grass of the cemetery grounds. Without Cassandra the Pines were indeed barren. Yet no other place had throbbed with her life. No other place marked her indomitable path. No other place, even in the stillness of its forests, echoed her passing. Only the Pines.